shadow of a huge red demon flared nd Jean-Marc like a firestorm

With Seeing altered by magic and pain, Jean-Marc saw flashes of black fangs, smoking horns and an enormous six-fingered scarlet hand, tipped with talons as sharp as scimitars, reaching for him. The stench assaulted him; sulfur and carrion, rotten blood, evil. The thing was Le Devourer, Lilliane's demon patron. His hand closed around Jean-Marc's soul, and its talons sliced through the radiant mass.

Jean-Marc rocketed past sanity from the violation. He had no thoughts, no emotions. He ceased, because being was too horrible. He didn't know where he was. He didn't know who he was. He didn't know what he was.

But one thing remained: a woman's name, and he shouted it with the voice of the possessed:

"Isabelle!"

NANCY HOLDER

is a bestselling author of nearly eighty books and two hundred short stories. She has received four Bram Stoker awards from the Horror Writers Association and her books have been translated into two dozen languages. A former ballet dancer, she has lived all over the world, and currently resides in San Diego, California, with her daughter, Belle. She would love to hear from readers at www.nancyholder.com.

SON OF THE SHADOWS

NANCY HOLDER

Silhouette® Books

nocturne™

 **SILHOUETTE BOOKS**

ISBN-13: 978-0-373-61793-7
ISBN-10:   0-373-61793-3

SON OF THE SHADOWS

Dear Reader,

One day last February, Belle, my eleven-year-old daughter, informed me that every time I kissed her, I had to pay her a quarter. The students at her elementary school could "send" chocolate Valentine roses for a dollar each to their friends, and she needed more cash. I knew she had a purse full of loot from her pet-sitting business, so I was very surprised to hear this.

It turned out that her very best friend, Haley, didn't have enough money to buy roses for her friends. So Belle made a secret list of the people to whom Haley wanted to send roses, but couldn't afford to. Belle's plan was to buy the roses herself with her kissing money and send them in Haley's name.

The most powerful magic of life is love. I am so proud that my very first Nocturne, *Son of the Shadows*, celebrates the essential truth that while love cannot conquer all, it can heal all. I believe this. Love can, and will, change the world. And love is priceless. It is the gift that Isabelle offers Jean-Marc. He has much to teach her so that she can survive in his world, but what she offers him can create a new world—their world.

I hope you enjoy this book half as much as I enjoyed paying my daughter oodles of quarters...for Haley's roses.

With my warmest wishes,

Nancy

For Belle, the most beautiful rose in the garden

Jean-Marc

I am Jean-Marc de Devereaux, Guardian of the House of the Shadows. As the leader of my ancient family, it is my duty to protect my people. We are Gifted—magic users—and we are under siege.

Through the centuries, Gifted families, tribes and clans the world over have walked among the Ungifted, our term for normal human beings. Few of them have any idea that we use magic as naturally as they breathe. Nor that we have served as their first line of defense against the Supernaturals—vampires, werewolves and demons.

For the most part.

The House of the Shadows—*La Maison des Ombres*—was founded in France during the Middle Ages, one of three French noble Gifted families. The other two are the House of the Flames and the House of the Blood. The Flames are descended from the Bouvards, once proud

warriors, now weakened and fearful. The Blood are the
Malchances, skilled in the darkest of arts. The Bouvards
fought beside Jehanne d'Arc—Joan of Arc—and she is
their patroness. On May 23, 1430, a Malchance captured
her and handed her over to her enemies. She was burned
at the stake.

My House, the House of the Shadows, stayed out of the
fighting, though we moved in the background, arranging
alliances and shedding friends who were no longer useful.
Yes, of course we killed our enemies, but rarely with
swords. That has changed.

My House is adept at invading dreams and creating
visions. We are master manipulators. Once we were the
diplomats of the Gifted world. I myself was called to serve
as the hated Regent of the Flames, when Isabelle, their
heiress, could not be found and their current *Gardienne*
hovered on the brink of death. Assassins targeted me. They
are all dead.

Like the Flames and the Blood, we Shadows are slow-
aging, quick-healing warriors. We are powerful fighters,
ruthless in battle.

Which is a lucky thing. Because when I finally located
Isabelle, I put her life—and my love for her—above my
duty, and I started a war.

It rages to this day.

Prologue

The Castle of the House of the Blood
Haiti

Down deep in the dungeons of Castle Malchance, Jean-Marc de Devereaux's soul thrashed inside the Chalice of the Blood. Although the golden, pulsing mass had been ripped from his living body, he could still see, hear, smell and feel everything around him. The pain was unbelievable. Half-mad with agony, he had to think through it, find a way to escape and get back to New Orleans. To Isabelle. By the Patron, what was happening to her?

Isabelle—who called herself Izzy—grew up in Brooklyn, unaware of her Gifted heritage, dreaming only of entering the Police Academy and perhaps marrying Pat, her boyfriend. Jean-Marc had been ordered by the Grand Covenate, the governing body of the Gifted, to track her down. She wanted no part of his world, and he understood why.

I brought her into this, he thought, cursing himself. *But I had to. Her enemies would have killed her. Who knew she had a twin, bent on her destruction?*

Jean-Marc's captor, Isabelle's twin Lilliane, danced in the dungeon torchlight. Wearing elaborate robes of black satin embroidered with red skulls, a black crown with silver skulls riding a black veil that covered her face, she laughed low in her throat like the madwoman she was and gazed down hungrily into the Chalice.

"Ah, *mon beau,* if we could have taken your magnificent body as well as your ferocious soul, I would give you such pleasure before I feed you to Le Devourer," she murmured, as she ran her tongue around the rim of the Chalice, her eyes heavy with lust. He could feel her heat, smell her desire.

"I have never slept with a Gifted male as powerful as you. Think of the child we could make, you and I. I am half Blood and half Flames, like my accursed sister. And you are Shadows. Our child would be a baby born of all three Houses—the Flames, the Blood and the Shadows. A child of Shadows born, destined to rule over thousands of Gifted."

She sighed with pleasure and threw back her head. "Such a dream," she whispered. Then her smile faded, and her features hardened. "Unfortunately you will never father children. In fact, your soul won't last another quarter hour. I have promised it to Le Devourer, and he always gets what he wants."

Not this time. Not this soul, Jean-Marc vowed.

It was difficult to stay lucid when he was in so much pain. He would sell this soul of his to have fists to fight with, a mouth to utter magical incantations and kill Lilliane on the spot.

He had seen soulless living men. He had listened to them shriek and jabber, drowning in physical pain and spiritual anguish. They begged for their souls, would promise anything, everything, if only it would stop, it would stop, it would stop.

Total oblivion was their best hope. An end to the agony. But he could not go into that good night.

I can't leave Isabelle to face the nightmare alone.

Mon Roi Gris, he prayed to his own demon patron. *Écoutez-moi.* Hear me. He strained for a sign that the Grey King was with him, but there was none. He was completely alone.

So be it.

"*Alors,* it's time," Lilliane whispered.

She plucked up the Chalice with one hand and lifted her skirts with the other, tripping barefoot up the dungeon stairs and pushing open the ornately carved ebony door. Her honor guard snapped to attention—dark, handsome Gifted men in full battle armor and helmets with their visors up. Uzis were slung against their chests, and they wore thick belts equipped with clips of ammo and grenades. Jean-Marc knew their magical arsenals of spells and fireballs were far more destructive than their Ungifted submachine guns and Magnum .357s. But when one was guarding one's queen, one took no chances.

Half a dozen torch-bearing *bokor* priests and priestesses joined the procession, regaled in their voodoo finery—billowing black robes sewn with mirrors, animal heads and chicken claws; headdresses of crow feathers, crocodile skulls and human bones.

The tallest, a man, stepped forward, his face hidden by a grotesquely carved wooden mask with a pointed nose, almond eyes and a rictus smile decorated with human teeth. Around his neck he wore a *gris-gris* of chicken feet. The priestess beside him held out a simple painted black gourd, and a noxious odor wafted from it. He dipped his fingers and flicked them at Lilliane, who curtsied.

"Merci," she said humbly, though she was convulsing with silent laughter.

The company moved swiftly down a foul-smelling corridor. Then they burst out into the moonlight, and the thirteen hundred members of the Malchance family—the House of the Blood—raised their voices in salutation.

"Lilliane!" they thundered. They could barely move, crammed as they were into the courtyard of the ancient medieval castle that was the family seat. The Knights Templar had abandoned it in 1301, after their leader had been burned at the stake for sorcery.

In the Devereaux way of Seeing, Jean-Marc's perspective shifted. Though he knew he hadn't left the Chalice, he looked down on the island as if he were flying. He Saw lines of zombies roped together beside the stone stairs that led to the voodoo altar. Voodoo drums pounded all over the island; *loa*—voodoo gods—slithered in their snake shapes through the plantation cane rustling in the night wind; and Ungifted danced around enormous bonfires blazing along the beaches. The island of Haiti had seen much death, but the death of the soul of a Gifted Guardian was a once-in-a-lifetime event.

Fly! Leave! Jean-Marc commanded himself. His soul batted the sides of the Chalice like a caged falcon. Then all his senses tumbled from the sky, confined to the Chalice, as Lilliane raised it, saluting her family. Their cries thundered and echoed over the courtyard.

"Lilliane! Lilliane!" The night shuddered with her name. A miasma of black magic saturated the air.

"Here we go, Jean-Marc," she whispered, dancing up the stairs with the chief *bokor* at her side.

With a flourish, she reached into the chalice and plucked up Jean-Marc's soul, giving it a shake that ignited every point of pain to blistering intensity.

"Devereaux is ours!" Her voice rang out. "We will feed him to Le Devourer and he will suffer eternally!"

"Oui!" the people cheered. *"Vive, Le Devourer! Vive, Lilliane!"*

The crowd surged forward, shrieking; the voodoo drums pounded. Overcome, clumps of people broke into gyrations, collapsing and writhing on the ground. Madness and evil infected the House of the Blood. They had pledged their loyalty to the Forces of Darkness, and sooner or later, that choice would destroy them. Of that, Jean-Marc had no doubt.

Lilliane and her chief priest approached the altar. Silver hands, crosses, X's, and silver eyes decorated the altar. Black mambo serpents and cockerels hissed in their cages on top of the shrine, upon which burned crimson candles.

A dead raven lay bleeding on the altar. Lilliane's ceremonial dagger, her athame, protruded dead center from its chest. She yanked the athame out of the raven's body. Blood dripped onto the stone.

In the courtyard below, the raised voices of the House of the Blood shook the stones of the temple and the ground beneath their feet shifted and tottered.

"Devereaux, là-bas! Fils des Ombres, là-bas!" Down with Devereaux, Son of the Shadows! Their enemy must suffer horribly, terribly. No compassion. No quarter.

"Adieu," Lilliane whispered to Jean-Marc.

Then she turned the athame tip down and stabbed Jean-Marc's soul with savage violence. The pain catapulted him out of the world and beyond the universe—the pain of soul mutilation was indescribable. She gave him no chance for recovery; her people pushed forward with their arms raised toward her, shrieking, weeping with hatred, urging her on.

"This is for my dead husband, murdered by this man and his woman!" she screamed. "By Isabelle, my own twin sister! I will do this to her next!"

"Isabelle là-bas!" the people chanted. *"Jean-Marc là-bas!"*

Then the shadow of a huge red demon flared around Jean-Marc like a firestorm. With Seeing altered by magic and pain, he saw flashes of black fangs, smoking horns and an enormous, six-fingered scarlet hand tipped with talons as sharp as scimitars reaching for him. The stench assaulted him: sulfur and carrion, rotten blood, evil. The thing was Le Devourer, Lilliane's patron. His hand closed around Jean-Marc's soul, and its talons slashed through the radiant mass.

Jean-Marc rocketed past sanity from the violation. He had no thoughts, no emotions. He ceased, because being was too horrible. He didn't know where he was. He didn't know who he was. He didn't know that he was.

But one thing remained: a woman's name, and he shouted it with the voice of the possessed:

"Isabelle!"

Chapter 1

The Bayou, New Orleans

Isabelle.

—Exquisite warmth grasped him as he thrust into silken moistness. Gentle and yielding, creamy and sweet, the rhythm surged through him; pleasure rode him, pleasure; arching for it, grasping and gasping. Oranges and roses filled his nostrils. He was dizzy with the scent and drunk on the honey taste of femininity, sweet and delectable—

—*ma vie, ma coeur, ma femme*—

—as it all came roaring back through him—lust and desire, wanton appetite and greed—for more, to have it all, to take what he wanted for as long as he wanted even if it killed her—

Die giving to me! I will have you until you are nothing!

He heard Isabelle sobbing and felt her weight against him as she collapsed, and then was silent.

Jean-Marc de Devereaux, Guardian of the House of the Shadows, was back.

Not all of me, he thought, flooding with awareness as his eyelids flickered. Deep in the center of his soul, a huge chunk was missing, seized by Le Devourer. He felt it as keenly as if someone had cut out his heart. But the space was not empty. Darkness—evil—had flooded in to take its place. He had been changed, tainted, and he knew what Isabelle had tried to do, for him.

"Ah, *non,*" he moaned in a ragged voice, as he gathered up the unconscious woman. She had fainted, her head hanging back over his arm, revealing her long, white neck. She looked exactly like her sister, Lilliane, except that her face was mottled and bruised, and her lips were swollen and bloody. Her riots of black curls were tipped in blood— his blood—black beneath the bone-white bayou moon.

"Why?" he whispered hoarsely against her temple as he cradled her. For he knew that she had magically halted his soul's total destruction over a thousand miles away, in Haiti. But at a terrible price.

His hands balled into fists and for a sweeping moment, he could hardly contain his anger. It was so overwhelming that he barely stopped himself from throwing Isabelle on the ground and choking her with his bare hands. She was not the one he hated with every fiber of his damaged soul, but the darkness was on him. He could barely control it.

Isabelle's eyelashes fluttered like hummingbirds against the gray circles above her cheekbones. She exhaled and turned her head. Her limpid brown eyes flecked with gold stared into his, and it calmed his fury just enough. He grabbed her hand and held it against his heart.

"How could you do that?" he growled, and, once more, his anger nearly got the best of him. He fought not to grab her shoulders and shake her until her teeth broke. "What were you thinking?"

Her lips moved soundlessly. Her eyes flashed opened and she blinked hard, staring at him in the gauzy moonlight. He tried to read her thoughts and couldn't.

With a shaking hand, she reached for something on the ground—it was a white satin robe embroidered with the entwined symbols of their Houses: three flames for hers and a dove for his. As she pulled the robe around her shoulders, she gingerly slid off his body. His penis slipped from inside her moist core of heat and droplets of his own seed dribbled onto his thigh.

Then she looked from his face to the black bayou around them, to the carnage and the blood. Not far from her, a man dressed in a black catsuit and body armor lay facedown in the mud, the back of his head covered by the fallen limb of a cypress tree. He was Malchance, the enemy. His submachine gun lay inches away from his limp hand. Another Malchance lay sprawled on his back, the deep gouge in his abdomen serving as evidence of a werewolf attack.

More Malchance casualties lay splayed around them, coated with mud and gore. A few floated facedown in the murky swamp water, not yet eaten by the gators. He wondered why they didn't sink beneath the weight of their armor, and his warrior's mind took note: maybe the Malchances had developed some kind of super-lightweight armor. He'd have to look into that later.

Hidden by cypress trees strangled with vines and moss, werewolves howled with grief and fury over their severe losses. Jean-Marc spoke their language, and he knew they were preparing for the second wave of the attack.

Cringing, Isabelle stared down at her own nakedness and back up to his face. Fear rolled off her in waves, and he reflexively wove a calming spell. The scents of oranges and roses billowed in the space between them. He created a sphere of light as well, and it floated above his palm as he approached her.

"It's all right," he whispered, although that was a terrible lie. He had never lied to her before, ever. "*Bon, écoutes,* listen, we have to get out of here as fast as we can. They're coming after you. We need to move *now.*"

She swallowed hard and took a ragged, deep breath.

"What are you talking about? Who are you?" she asked him.

"*Comment?*" he asked incredulously.

She looked even more frightened. Her hands shook as she clutched the robe around herself, glancing downward toward her thighs, then pushing to her feet and stumbling backward in the mud, away from him.

"Did you just…you *raped* me…*who the hell are you?*"

Then she screamed as she nearly fell on top of Pat Kittrell, her NYPD detective lover. Pat had tracked her down in a misguided attempt to help; for his trouble he had been severely beaten, and he lay near death.

"*Calme-toi.* I'll explain. You've had a terrible shock," Jean-Marc said as she stepped around Pat, backing away. He was surprised at her seeming indifference to his grievous condition; she loved Pat.

Almost as much as she loved him.

He walked toward her, aware that his nudity was upsetting her. The darkness in his soul reveled in lust and his body began to respond. Pulling himself back down, he snapped his fingers and dark blue Devereaux body armor appeared over a catsuit. She gaped at him as if she'd never seen magic in her life. He started to pick up Kittrell's Uzi, then realized how that would look to her, so he left it in the mud, and sent more calming energy in her direction, although he felt anything but calm himself.

"You've had a shock, Isabelle," he repeated. "You need to collect yourself. We need to plan."

"Jean-Marc!"

It was his dusky-hued cousin, Alain, who broke from the tangles of trees and ferns. Alain's white teeth seemed to float in the ebony shadows. "You did it, Isabelle! *Ma belle!* You are magnificent!" Overjoyed, he flung his arms around Isabelle and kissed her cheek, his dreadlocks flying. She went rigid, her eyes enormous, her mouth an O of utter shock.

"Get away from me!" She angled a karate-style knife-hand strike at Alain's windpipe. Alain's magical aura of deep indigo flared, protecting him as he darted out of her range. She pursued, lunging at him, slipping and sliding in the mud, glancing around as if she were searching for a weapon.

"Touch me again and I'll kill you." It was an empty threat, but Alain was clearly no less stunned. He looked from her to Jean-Marc and back again with palms held up in front of him.

"You're confused. It must be the toll of the spell," he said slowly. "It's me, Alain, remember me? You've done a wonderful thing. You brought him back. *Merci, merci bien, Gardienne.*"

Waves of tranquilizing magic flowed from Alain's palms in Isabelle's direction, and the scent of oranges and roses intensified. Jean-Marc watched her fight it. First she remained stiff, giving her head a shake, then she swayed, enchanted, as her lids grew heavy and her lips parted. Allowing himself to be affected by Alain's spell—he needed soothing; he was a mess—Jean-Marc's aura became visible as well—deep, vibrant blue…until streaks in the color shifted and darkened—a blacker shadow, a pall of pure evil.

Alain stared at him in horror, lowering his hands, forgetting what he was doing. "My cousin…" he whispered.

"You see it." Jean-Marc held out his hands. The blackness played over his aura, smearing the vibrant Devereaux blue.

"Ah, *non*. What went wrong?" Alain asked in an agonized voice. "We moved fast to recapture your soul."

Idiot! the darkness inside him growled at Alain. *Have you no imagination, no idea what your bungling has done to me?*

"Lilliane moved faster, to sacrifice it to her patron," Jean-Marc replied, ignoring the damning voice inside his head. "He's called Le Devourer, and he is an eater of souls. He tore out part of it, and the void filled with his essence. Demonic evil."

"That cannot be," Alain protested, his voice hollow with disbelief. "Such things…they don't happen."

"It *has* happened," Jean-Marc replied, as the horrible presence throbbed and pulsed inside his being. He had been mutilated, violated…by Isabelle's own sister.

"Isabelle is half Malchance," Alain said slowly. Perhaps he heard the echo of her name in Jean-Marc's thoughts. "Could it be possible she gave you part of *her* soul?"

"The Malchances walk with darkness, it is true," Jean-Marc answered. "But this is beyond even them."

Jean-Marc studied Isabelle, whose head bobbed toward her chest, starting at the crown of her head, to her cheeks slashed with blood like war paint, to the cleavage of her breasts and her delicate hands. He moved his hands in a spell of his own, willing her aura to reveal itself. But there was nothing. He tried again. He couldn't believe it. *She had no aura.* There was no such thing as a Gifted person who didn't have an aura.

"Alors," Alain choked out, his hand covering his mouth. He looked as if he might be sick.

Fresh rage surged through Jean-Marc at his cousin's stupidity and weakness. He raked his hands through the matted curls of his shoulder-length black hair, pulling it away from his left cheek, where it was plastered with blood. He took deep breaths, forcing himself to remain composed.

"Sex magic is the strongest magic we have," he said at last. "She took me when I was mindless and soulless. It's done something to her, too." He bared his teeth at Alain. "How could you tell her to do that?"

"I…" Alain swallowed hard and licked his lips, his body language alone betraying the fact that he knew he was at fault. But Jean-Marc could read his emotions, too, and he stank of guilt. "I didn't know…"

"Don't lie to me!" Jean-Marc thundered. And a voice inside him whispered insidiously, *Kill him.*

He ignored it, balling his fists, weaving a spell around the ravages of his soul to keep the voice at bay. *Oui,* he wanted to kill Alain. He wanted to maim him, torture him, make him beg for death—

"Alain," he said evenly, "don't lie to me."

Alain lowered his head in shame and nodded.

"You are not only my cousin, Jean-Marc, you are the leader of my family. How could I stand by and watch you suffer? You are my blood. I would have done anything to bring you back."

"Including risking her," Jean-Marc said.

"Oui," Alain confessed, raising his head. "Including that."

"Bâtard!" Jean-Marc bellowed. Hatred coursed through him like a live wire. He lost what little control he had achieved; he knew he was going to kill Alain here, now. And he was going to enjoy it.

His aura flared around his body like a nuclear detonation, and he hurled a fireball at Alain, who instantly held up his palms and created a protective barrier of shimmering blue. The fireball exploded against it, then disintegrated into sparks that winked out before they touched the ground.

"Jean-Marc, listen to me," Alain said, moving with his hands and body, strengthening the curtain of indigo that hung in the air between him and his cousin. "We'll get rid of the evil in your soul. We'll make you well and whole. But for now, you must fight it."

"I am trying," Jean-Marc said through clenched teeth. Sweat beaded his brow. "Oh, gods, I can hardly bear this."

"Bear it," Alain begged him. *"Écoutes,* I've been on recon. It's as the werewolves say. We've defeated the Malchances that were here in the bayou, but the Malchance troops inside the Flames' headquarters are escaping. They're on their way here, and the House of the Flames are pursuing them. The Flames may be loyal to Isabelle, but then again, since she is half Malchance, they may not. And if not, there's no telling what they'll do to Isabelle if they capture her."

And to us, Alain could have added, but he and Jean-Marc were soldiers. It went without saying that they stood in harm's way.

Jean-Marc nodded. *"Alors,* Isabelle," he began, then

looked around. She was gone. "*Putain de merde,* where is she? Isabelle!"

Both men broke into a run. The noise in the bayou ratcheted up, as if sensing that something more had happened, something worse. Nutria screamed from the cypress trees; a gator rushed a floating body and dragged it underwater. Crashing through the undergrowth, were-wolves howled.

We have dead, and we will kill our enemies! Stay out of the bayou unless you're one of us!

Jean-Marc howled back, telling them to find Isabelle. Find her, subdue her and get her out of there by any means necessary.

Dizzy and nauseated, she fled as wolf howls chased after her. He had hypnotized her but she'd broken out of it; there was no telling what he'd planned to do to her next. He and that guy with the dreadlocks—Alain—it was like a horror movie, with men in armor slaughtered all around her, and that man raping her....

Tree branches whipped her face. She fell into the mud on her hands and knees, twisting her ankle, and the pain shot up into her hip socket. Grunting, she got back up, losing the robe she'd covered herself with. Now she was completely naked, lost in a swamp that shook and screamed like a living creature. She didn't know who she was, or where she was, but she knew she had been violated, and she was still in terrible danger.

They called me Isabelle, she thought, *but that's wrong. That's not my name. My name is...*

She couldn't remember. Why couldn't she remember her own name? Trauma. From the rape. And whatever else had happened to her. Those two men...what had they been talking about? What had they done to her?

Run for your life. Get out of here, she told herself. *You're all alone, and you don't know who you are. You're all alone, and—*

No.

She wasn't alone. Someone had come here to save her.

Suddenly the face of the man she had almost fallen on top of blossomed in her mind. The man with the white-blond hair, so terribly wounded she hadn't been certain he was alive. He had come here from somewhere else to help her. He wasn't part of this. He was like her.

And when he smiled the world was brighter, and he made love to her as if she were a goddess.

And he calls me Izzy. That's my name. Izzy. I'm in love with him. I have to go back for him.

She had to get him away from those rapists and murderers. And the others who were coming. For there were others, searching for her at this very moment. She knew that, too. And they wanted to destroy her.

"Isabelle!" It was the man who had raped her, the one called Jean-Marc. His voice sent a frozen flash fire down her spine, and she whimpered, panicking. He was coming after her.

"This is just a dream," she whispered aloud. "Just a terrible dream. I'm going to wake up."

But it was no dream. She was hurt, and cold. She felt the sharp prick of a twig beneath her insole as she staggered forward, searching the wild landscape for an escape route. The trees were dripping with cold water. It had rained. Why couldn't she remember the rain?

"Isabelle!" Jean-Marc's voice chased her. Wolf howls rattled her bones. They were raging, shrieking…and they were coming closer.

"Oh God, oh God," she blurted, grabbing up wild riots of hair away from her face. Her teeth were chattering.

Get it together, she ordered herself. *There are dead soldiers everywhere. Get a gun. Blow their heads off and save the blond man.*

Izzy thrashed through a wall of vines and tree limbs, arms flailing, legs kicking, until she broke through. Then she skidded to a halt at the horrifying spectacle before her: spread-eagled on a large fallen tree trunk, his arms and legs dangling, a gagged man lay whining like a wounded dog with his eyes wide-open—eyes that were a milky-white, with no color in them, no sight. The tatters of a shredded windbreaker with NOPD—New Orleans Police Department—stitched over the breast fluttered in the night breeze. There was a thick gash across his chest and dried blood on the tree trunk.

She turned and retched. On the ground in front of the tree trunk, another man, this one unnaturally handsome, with short, tawny hair, lay limp in black leather battle armor with a patch on his biceps of a black Chalice decorated with black and red skulls. His eyes were closed. There were some singed books scattered beside him, and some knives, bells, pieces of crystal and what smelled like very foul incense.

And a gun.

It was a wicked black revolver. The grip was ivory, etched with the image of a short-haired young girl in medieval armor, her helmet under her arm. Izzy felt a tug in her mind. The eyes of the girl caught her gaze, held her, and her chest tightened with inexplicable emotion—despair, and loss. Tears welled, but she shook them away. She had to stay focused if she wanted to live…and to save the blond man.

This is my gun, she knew suddenly. *It's called a Medusa.*

"Isabelle!" Jean-Marc called, closer still. The other man—Alain—joined him. She heard them crashing through the forest, hunting her. Jean-Marc thundered at Alain in French, and she realized that she could understand him. He was threatening to kill him, kill Alain, and send his soul to hell.

He's insane, she thought, crouching down behind the tree trunk. She cracked open the gun, and saw that the cylinder was empty.

Ammo. I need ammo.

Laying the gun in her lap, she rooted around, lifting up the books, then gingerly raising the right arm of the dead man. *Yes.* It was almost as if he had been trying to hide the olive-green box of 9 mm cartridges, but it was hers now. She didn't know how she knew the caliber of the ammo, or that it would work in the Medusa. Right now, she didn't care. Moving rapidly, as if she had done it all her life, she loaded six cartridges into the empty chambers with surprisingly steady hands. Then she slipped the cylinder back into the frame with a click and rose to a high crouch, staring into the darkness for the first sign of the madman.

A hand clamped on her shoulder. Without even thinking about it, she windmilled around, breaking contact and fired. The report echoed like a whip crack through the swamp.

Her attacker was a dark-skinned woman with platinum hair; she threw back her head and howled like a wolf as the force of the bullet flung her backward, then slammed her against what appeared to be an enormous conga drum painted with black and red symbols. She landed in a pile of ashes, eyes wide-open, mouth working as blood streamed down her chest. Then she began to whimper and pant like a wounded animal as her eyes rolled back in her head.

"Oh God," Izzy whispered, nearly dropping the gun.

For a moment she stood transfixed, unable to process what she had just done. Clutching the revolver, she ran to the woman's side and stared down at her. The woman's breathing was fluttery and labored. Her face was shiny with perspiration and her dark skin was turning a deep shade of gray. As Izzy looked down on her in the moonlight, she began to jerk as if she were having a seizure.

Whether friend or foe, she needed help. But Izzy debated, worried that her victim might still be able to hypnotize her the way Jean-Marc had done, or hurl a ball of fire.

Cloaked by the forest, howling and shouting made her ears throb and she bolted, grappling with another tangled web of slick vines and twisting tree branches.

The wounded woman's whimpering grew louder, like a plea for help, panic at being abandoned. Izzy's heart caught and sank to her feet. She couldn't let this woman die. No matter the cost to her, the danger…

They're coming. They'll take care of her.

But they weren't here yet, and the woman might not have that much time. She was bleeding badly.

"Damn it," Izzy whispered, turning around.

She looked at her. The woman was gurgling and gasping. Blood pooled beneath her in the ashes, and her eyelids flickered. Her lips pressed together; dark bubbles foamed at the corners of her mouth.

I can't stay. I have to get back to the man, Izzy thought. *I have to save him from those evil men.*

But this woman needed her now.

Moaning a feeble protest, she dashed back to the woman's side and dropped down to her knees. She saw the bullet hole above her heart and knew that the exit wound would be much worse—how she knew, she had no idea—

but she had to stop the blood flow. She clasped her hands one over the other and pressed them over the wound. Hot blood pumped between her fingertips, the force of it startling her. Rising on her knees, she clamped down harder.

The forest rustled and shook, as if something enormous was on its way. She crouched over the woman, naked and terrified, and she began to lose it, shaking, panting.

Stay with it, she ordered herself. *You're her only hope.*

But I have to get to the man.

She began to spin out of control, confronted with two equally high priorities. *He was lying so still...his body can go for four to seven minutes without oxygen, and then he's dead...*

"I have to go," she said aloud.

The woman groaned and half opened her eyes. They looked strange, unworldly, with dark irises that swallowed her pupils. Still, there was light in them, and Izzy studied the pain and fear in her gasping, grimacing expression.

I put that pain there. I shot her.

The woman's mouth moved. "Andre," she whispered faintly, as her eyes rolled back in her head.

The world tilted and shifted as Izzy swallowed hard. For the time being, her decision was made.

"All right, then. I won't leave you," Izzy promised.

Chapter 2

The gunshot and the howls startled Jean-Marc out of the murderous tirade directed at his cousin. He shifted his direction toward the sound, realizing that Isabelle had found a gun, and that she had shot one of the pack. Her victim was in bigger trouble if it was her Medusa, a versatile weapon whose barrel could hold multiple calibers of ammunition—ammo that carried not only a physical payload, but magical spells that could kill demons and stop hearts.

"*Vite,* Alain!"

He crashed through the underbrush, the faces of his werewolf friends racing through his mind. Leaping over a tree root, he launched his perception into the air and looked down on the bayou, searching for her, then Seeing her head bent over a prone figure. He couldn't tell who it was; but he—or she—wore no armor. A werewolf most likely, then.

Non, non. He was sickened, enraged…and filled with
horror. He had sworn to protect the werewolves of New
Orleans. No one ever had, despite the centuries-old pledge
of the House of the Flames "to stand between *le loup-
garou* and *le Diable* Himself." Like so much else, the
Bouvards had failed to honor their word, but, when Jean-
Marc arrived to serve as Regent, he had immediately put
the Cajun werewolves under his personal protection.

"Alain! Damn you, hurry up!"

As he loped through the dense live oaks and cypresses,
sloshing over loamy bayou earth, he prepared a fireball and
clenched it in his fist like a grenade, knowing that he would
never use it directly against Isabelle herself. But he might
have to slow her down if she tried to shoot him with the
Medusa. And if a battle-maddened, grief-stricken
werewolf came after her, he knew what his choice must be
there, too, although he was as close to the Cajun pack as
if they were his blood family.

But she…she was his life.

And then he pushed himself into Isabelle's mind and
Saw her surroundings as she saw them. He knew where she
was lurking—behind the makeshift sacrificial altar where
an unsouled New Orleans police officer writhed in agony
at this very moment. There was someone on the ground,
lying in a pool of blood, and she was trying to staunch the
wound— *Ah non, it's Caresse!*

Fury roared inside him like a demon. Caresse was the
mate of Andre, the alpha werewolf, and this crazed *bitch*
had shot her. She deserved to have her neck wrung.

Do it, said the voice inside his head. *Kill her.*

Calme-toi, he told himself as he clenched and un-
clenched his fists. *The blackness is on you. Calme-toi.*

He knew she might shoot him. He could stop her with

a burst of magical energy, but the first time he had done such a thing, he had stopped her heart.

He eased into her line of sight, muscles tensed for battle, fireball in his fist.

"Stop! Stop right there!" she ordered, grabbing her Medusa and rising just enough to rest her elbows on the trunk so she could take aim. Moonlight dappled her face as she stared him down. Her chest was heaving. She was naked, covered with blood and mud, and her hands were shaking.

"Mes amis!" Jean-Marc called, hoping to get through to any werewolf who was coming after her. *"Je suis Jean-Marc! Je suis là!"* My friends, I am Jean-Marc. I am here. He howled in the werewolves' language, warning them, preparing him.

Then Andre, the wolf pack's alpha, staggered into the clearing in his human form. He took one look at Isabelle, and Caresse bleeding beside her, and rushed toward them.

"Caresse, *ma femme,*" Andre said. "Ah, *non. Non, non.*" He took a step forward. Another, each one a lurch of traumatized outrage. "Who did this, *ma petite?*"

Isabelle gestured at him with her gun.

"Stop right there," she ordered. "Both of you. And raise your hands."

"Andre," Jean-Marc warned, eyeing the Medusa, "keep back."

"Jolie, what are you doing?" Andre gasped at Isabelle. "What happened?"

"Back," she said, aiming at him. To Jean-Marc, "Get rid of that ball of fire. If you do *anything,* make one move, I'll shoot him."

"Jean-Marc, what is wrong with her? Is she bewitched?" Andre demanded. "Isabelle, it's *us.*"

"I am. I'm what's wrong with her," Jean-Marc said dully. He was sorry he had taught her how to defend herself so well. He lifted his hands above his head. The fireball floated for a second or two, then extinguished. He heard the poor, gibbering police officer on the altar and sent out a spell to quiet the man. He could do nothing more to give him peace. If the man died without his soul, he would thrash throughout eternity in mindless anguish.

That would have been my fate, he reminded himself, *if Alain and Isabelle had not intervened.*

Non, a voice whispered inside his head. *Your eternity would have been glorious. An unending existence of pleasure. They stopped it. They robbed you.*

He shut out the insinuating whispers and focused on Isabelle. By his patron the Grey King, despite everything, she was uncannily beautiful, possessing a light that had long ago abandoned Lilliane, if it had ever been there in the first place. He had no idea why his calming spell on her had lost its potency, allowing her to run from him. Perhaps it was because she was half Bouvard and half Malchance, an unknown quantity to him.

"And now?" he asked her. "They are coming, Isabelle."

Her chest rose and fell. Her nostrils flared. He honed in on her, intent, trying to See inside her.

I need to get to him, Isabelle thought.

Jean-Marc knew she wasn't sending out her thoughts. Maybe she had forgotten that he could read her mind if she neglected to cloak it. But he received a clear image of Pat Kittrell's face and absorbed Isabelle's intense fear for his life. So something of her past had resurfaced. Perhaps that was a sign that the shock was wearing off. He tried to push Pat's image more firmly into her mind, cloud her actions with an overwhelming urgency to get to him. He would manipulate her without compunction if it served his ends—to keep her alive and save Caresse.

"Let us tend to her," Jean-Marc said. "Then I swear I'll find Pat for you." He sensed her confusion and sent out more images into her mind—Pat, struggling for breath, calling her name, *Izzy.* "Pat. Your lover. The man you need to save."

She wavered. He felt her anguish, her bewilderment, as if they were physical entities tearing at his skin, his hair, and he knew that while the connection between them had weakened, it was not gone. He concentrated, trying to strengthen it with magical energy, make her trust him, make her listen.

"He doesn't call me Isabelle," she said tightly. "*You* do." She was quiet a moment. "He calls me Izzy."

So she had some memory, then.

"Put the gun down, Izzy," he said, as calmly as he could manage. He glanced back down at Caresse, whose face was turning blue. His heart skipped a beat. The Shadows weren't healers and never had been, but even he could see that Caresse had little time left. "She needs—"

His words were cut off as the world exploded.

Izzy screamed.

The mud to her left geysered upward in a plume; the bayou water to her right shot straight up as if from a broken fire hydrant. The ground beneath her feet shook so violently that she dropped to her knees. Instinctively she flattened against the mud, shouting, "Incoming! Incoming! Duck and cover!" As soon as she was stable, she made a tripod with her elbows and shot off another round with her Medusa.

Its report was soundless, but she'd hit a target: something in the darkness bellowed with pain. As if in reply, scarlet pinwheels of light blossomed above drooping cypress treetops, obliterating the moon. White and red flares peppered the landscape like dueling fireworks. She shot off more rounds, having no idea what was coming yet sure that they meant to kill her.

They who? What's happening?

Something sizzled along the length of her body, breaking her concentration. She looked down as a catsuit and body armor appeared fully formed on her body. She yelled and batted at it, but it was on to stay, and after a couple of seconds she realized it wasn't hurting her in any way and was preferable to being naked. It was identical to Jean-Marc's except that on the bicep of the clinging second-skin, there was some kind of patch depicting a trio of white flames that looked very familiar.

I belong here, she thought, jerking as a layer of deep indigo light completely surrounded her. *Oh, my God, is that my aura?*

"Protect yourself!" Jean-Marc leaped in front of her, his back to her as he spread his legs wide and shot off rounds from an Uzi he hadn't had before. He followed them with one of the balls of fire he could make with his hands. "Make a shield *now!*"

She had no idea what he was talking about, and no time to wonder about it, as an incoming blur of white light slammed into the field of blue. Panic turned her blood to ice as she caught her breath, ducked her head and pulled the trigger—realizing too late that Jean-Marc stood directly in her line of fire.

"Arête!" he yelled at her, as he dove for the mud. Landing on his belly, he rolled onto his left elbow, his face contorted in a combination of terror and fury. A ball of fire erupted from his right hand, engulfing the space between them. Heat slapped her icy face and she reflexively looped

her finger around the trigger as he lobbed a second fireball. A tiny object pierced the center of the fiery globe and exploded—it was her 9 mm cartridge—and he chanted in a language she didn't understand, speaking rapidly and firmly as he pointed his fingers at her.

Invisible hands grabbed her and propelled her into the air. Five feet above his prone body, she hovered in smoke for a few heartbeats, and then she plummeted, landing beside him in the mud. Shifting patterns of blue and black undulated in her field of vision as he flung his arm around her and pressed her to the ground.

"Don't shoot at me!"

She smelled oranges, roses, hot metal, oil and something else—blood and death. He moved his fingers in a circle and the gun shot out of her grasp. She lunged for it as he grabbed it out of the air.

"Give that back!" she bellowed, lunging at him, slithering and sliding in the mud as she scrambled over his body and grabbed at the gun. He wrapped his free hand around her forearm, pushed himself to a standing position and dragged her toward the closest tangle of bayou undergrowth. When the catsuit and armor had appeared, so had boots; inside them, her stockinged feet were cut and bleeding. He turned to her, rage spinning in his dark, hooded eyes. His white teeth were clenched and he looked horrifically feral, more like an animal than a man. His chest began to heave, his hand to tighten around her arm. Painfully.

"Ow," she blurted, her knees buckling.

Glaring at her like a madman, he held her upright and shook her hard. Her head snapped back and forth; blindly she batted at him, then began to kick at his shins, slipping and sliding over wet leaves and wetter earth as he kept her gun out of reach. His hard features blazed with fury and he shook her again, hard.

"You shouldn't have done it. He shouldn't have let you." He was growling the words at her. "I could just…by the Grey King…*je suis fou…*" He bared his teeth and cold, hard fear smacked against each vertebra in her spine like a steel mallet on ice cubes.

He's inhuman, she thought. *Werewolf. Monster.*

"Jean-Marc, *calme-toi,*" said a voice behind them—the dark-skinned man with the dreadlocks, Alain, had appeared and was sprawled on the ground beside the woman she had shot. The other man, Andre, had fallen down beside him. "Find your center. Pull yourself out of the blackness. I need help here. Caresse is dying."

Jean-Marc whipped around, whirling her behind him like a rag doll as Andre erupted into an eardrum-shattering barrage of howls. His face began to lengthen; his eyes, to glow golden and fierce. His backbone popped through his skin as glossy, silvery-black fur sprouted in tufts along his face, his chest, his abdomen, his thighs. His fingernails stretched into claws.

Weaving and transforming, he lurched toward Jean-Marc and her. Where a man had stood, a hunched, demonic creature covered with glossy black fur roared at her and clacked the air with its elongating jaw.

Jean-Marc remained in front of her as deep indigo surrounded her. She looked through it, as if it were a veil draped in front of her face; then wisps of black drifted across her field of vision, like tattered lace or lazing smoke. Her ears buzzed; her skin burned and tingled as if she had fallen into a snowbank. Acid flooded her mouth. Rigid with fear, she stiffened and stumbled backward.

Hide, stay away, a voice whispered urgently.

She knew she mustn't let the blackness touch her. And yet something from deep within her urged her forward, tempted her to reach out her hand to it, let it taste of her, caress her…

It will feel wonderful, said a different voice, with velvety softness overlaid with lush desire. *There is nothing in this world that compares with it…let it have you….*

The tendril of black hovered at eye level between her and Jean-Marc's back; it turned itself toward her, revealing itself: it was an ebony serpent with glittering, jet-black eyes that blinked at her as it pulled back on itself, eyes gleaming, as if to strike—

Yessssss, you are ssssomewhere near, Issssssssssabelle…

She caught her breath and leaped backward, half falling out of the indigo as energy sizzled over her shoulders and the back of her head like steam. She had moved out of the bubble. The black snake struck, smacking against the blue barrier, and vanished with a hiss.

Blinking her eyes rapidly, she watched as Jean-Marc pointed the Medusa straight into the air, telegraphing that he had it, but was not going to immediately use it. Ten feet away, the creature that had been Andre wagged its enormous head back and forth, as if in refusal. It took another lurching step forward. Its growl vibrated through Izzy's boots.

"Andre, *c'est moi,*" Jean-Marc said in French. Then he himself growled, the implied threat laid over a warning. The werewolf answered, deep and angry, lowering its head as it stared at the woman lying in blood on the ground.

"Jean-Marc is trying to remind him that you didn't mean to hurt her," Alain translated. "And that she needs healing magic now, or she will die."

So she's not dead, Izzy thought with relief.

"I didn't mean to shoot her," she told him. "I know her, don't I? I know all of you." She ticked her head toward the werewolf, although she was too frightened to look directly at it. "I know him."

"Andre has risked his life to save yours more than once," Alain replied. "He promised to watch out for you, always. My cousin is reminding him of that now."

"I don't remember," she whispered, her mouth as dry as dust. *Who would want to remember any of this?*

Jean-Marc kept speaking to the werewolf, even, calm, firm. Alain moved his hands over the bleeding woman, never taking his eyes off the scene as it played out before him.

"Jean-Marc, I am at a loss. We need Bouvard magic." Alain shifted his dark eyes to Izzy. "Can you not help?"

"*Non,* she cannot, thanks to you," Jean-Marc replied bitterly. "Maybe I can."

He lowered the revolver to his side as he strode past the towering werewolf, which watched every move and kept growling, hunkering down slightly as if it were about to pounce. Jean-Marc ignored it, although Izzy had no idea how he could.

"Andre, I am attending to your mate," Jean-Marc said in English. Then he repeated the words in French. Next, he growled. The werewolf growled back, but it remained taut, its eyes darting around, its huge teeth glistening.

Jean-Marc moved his fingers and a bandage appeared— simply appeared—out of nowhere. He placed it against the wound and turned to Andre.

"*Et voilà,*" he said. Then he looked up at Izzy. "I'll make another shield for you. Stay inside this time." He began to move his fingers again.

She shook her head as she gestured at the still-glowing

layer of light, blue and ethereal. "There's something in it. Something bad."

"The Devourer's taint." He sighed heavily. Beside him, Alain steadfastly looked down, pressing his hand over the bandage. Blue light emanated from his palm. "The good news is that the 9 mm rounds must not be magical," Jean-Marc said. "Caresse's heart was not stopped."

A second explosion nearly shook Izzy off her feet. A third followed immediately after. She reached out and grabbed onto a tangle of vines, remembering then that she had hit someone with her second bullet. She darted into the thick tangle to find a man dressed in a black catsuit like hers, with black Bouvard body armor and their trio of flames insignia on the breast. He was lying on his back with his eyes open.

"Jean-Marc," she called.

He came to her side immediately, looked where she pointed and aimed his Uzi at the man. Kicking at him with his boot, he grunted, then kicked him hard. She flinched. The man did not.

"Dead." Jean-Marc was pleased.

She fell against the tree with a sob.

"Stay calm." His voice held no warmth. "This is a crisis situation. There are going to be casualties."

"This man. Caresse," she rasped.

"Caresse was a mistake. She frightened you. I think this man was trying to shoot you. The Bouvards are fanning out from their headquarters," he continued without pausing to indicate that he had moved to a new topic. With a jerk of his head, he looked over his shoulder. "Find a *Femme Blanche* if you can. That's Caresse's best hope."

He was speaking to the werewolf, which had begun to change back into the man, Andre. His muzzle shortened

and the fur covering his body began to recede—as if
sliding back inside his skin—before her eyes.

She said to him, "I'm so sorry."

The wolf growled low in its throat. She saw Andre's
eyes glistening in the mats of silvery-black fur.

"Stay in wolf form," Jean-Marc cut in. "You'll move
faster."

The werewolf threw back its head and howled to the
moon. It paced back and forth, like a gliding shadow, then
its muzzle stretched out again and the spark of humanity
in its eyes faded. With a heaving grunt, it dropped to its
forepaws and flashed into the brush.

Jean-Marc lingered beside her. Blood and moonlight
tinted the tight curls cascading to his shoulders, his large,
deep-set eyes drawing in light, returning nothing but steely
resolve. She smelled sweat and leather on him, a not un-
pleasant combination, and studied him, trying to remember
the past she shared with him.

Behind him, Alain lifted his palms and blue light
swirled in the centers, as if he were holding two flat
glowing discs. Flashes of azure glazed the high planes of
his cheeks and wide mouth with a purplish glow.

"Jean-Marc, I need you," Alain insisted. "I need help.
Please pray with me."

Pray?

He said to her, "Don't move. Don't run."

"Can I help?" she asked.

"Not with this," he replied, his voice emotionless. He
held his body taut as he strode to his cousin's side. He
lowered his head, his hair streaming crazily over his shoulders. Alain did the same, and both moved their lips as she
looked on. She wondered if they were praying to God.

She wiped her forehead with bloody fingertips and

leaned against a tree trunk, watching them. She was acutely aware that a man lay dead behind her—a man she had killed. Her stomach lurched, and she bent over, sickened, with an attack of dry heaves. How long had it been since she'd had anything to eat or drink? She had no idea.

Why can't I remember anything?

There was a rustle in the trees to her right, and she reached automatically for the gun—which was not there. Andre the silvery-black werewolf parted the underbrush, its eyes gleaming with moonlight as it stared at her for a moment, then chuffed at someone behind it.

A young, frightened woman dressed all in white appeared. She had gathered up the hem of a long, white satin robe in her hands, and her head was covered by a white veil. When she saw Izzy, her eyes filled with joy. She curtsied and lowered her head.

"Ma Gardienne," she said in a voice filled with awe. "I'm so glad to see that you're alive."

"Thank you," Izzy said, then, *"Merci."*

"We took back the mansion," the woman continued, with a flash of pride "But the Malchances have scattered into the bayou. It's not safe here, madame."

"Viens-ici," Jean-Marc called to the woman.

She raised her brows questioningly at Izzy. "With your permission?"

"Wait," Izzy said, and the woman froze. *What am I to her?* she wondered. *Some kind of leader, or queen?*

She turned to Jean-Marc. "You promised to take me to Pat."

He narrowed his eyes. She could almost feel his hatred—directed at her, or at Pat?—and she took a deep breath and raised her chin.

"I won't give this woman permission to help unless you come with me now," she said.

The werewolf growled menacingly as the woman in the veil stared in astonishment at Izzy.

"Madame, I must help her. I can feel her life force ebbing," she reported. "She is dying."

The werewolf slunk toward Izzy. As it came closer, the hair on the back of her neck prickled. Her heart thumped wildly. Biting her cheek, she forced herself to remain silent. She had thrown down her gauntlet, and it was the only weapon she had.

"There will be plenty of dying. This is the world of the Gifted. All we do is die. Or kill," Jean-Marc said angrily, rising and stomping past the werewolf. He patted the creature, then he whirled around and hurled a fireball directly at Izzy. She felt an electric shock run through her as she fell backward, landing hard on the soggy ground.

Just as unexpectedly, Jean-Marc straddled her, hands held over her face, glowing and white.

"Wh-what?" she managed.

"Good. You're breathing. Attend to her," he said to the woman in white, pointing at Caresse. "I'll fulfill the request of your beloved *Gardienne. Vite!*"

"Let go of me!" Izzy yelled, struggling, as he grabbed both her wrists in one of his.

"Tais-toi," he said. He scowled at the woman. "Do as I say! I am Jean-Marc de Devereaux, of the House of the Shadows!"

The woman looked questioningly at Izzy. *"Gardienne?"*

"Yes," Izzy managed. "Help her."

The veiled woman dashed over to Caresse. The werewolf followed, rising up on its hind legs, beginning the transformation back into Andre the man. Taking no notice, Jean-Marc hoisted her to her feet, his hand around her wrists so tight she could almost hear the bones in her wrist snap.

"Now, we'll do it *my* way," he said.

Chapter 3

Jean-Marc dragged Izzy through the bayou. She could barely keep up; when she stumbled over a tree root, he simply dragged her along behind him.

"Stop! Let me go!" she protested, scratching at the back of his hand with her fingernails as they splashed shin-deep in stinking black water. Smells roiled around her like living things—decay, blood, death—and she worked to plant her feet, fighting his momentum. But she kept sliding in the ooze, and he didn't even seem to notice she was trying to fight him.

Then several figures darted from behind a cluster of trees hanging low over the water. They were seven, all men, wearing body armor emblazoned with the by-now familiar trio of flames on their breastplates. Their faces were smudged with smoke and blood, as if they were wearing masks, and the one in the middle looked familiar. Dark hair, dark eyes, very straight nose.

"*Gardienne,*" he said breathless, ducking his head. "*Grâce à Jehanne,* you are alive. We heard all that howling…"

She stared mutely as the other soldiers also lowered their heads. Submachine guns dangled around their necks. Behind them, to the left, to the right, projectiles impacted and gouged the earth. Water sloshed; herons burst out of the cypress trees and animals shrieked in panic.

"Michel," Jean-Marc said. "*La situation?*"

The man—Michel—raised his head. "The Malchances panicked when they heard that Luc de Malchance was killed. We took the offensive and won back the mansion. They're retreating and we are on them. They're coming this way. But word has spread—a rumor only, I hope…" He took a deep breath, his dark eyes searching the woman's. "Did Madame raise a demon?"

Her mouth dropped open. Had she heard him right?

Jean-Marc stepped in front of her. "There's time for that later. We need to get her out of here." He raised his hand and showed the other man—Michel—the Medusa. "The werewolves are with me. The bayou is ours. Your people can be my hostages or my allies."

The men with Michel glanced at each other and put their hands to their Uzis, then looked at their leader for orders. He swiped the air, signaling them to back down.

"Our *Gardienne* is here," Michel argued, looking straight at Izzy. Her stomach flipped. "She can speak for us."

"*Non,*" Jean-Marc replied. "She cannot. She has sustained magical injuries and she is healing herself. I was her Regent, and I served your family well. Deal with me in that capacity."

Michel raised a brow. "Madame, you are incapacitated?"

She caught a nuance in his use of the word "incapacitated," and guessed that Jean-Marc's authority rested on her answer. She didn't know if she wanted him to speak for her. For this magical House of the Flames, of which she was the leader, so it seemed.

She didn't like him. She didn't trust him. But he was the devil she knew.

"I'd like Jean-Marc to speak for me," she said, mentally crossing her fingers that she wasn't making a terrible mistake.

Michel glowered at her. "I *knew* it. Half Malchance, conspiring to take over our family, and you're probably allied with the House of the Shadows for battle strength. What did our dear Regent promise, that he would marry you? More half-breeds destroying centuries of tradition?"

"Take care, Michel de Bouvard," Jean-Marc said, raising the Medusa and pointing it directly at Michel. "You are speaking treason. And you know I dealt harshly with traitors, when I wore the signet ring."

His men stirred. The two farthest away grabbed their Uzis and aimed them at Jean-Marc. Another projectile shrieked through the sky and lit a canopy of trees across the water on fire. Michel ducked. Jean-Marc didn't move at all. There was a second, closer. A third, closer still. In the firelight, Michel exhaled heavily and straightened.

"Where is the ring now?" Michel demanded, looking from him to Izzy.

"It is safe," Jean-Marc replied, his arm never wavering. The contours of his catsuit highlighted corded muscles. He looked strong enough to keep the heavy weapon in place all night.

"No one saw this coming," Michel said, sounding more lost than angry. "Our new *Gardienne*—our queen—the child of our deadliest enemies." He studied her, as if the answers to his questions were written on her face. "Did you know what you were?" he asked in an agonized voice. "We welcomed you as our protector. Well, some of us did. *I* did. But then I saw the proof of your tainted blood. And this talk of raising a demon…"

She remembered nothing like that. She didn't even know the name Malchance. She had no idea what a *Gardienne* was. The only things that were familiar were the logo of the triple flames, Michel's face and Pat. And those only felt like ghosts of memories, and not memories themselves.

"She did not know what she was. You know that she didn't," Jean-Marc said. "Of all the Bouvards, you knew her best. She came here in ignorance. And she's suffered for it. You are witnessing the results as we speak."

Michel took a breath. "But—"

"You know she didn't want to come. She didn't even know that she was Gifted."

"A ruse," said one of Michel's men—a tall man, his hand hovering beside a Glock in a holster.

How do I know the makes of their weapons?

"I'm surprised you were able to take back the mansion from the Malchances," Jean-Marc continued, changing the subject again.

"What are you suggesting?" Michel snapped.

"You're so weak," Jean-Marc observed, "and the Malchances created that dampening field to make your magic ineffectual. They walked right in and took over. I can't imagine how you turned the tables so easily."

Michel bristled. "You don't know everything about us, Devereaux."

Jean-Marc raised a brow. "I know more than most," Jean-Marc countered. The arm holding the Medusa was as steady as if it were made of marble. A muscle jumped in his cheek. His eyes blazed as he narrowed them, contempt and hatred dripping off him like poison.

"I know that your House is weak. Your magic is fragmented and unreliable." Jean-Marc cocked his head, his eyes mere slits. "Have *you* perhaps allied yourselves with the Malchances? Did *you* make a deal—the House of the Flames could still stand, if you hunted down Isabelle de Bouvard and handed her over?"

She could feel the wrath surging through him, *feel* it, like icy heat. It stung her, physically. One of Michel's soldiers— tall, thin—spat into the mud. He seemed unaware that Jean-Marc was about to explode like a live grenade.

"That would be a bargain *your* House would make." Michel sneered. "The House of the Shadows, loyal to no one, waiting to see which way the battle goes so they can loot the bodies—"

Another mortar splashed into the bayou, shattering into a thousand purple flares that streaked straight at them in a collective cloud. This time, Michel and his soldiers whirled around and shot off their weapons, issuing streams of white light that crashed into the purple glow. The sky filled with a mushroom of white and purple, then lavender.

"Hostie!" one of them shouted as they shot again, and the light did not change.

Then Jean-Marc joined in, raising his hand toward the moon and lobbing off a huge mass of fire about the size of a basketball. An answering volley landed much closer, shaking the tree branches and wafting their collars of Spanish moss. Michel swore in French.

"Allons! Vite!" he shouted, ordering their retreat.

Without missing a beat, Jean-Marc bent down and scooped her into his arms, his empty left hand curling around her shoulder, his right hand, filled with her gun, positioned under her knees.

"Hey, put me down!" she protested as he bolted for the

shadows, sloshing through the loamy earth toward the fetid bayou deep. She felt his muscular chest through her armor, the strength of his hands gripping her under her arms and knees—and the cold heat of his fury sizzling into her flesh.

He raped me, she thought, remembering those first few moments when she woke up and felt his hard length slipping from her body. Or did he? As he carried her out of the battle, her body reacted to his touch with sharp, undeniable hunger—despite their dire situation and her amnesia, despite everything. It was all she could do to keep her face averted as his hot breath panted against her cheek.

Michel caught up with him. He was free of burdens. He could shoot Jean-Marc and her in an instant.

"They're coming," Jean-Marc said. "They'll take her if they find her. If you're with us, tell me now."

"And yet," Michel replied sarcastically, holding his Uzi barrel with his left hand as he trotted beside Jean-Marc, "the bayou is yours."

Before she realized what she was doing, she took a deep breath, held it as if she were preparing to recite lines someone else had written and spoke. "Fair warning—if you've turned against me, you're in enemy territory, and you're dead." It was bravado, all for show, but it had its desired effect: the other man—Michel—gave his head a shake.

"*Mais non.* We are here precisely because we are loyal."

Jean-Marc gazed down at her, blood smeared on his cheek, eyes glimmering with private amusement.

"Well done, Izzy from Brooklyn," he said under his breath.

Whatever reply she might have made was lost as a hail of red light streaked toward them, screaming like Roman candles on the Fourth of July. Two of Michel's men raised their Uzis and fired at it while Michel spread open his hands. White balls of fire rocketed from his palms against the cannonade.

Then incoming white light joined the fusillade of crimson and Jean-Marc swore under his breath, dashing beneath a thick canopy of trees just as they burst into flame. Blazing branches dropped like stones, hissing into the mud. She smelled charred leaves and saw sparks. A barrier of deep indigo flared around him and he zigzagged beyond that tree to another one, but the entire tree exploded in a shower of fiery wood chunks. They bounced off the shield of blue as he ran on.

Werewolves howled. Submachine guns pulsed *one-two-three, one-two-three.*

I really hope, she thought, clinging to him, *that I live long enough to find out what's going on…and who I am.*

"Damn them," Jean-Marc grunted, as he raced through the bayou. His first priority was to protect Isabelle, but that kept him from the battle—and his help was sorely needed. He carried her through the burning forest, seeking escape routes, weaving magical spells to shield them both. He knew she had seen menace in his aura—the blackness that had invaded his soul—and so he guarded against enclosing her within its protective influence. He kept it thin against his own body like a coating of wax, flinching when the streaks of evil ran over him like a strangely pleasurable cut.

Then a bone-searing burst of magic pierced his aura and ripped through his armor, imbedding itself in his shoulder as if someone had sliced him open and pushed in a charcoal briquette. The pain sent him stumbling; it took him back to the place where Lillianne had taken his soul. The blackness rose up inside him—the fury of the indignity; the danger—*her fault, she has ruined my life, I'll kill her now*—and he forced himself to ignore it and run on.

"You're hurt," she said, his blood spattering her forehead and cheeks.

Just drop her in the mud, a voice whispered. *Be done with her.*

He faltered. He knew he was badly wounded. He needed help.

"Heal me. You're the Daughter of the Flames. You have that power."

Her lush mouth worked as if he had told her the most unbelievable lie in the world. Then her lids flickered shut, her lashes brushing her cheeks. She grew still. He felt worse. After a few more seconds, she opened her eyes.

"I'm sorry," she said. "I don't know how…I…I don't remember…."

"Find your center. Try to focus. We have time." He was lying to her again. "Allow yourself a moment, and it will come back to you."

He pushed one leg forward but it wouldn't bear his weight; his ankle gave way and he almost dropped her. The pain began shooting through his veins. He knew what was happening. He knew how long it would take. It would reach his heart in less than three minutes, and stop it from beating. He would drown in his own blood.

What would happen to her then?

"Isabelle, *écoutes,*" he said, and he could hear his words slurring. "You have the power. Somewhere. Find it. *Now.*"

She paled and shook her head, parted her lips to speak as a wall of flame erupted about forty meters ahead of them, cutting off that route. He glanced left, right; the world was blurring to blackness. Waves of cold, dark shame crashed over him, sucking his energy down to a black place; he was failing her, with his weakness and his slowness—*I should have dodged that bullet*—he was inept; he was a liar; he could no more protect her than that half-dead cowboy detective of hers.

Yet pride and anger kept him telling her that he was sorry, and a horrible, engulfing sorrow smothered his shame. He was going to die and all that could have been would never be.

By the Patron of my life, but I loved you. You were not for me—I would make your life so difficult if I took you as my woman. But I wanted to. I never told you that. I wanted to save you from what would happen next. From what I would bring to your bed...

And that speck of love filtered through the hard, flinted evil in the middle of his soul, and gave him a bit of peace as he continued to die. He rallied his strength, gazing down at her as she clung fearfully to him, his once-proud warrior queen reduced to confusion and terror.... He forced himself to keep moving, arrowing to the right, where he saw no flames, no smoke, no barrage of enemy magic. Moonlight filtered through the trees, promising a clearing.

Jean-Marc threw back his head and howled to the wolf pack. *Come to me. Come now.* His voice was packed with the urgency of one dying. *I need help.*

"Let me down," she insisted, pushing on his hands. "You shouldn't be carrying me."

As his mind began to shut down, he couldn't speak with words anymore. He didn't know how to tell her that his hands were spasming and he couldn't let go.

He lumbered past two live oaks, pushing through the streamers of Spanish moss swathed between their trunks as if the tree on the right were choking the life out of the tree on the left. Their leafy canopies shook as if with their own death throes. He pushed past them, staggering, and groaned aloud as silvery moonlight highlighted Isabelle's dark cascades of curls.

"Jean-Marc!" she insisted, scrabbling out of his embrace, grabbing his arm to keep him upright as he contracted from the pain. He felt his protesting heartbeat, and he wove a spell of strength around himself as best he could.

My patron, the Grey King, I call on you, he thought. *Save me, and I will be a faithful son. I will do whatever you ask. At least, keep me alive until I get her out of here.*

He felt something move inside his being, a presence, a force, and he knew it was the Grey King. All faithful Devereauxes revered their patron, who was himself a demon. Those with strong Gifts, like Jean-Marc and Alain, were able to call on him directly. Hours before, the Grey King had appeared in the bayou and destroyed the demon Izzy had called—a fierce, fanged female creature with glowing, almond-shaped eyes and necklaces of skulls around her neck.

There will be a price, the Grey King informed Jean-Marc. *A high one.*

I will pay it gladly, Jean-Marc replied, *if it keeps her safe.*

Then it is done.

The presence receded, and Jean-Marc felt a solitary moment of fear. His patron was just, but he could also be merciless. Sometimes he moved in ways Jean-Marc couldn't understand.

Yet, in the clearing, he saw a miracle: the werewolves' crazy, black Cajun van. The passenger panel was slid back, revealing the garish interior studded with voodoo *jujus* of silver and brass, the strings of chicken's feet and glittering mirrors and ankhs. And more wonderful, the *Femme*

Blanche Andre had brought to heal Caresse poked her head out of the van. She took one look at Jean-Marc and hopped out, racing toward him. Another *Femme Blanche* peered out at them but remained inside the vehicle. So they had two. *Magnifique.*

I thank you, my patron, he thought, even though, of course, the patroness of the House of the Flames was Joan of Arc, and these women were her acolytes. He might have more properly thanked her, but he didn't. He was certain that his patron had brought the van to him.

The window on the driver's side rolled down, revealing Andre, now dressed in a plaid shirt. He threw open the door and leaped out, racing toward Isabelle and Jean-Marc, reaching out his arms.

"You've been hit. Denise, *vite!*" he bellowed.

"I'm coming," said the *Femme Blanche,* unable to keep pace with the burly Cajun werewolf. "Sir, give the *Gardienne* to Andre."

"We've got three *Femmes Blanches* now. They saved Caresse," Andre said, jerking his head toward the *Femme Blanche* named Denise. "They can spare some time for you. Lucienne! Sara! Come now! *Ils sont Jean-Marc de Devereaux et la Gardienne!*"

"Bon," Jean-Marc said, relieved to his soul that Caresse was better. Then his legs gave way as the ground rushed up.

It would be a relief to die—he hurt so badly—but he heard Isabelle cry out, "Take care of him. Then have someone come with me. I'm going back for…for…him!"

Jean-Marc's mind was fragmenting; the kaleidoscope bits shattered and reformed into the face of Pat Kittrell. *Leave him there,* he thought, jealous rage mingling with battle-hardened common sense. *I won't risk your life for his.*

"Her lover," Jean-Marc gasped. "You know, that man

from New York. The detective. Also, there are Bouvards loyal to her. Michel is with us. They should be found."

With Isabelle in his arms, Andre turned to the *Femme Blanche*. "Goddamn it, fix him!" he shouted. "Alain!" He looked past Jean-Marc. "We gotta find *la jolie's* boyfriend."

"The Bouvard special ops are circling back to get some vehicles," Alain reported. His voice dropped as he came around, staring in horror at Jean-Marc. "*Mon cousin,* what has happened?"

Then the two cousins spoke telepathically, which was a blessing, because Jean-Mark could no longer make his mouth work.

Je regret. *I couldn't stop myself from attacking you. I have been poisoned. I'm going to die with filth in my soul. I'll go to a place where I can harm no one…*

With a gasp, Alain slung his arm under Jean-Marc's and half carried him toward the van.

Non, he protested. *You will not die, Jean-Marc. You cannot die, and especially not in this condition.*

The *Femme Blanche* named Denise approached and dropped her veil over her face. She raised her hand, glowing with white healing energy, and placed it directly over Jean-Marc's wound. Fire as from a white-hot poker blazed from her palm into the ravaged sinews of his bicep, searing down to the bone; he hissed and doubled over. His cousin lowered him to the ground as Denise knelt, steadfastly poured healing magic into his body.

"Let it happen, let it be," she murmured aloud to him in French. He knew it took her supreme effort to speak while she was working and he dipped his head, the closest he could come to a nod.

The second *Femme Blanche* from the van joined them,

placing her palm over her sister's. Then a third. Jean-Marc detected no change in his death throes. Perhaps he was too far gone, even for Bouvard healing magic.

"You have to find him." Isabelle's voice carried over the pain and a fresh round of mortar fire. "I won't leave without him."

His drowning heart sank; he was dying, but her thoughts were of Pat. Jean-Marc tried to tell himself that she probably didn't realize how little time he had left. Magical wounds often appeared less severe than they actually were.

Or perhaps because her memory was gone and her Gift was dormant—*her magical power can't be gone; that is impossible*—she no longer felt the incredible electricity between them. As his body began to quit, he could feel her, sense her, practically taste her. He almost managed a chuckle as his shaft hardened in response to her. *I'm a dog,* he thought wryly.

I'm a man.

A shrill whistling thrummed through his bones—incoming!—and he signaled to Andre to get Isabelle to the van. He was nearly blind now, as death came, but he could see her arms and legs flailing as Andre carried her around to the other side of the van. Then he lost sight of her as the *Femmes Blanches* intensified their magic and Alain chanted in the Old Language beneath his breath, praying to the patron of the House of the Shadows, the Grey King, to care for his devoted son.

He almost blacked out; nearly came to. Shadows wove around him as Alain eased him into the panel van. It was bulging to capacity—battle gear, wafting white robes, sweat, blood, dirt. And the sharp musk of werewolves, changed back to human, but with their natures wrapped around them like invisible pelts.

As soon as Andre gunned the engine and the vehicle

roared into motion, a magical burst slammed into the ground where it had sat, rocking the chassis back and forth on its wheels. Two seconds later, and it would have landed squarely on top of the van.

Jean-Marc concentrated on Alain's voice as his cousin magically willed him to live. He heard Andre arguing with someone over the roar of the battle and the engine. It was Isabelle, who was screaming at him to get Pat.

"It's too dangerous, *chérie,*" he said. "I'm sorry."

"If it was someone *you* loved…" she retorted, obviously not thinking clearly. Because it *had* been Caresse, and she herself had not only shot her, but refused to help her in favor of Pat. Jean-Marc inhaled the scent of werewolf musk and Caresse's spicy perfume, knowing she was nearby in the van. He tried to lift his head to find her, see how she was doing. He tried to send out healing thoughts, but that was not his Gift.

"Shh, don't move," Alain insisted. And then in thought, *Are you in much pain?* Alain ticked a worried glance at the veiled *Femmes Blanches* seated on the floor beside Jean-Marc. They had all lowered their veils to keep out distractions as they worked on him. The palm of the one closest was pressed against his shoulder, cauterizing his wound, or so it seemed to Jean-Marc. If anything, the pain intensified. But he had been trained from birth to be the master of his behavior, and so he forbade himself to writhe or cry out. What she did, she did to heal him.

Without answering, Jean-Marc slid his gaze down his body, finding the second *Femme Blanche* at his side and the third crouched at his feet, knees pressed against her chest beneath her dress. The three women were holding hands, transferring healing energy like a conduit through themselves to him.

"Caresse," he whispered. "New Orleans PD. Unsouled."

"She is stable. We have him. It is your turn," Alain said.

The van bounded and bounced along, all the shiny metal objects shimmying and shaking. The *Femme Blanche* held on tight to his shoulder, grinding her fingertips painfully into torn muscles as if for purchase; he doubted she realized what she was doing.

A thunderous roar like a sonic boom jerked him out of his languor. The vehicle rocked hard to the right, sending everyone sliding, including Alain, the *Femme Blanches* and him. Next it ground to a halt and the panel door slid back. The noise outside was deafening.

He tried to sit up. With a fierce expletive, Alain held him down; then he saw a flash of facial features as three uniformed Bouvard special ops carried Pat Kittrell between them. Pat's head was thrown back, his mouth was slack, the flesh of his silhouetted face gray and mottled. He looked as if he had been dead for a week.

They handed him in, other figures scrambling to help. The panel slammed shut. In the front seat, Isabelle called out to him. Jean-Marc dimly heard the sounds of movement and arguing: she was trying to climb over her seat to Pat.

Pat was laid down beside Jean-Marc. Jean-Marc turned his head and studied the brave man who had flown blind into this hell storm for love of his woman. Jean-Marc willed him to live.

Non, Alain told him telepathically. *Stop exerting yourself.* And then, *Sleep.*

I have to protect her, Jean-Marc replied. *And he is part of her.* It was so much easier to communicate without speaking. *I have to...not sleep...I have to keep him from dying....*

You *have to not die yourself,* Alain retorted. *Or I'll have risked your wrath for nothing.*

I'll take my wrath to the grave, Jean-Marc promised him, *and use it to haunt you forever. I will never forgive you for what you did.*

Alain grunted. *And yet, I would do it again. Such is the nature of my loyalty, and my love for you, cousin. You would do the same, would you not? For Isabelle?*

Chapter 4

Seated beside Izzy in the van, Andre answered his cell phone and spoke in a strangely accented, rapid-fire version of French that Izzy could barely understand. But she got the drift: They were in trouble.

She peered through the windshield. After dodging explosions, enemy forces with rocket launchers, grenades and submachine gunfire, they had met up with several Humvees and white vans emblazoned with the three flames. Now the parade screamed without headlights through ebony rain on an obsidian highway, out of New Orleans.

Andre disconnected and set down his phone. "Alain," he called, "that was Michel. We need to get off the main road. The bad guys have choppers in the air."

"D'accord," Alain replied. "I've warded the van, but you never know."

"Helicopters?" Izzy leaned forward and craned her neck

to see up. Streaks of pastel melted the darkness, signaling the approach of dawn.

"Oui," Andre grunted. "That may mean air-to-ground rocket launchers. The sun will rise soon. At least there won't be any vampires coming after us." He crossed himself and kissed his thumb.

Her stomach twisted as she studied him, trying to see if he was joking. Rocket launchers and *vampires?* What kind of world was this?

"Bon," Alain replied. "Can you get us other cars? We'll ditch these."

"Already done," Andre said. He smiled grimly. "We Cajuns got a lot of cousins, us. The cars won't be as nice. But they'll be harder to track." He turned to Izzy and gestured to the glove compartment. Comprehending, she opened it.

"There's a big wooden box. Remember that *juju* I gave you? There's more in there. We'll take those and hand them out to our people. Should have done it before."

She didn't remember the *juju* he gave her. She didn't even know what it was. Flipping open the glove compartment, she found the box and opened it. Strings of bird claws, tiny blue bags and silver charms lay heaped inside. She tried not to let her disgust show as she picked up a string of claws and dangled it in front of her face. Sensing his eyes on her, she draped it over her shoulders.

She turned to him. "I'm sorry," she said thickly. "I didn't mean to shoot her. And…and that I wouldn't let anyone help her until I got what I wanted."

The burly man leaned over and patted her chilly hands. *"D'accord,"* he said. "You're going to be all right."

"Me? But how can you forgive me so easily?"

His eyes crinkled with real affection. "Because I know you. I know that you poor Gifted have all kinds of problems. You'll come back to us. Then we'll kick some Malchance ass and have a *fais-dodo*. Now pass out the mojo, *chére*. Everybody needs help."

Izzy began to sort out the coils of charms and claws. She handed one to Andre, who grunted and pulled a string of claws and silver charms from inside his plaid shirt, showing that he was already taken care of. Then he looked in the rearview mirror.

"Alain, I'm turning off the road, going for the trees. Cars are waiting for us already." He took a breath. "How is my *bebe?* You hold onto her, *oui?*"

"She's better and better," Alain replied. "The *Femmes Blanches* have worked good magic for her, *mon ami.*"

"Merci, merci bien, mes jolies," Andre said. He raised a bushy brow at Izzy and she saw a tear sparkling in his lower eyelashes. "You see? It's gonna be okay. Now pass them things out. We gotta hurry, us."

She was grateful to have something to do as she handed the necklaces one at a time to Alain, who took them from her and draped one each over Jean-Marc, Caresse and Pat. Three more for the *Femmes Blanches* and three for the soldiers. There was no room to move in the back; everyone was wedged in like victims of a shipwreck in a lifeboat.

Adrenaline was pumping through her body like a river. She had a wild moment where she considered bolting from the van and running away, but she knew how irrational that was. And of course she would never desert Pat. But vampires? Demons? *Juju?* Mojo? Words from horror movies, not real life. Her heart pounded so hard she could hear the rhythm.

Andre's cell phone rang again. He grabbed it, grunted and said, *"Oui."* After he hung up, he yelled, "Okay, this is it!"

A second later he downshifted, swung sharply to the right and the van left the road. After they breached the roadside berm of dirt and vegetation, they tilted sharply downward. The low beams revealed branches rushing up as he kept his foot on the gas and his hands on the wheel. She heard the *whum-whum-whum* of a helicopter. He swore in French and turned off the headlights. She held onto the armrest and the dash, holding her breath.

Then the van slammed hard into what had to be the trunk of a tree, throwing her forward against her shoulder strap, and Andre immediately killed the engine.

"*Merde!* Everyone good?" Andre called.

"We're good," Alain reported. "The wounded are stable."

"*Vite, vite,*" Andre said. Movement filled the compartment behind them. "You wait, I'll help you out," he told Izzy.

She gave her head a shake and tried the door handle. It opened and she hopped out onto hardpacked earth. Several low-slung, rusty sedans, minivans and station wagons wheezed beneath a stand of live oaks trees, exhaust puffing from their tailpipes. A van lumbered up, followed closely behind by a pickup truck embellished with a gun rack.

"You have got to be kidding me," she muttered, as a rangy man wearing a baseball cap and a jean jacket popped out of the nearest car. But that wasn't her immediate concern. She had to see how Pat was doing. She knew he had been in her life before all the madness. He was the only normal person here, and he had come for her. She didn't know how she knew that, but she did.

She circled around to the left-hand side, pulled open the panel and looked down at Pat. His face was gray and slack.

His chest isn't rising, she thought in a flurry of panic.

"Hail Mary, full of grace," she whispered automatically, placing a hand reverently on his forehead. *So I'm Catholic,* she thought. "Blessed art though among women."

The other passengers stirred as if she had said something very odd. Then her mind filled with the image of the medieval woman with the short dark hair. Deep emotion gripped her hard, as if someone had gathered up her heart and given it a squeeze. She touched her chest as she missed not one but several beats. Then the sensation passed.

And she could no longer remember the words of the prayer.

Anxiously she licked her lips and put both her hands on Pat's forehead. The van boiled with tension; the others were watching, waiting to see if she had the power to help him. She closed her eyes, willing herself to have that power. But as before, with Jean-Marc, she felt nothing.

"Allons," someone said—one of the soldiers—and Izzy felt movement as people exited the van on the right side. Feeling useless, she cupped the sides of his face with her hands. He felt so cold.

Beside him, flat on his back, Jean-Marc watched her with half-open eyes, and she felt a moment's awkwardness that she hadn't done anything for him. If their past was half as complicated as their very short present, it would take some sorting out to see how she felt about him. She opened her mouth to speak to him, but Andre tugged hard on her elbow.

"Chére, we need to get them out of here."

"Be careful with them," she pleaded with Andre, then backed out just as lightning zigzagged across the sky and rain poured down as if a dam had broken.

"Hostie," Andre swore. He held a hand over her head as if it would do any good at all. On boneless legs, she wobbled beside him to a dark-colored station wagon. "Get in the back. It's safer there."

She wanted to do something heroic, like insist that she didn't want to be safe, but of course she did, and of course she knew that she had been expected to help, and had repeatedly failed, that this was happening because of her, but she didn't know why.

The only thing she could do was not slow them down. So she climbed into the seat behind him and let him shut the door, then scooted to the far side so others could climb in. Craning her neck, she watched to see where they took Pat and Jean-Marc. Dark shapes moved in the darker rain. Lightning threw white light against the scene as a van rolled between her and Andre's vehicle. There was a little boy sitting in the front, holding a little black stuffed animal.

No. It's a kitten. It's my kitten, she thought in a rush. *It's got a name, a funny name. It's...* She held her breath, waiting. Nothing popped into her head.

Then her door opened and Michel slid in, followed by a chisel-faced, dark-headed man in dark blue body armor, with a design in a patch on his biceps. She stared hard at it, trying to make it familiar. It was a tower made of stone. A gauntleted hand extended from it, either reaching for a dove that was flying out of the tower, or releasing it.

"I am Dominique de Devereaux. Jean-Marc called us in, *Gardienne*," the man said, inclining his head deferentially. His accent was very thick, very French. "Lucky, Georges and Maurice. None better. I'm sorry we couldn't get here any sooner." He flashed her an almost boyish, lopsided grin, a startling bit of sunshine in his hard warrior's face. "No one will get close to you, now that we're here."

"Thank you," she said, faking a calm response as she wondered who "we" were, and how many. *"Merci bien."*

"We have to go," Michel insisted, pulling a pistol from

a holster under his arm and cracking it open. "I have no idea why the ammo in your Medusa carried no magical payload. We've got several footlockers of different calibers of ammunition with us now, and everything tests out as fully loaded."

"That's good." Another faked response. She was glad her Medusa hadn't carried "magical payloads." From what she understood, if she had shot Caresse with such a bullet, her heart would have stopped instantly.

The front passenger door opened and a dusky-hued woman in a loose-knit sweater and a long skirt sat down, slammed the door and put on her seat belt.

"Bon," she said, trying to smile at Isabelle. "I'm glad you're okay, *chére.* A bad business, this. I hope there's room in your place in New York for all us Cajuns."

My place in New York? Isabelle thought, wondering who this woman was and if she was a werewolf, too. "Of course there is," she replied.

Jean-Marc did not die. He, Pat and the unsouled police officer were carried on stretchers into another van. One of his trusted Shadows lieutenants, Georges, got behind the wheel and took it down unpaved side roads that quickly became muddy gulleys as the rain poured down. Lying on his back with Alain hovering over him, he spoke to his cousin telepathically and the two assessed their situation.

Are the Bouvards among us aware that Isabelle has lost the use of her Gift, and has no memory of anything except Pat Kittrell?

Alain made a Gallic shrug. *I don't know. I don't think so. But whether they do or not, I don't like having Michel around. I don't trust him.*

I've never liked him, Jean-Marc concurred. *He's by the book, and there's no book for what is happening here. Since the Middle Ages, our three Houses have maintained clear boundaries. There has never been a child of two Houses before—and of Bouvard and Malchance, of all things. Those two are mortal enemies.*

Unlike we Shadows, who have no enemies, Alain observed dryly.

And fewer real friends, Jean-Marc pointed out. *I was going to change all that after I became Guardian. I dreamed that I would rein in our manipulating and scheming.*

Alain smiled grimly. *You might as well have told our entire House to leap off a cliff. That has always been our way. Had he the chance, I'm sure Machiavelli would have chosen to become a Devereaux in a heartbeat.*

He would be Malchance, Jean-Marc argued. *He had a taint of evil, or so our grandmother said.*

And she should know, his cousin replied, *since she was his mistress for a time.* A beat, and then, *Thanks be to the Grey King that you did not die, cousin.*

I haven't forgiven you for what you did to Isabelle, Jean-Marc reminded him.

Better that you never forgive me, than that I did not dare anything and everything to get you back your soul.

A soul that is unclean.

We will remedy that, Alain promised. *On this I swear a blood oath.*

Jean-Marc lifted his right arm at the elbow. Alain clasped his hand, sealing the bargain. But Jean-Marc was not convinced that they had agreed to the same thing.

Alain, you must temper your loyalty to me. Promise me this. If the darkness overtakes me, and I become dangerous to those around me…to her…that you will end me.

Alain set his jaw and shook his head, his dreadlocks bobbing. *You can't ask that of me. I'll never do it.*

Jean-Marc sighed heavily, frustrated and wary.

She's safe for now, Alain reminded him, laying Jean-Marc's arm down by his side. *Maybe this loss is her patroness's way of releasing her from our world.*

As patroness of the House of the Flames, Jehanne d'Arc had to know that Isabelle is half Malchance. And yet she allowed her to rule, Jean-Marc argued. *Perhaps Jehanne was testing her to see which half was stronger.*

I would argue for Malchance, Alain replied. *After all, Isabelle lost her Gift after she raised the demon. A Bouvard can't raise a demon, and even if one could manage it, they would rather die first.*

And now she is defenseless. His temper rose and he struggled to sit up. *And she lost her Gift because she performed sex magic to get back my soul.*

We don't know that's why she lost it, Alain replied, pressing gently on his chest, first with his hand, and then, as Jean-Marc pushed angrily against it, with magic. *Just before that, she conjured a demon. Her patroness is a martyred saint of the Catholic Church. Joan of Arc forbade the raising of demons, and abjured Isabelle from going through with it. It is possible she withdrew the Gift herself.*

We must get it back for her. Immediately. Jean-Marc pushed on his elbows, then contracted, hard, as pain shot through his body.

Lie down and get better while you can. There is no rest for the wicked, Jean-Marc.

Your sense of humor is highly inappropriate, Jean-Marc snapped.

Then get up and kick my ass, Alain replied with a crooked grin.

I intend to. Jean-Marc didn't smile. He felt himself losing consciousness…whether his cousin's doing or his own exhaustion, he couldn't tell.

When he woke up, he was lying on something wonderfully soft. There was a flickering glow against the ceiling and Denise, the *Femme Blanche,* sat in a simple wooden chair beside his feather bed. He was in a house, in a bedroom. She was holding his hand, sharing her energy with him, and when he stirred, she jerked and half stood, knocking over her chair. It clattered against stone.

"*Monsieur Gardien,* I'm sorry. I didn't mean to awaken you," she whispered, whirling around and retrieving the chair. She set it down, clasped her hand against her chest and took a step backward. Her dark eyes—Bouvard eyes—were enormous, her cheeks pale. She was afraid of him.

"It's all right, Denise," Isabelle said from the doorway. She was wearing a scarlet velvet skirt that swept the floor and a black boat-neck sweater that was too big for her— clearly castoffs from someone else. Her hair was gathered up and held in place with a black velvet comb. Tendrils caressed her temples and cheeks. She looked like a nine- teenth-century Spanish dancer.

Denise dipped a curtsy in Jean-Marc's direction, then hurried to the doorway like a little white bird greeting its returning mother to their nest.

"*Ma Gardienne,*" she murmured. "He's awake." She spoke the words as if they were a warning.

"It's all right," Isabelle said again, dismissing her. Denise moved around the room, which was decorated in fifties' retro-chic—black-and-white-checked linoleum on the floor, and white walls decorated with old monster-movie memorabilia. There were a lot of monsters from Lon Chaney movies—werewolf movies.

Then he looked down at his naked chest—and the large scar across his heart, where he'd been previously wounded—and realized that beneath the bedclothes, he'd been stripped naked.

"Why is she so afraid?" he asked her.

"She said you were muttering things in your sleep…terrible things. She was afraid you were going to cast a spell that would kill us all."

"Hostie," he grunted. "And yet she stayed."

"She is a very dedicated healer."

"She's loyal to you, Isabelle. You asked her to remain," he guessed.

"No," she replied coolly. "I told her she could leave the room if you got too scary."

"Ah." They had never pulled punches with each other before. Why should he expect her to be different now? She had lost her memory, not her personality.

"Has this place been warded? By warded, I mean—"

"I know what it means," she replied. "It has."

"You've gotten your memory back," he ventured hopefully.

She shook her head. "Alain explained it to me. Magical barriers have been put in place to lessen the chance that we'll be found and attacked." She spoke calmly, but he sensed her anxiety. She'd be a fool not to be terrified.

He smelled herbal shampoo and lavender soap and body lotion as she walked toward his bed, placing her hands on the back of the chair as if it were a shield. Her hands were trembling. So she was afraid of him, too.

"We're in a safe house," he guessed. "Where? Whose?"

"Virginia. We drove straight through, changing drivers.

It's been about twenty-five hours. The house belongs to friends of Andre's." She cleared her throat. "A werewolf named Bobby."

"How is Caresse?"

She took a deep breath before answering. "She's doing very well. That police officer…they knocked him out. Alain told me that he's deteriorating badly and may die. I tried to help. The Femmes Blanches are shocked that I can't heal anyone myself. The Bouvards are known for it." Her expression clouded. "I…not so much."

"You've had your moments," he said.

She nervously tapped the chair with her fingertips. Some spells were tapped out like that. He wondered if she remembered the danced spells he had taught her—moving together as if they were practicing tai chi, spinning slowly like dervishes in sweats and T-shirts. She was as graceful as a fawn.

"Alain and Michel have been filling me in." She shook her head. "It's quite a story."

"It must be hard to take. The first time I told you about the world of the Gifted, you thought I was insane."

"I don't remember the first time you told me, but if it makes you feel any better, I still think you're insane." Her gaze traveled from his face to his chest and lingered there. From the softening of her expression, he guessed that she was wondering about the scar. Then she saw that he was watching her. Flushing, she came around the chair and sat down, crossing her arms over her chest and her legs over each other—another shield.

"Alain said that you, he and I were taken prisoner by the Malchances in the bayou," she went on. "They invaded my headquarters and created dampening fields so that the Flames couldn't fight back with magic."

"It didn't take much to disarm your family. The magical

potency of the House of the Flames was already very weak," he replied, pulling no punches. "No one knows why, but I think it's because your mother slept with the Guardian of another House, and had children with him. It damaged her beyond repair."

The color in her cheeks deepened, as if she were ashamed. Of course she had no reason to be—she'd had no part in what her parents had done. He felt for her—all the jolts, the revelations. He was surprised she hadn't lost her mind altogether.

"I don't remember my mother," she said. "Or my sister."

"You were both taken from her as a baby. You were adopted, hidden until recently. I found you."

"So I've been told. I don't remember my adoptive parents, either."

He tried not to read her mind, but anyone with an ounce of Gifted blood in his veins would be unable to ignore the anguish washing over her. He couldn't imagine how frightened she must be.

"In the bayou," she continued doggedly, "your soul was stolen. I...I performed sex magic with you to get it back. And now here we are. As we are." She stared at him. "Screwed up."

Anger boiled instantly to the surface. He had always had a temper, but years of discipline and adhering to duty had long ago taught him to restrain it. Now he could barely stay in control. It was the darkness in him, he told himself, and not his fear for her.

"Alain shouldn't have—"

"I think that I was the one who suggested it," she interrupted. "I'm not sure why he's taking the blame."

"Because he should. It's not something you could have done on your own. He had to guide you, to weave spells around us both. Just as the Bouvards forbid the raising of demons, we forbid any contact with the unsouled. It's anathema to us."

"That's too bad for you," she bristled. "As far as I'm concerned, he did me a favor. I've lost my so-called 'Gift' and now I'm a regular human being. And as soon as Pat is well enough to travel, we're leaving, thank God."

"We're all going to New York," he said carefully.

"I mean, we're leaving you people. I don't ever want to see you or hear from any of you again." He saw the tension in her face, the stiffness of her shoulders. He could will that out of her, make her less stressed. But he knew that she needed her anger. It was giving her some power and his Isabelle needed some of that.

She is not my Isabelle.

"You can't do that," he informed her, pitying her, wishing he could tell her that she could wash her hands of them and return to the world of the Ungifted. "Your sister is named Lilliane. She was married to your cousin, Luc, and you summoned a demon that killed him."

"So everyone keeps reminding me," she snapped. "I have no recollection of that, and if I did it, I'm sorry. I'm different now. I'm not a threat to anyone. I'll send her a message—"

"She'll never accept your apology. She wants nothing less than to feed your soul to Le Devourer. She's mad, Isabelle. *Folle.*" He underscored, leaning toward her. "Your common blood won't spare you. If anything, it condemns you, in her eyes. You killed the *Gardien* of the Malchances, and you are half Malchance yourself."

She looked away, eyes darting for a few moments, then focusing on the candle beside the bed. The light played on her skin, caressing the planes and hollows of her features, reminding him of the exquisite oil portraits of Devereaux duchesses on the walls of his mansion back in Montreal. But she was not Devereaux. And despite that, they had once been so close; their connection ran deeper than any he had ever shared, even with Callia, the woman he had been expected to marry.

He remembered his Shakespeare: *She doth teach the torches to burn bright.* His chest caught; his sex stiffened.

Take her. Throw her down and take her. Show her who's in charge here. Claim your right. You are a king...

"Isabelle, *écoutes,*" Jean-Marc said, shifting the coverlet to conceal his erection. "I know you don't remember, but an assassin came for you in New York. It was tracking you everywhere. You would have died if I hadn't found you and shown you how to use your Gift."

Her shoulders stiffened and her fingers stopped tapping. She kept looking at the candle. He could see her tuning him out, because she was afraid. He leaned farther toward her. He wanted to grab her by the shoulders and make her understand. Her life depended on it.

"You're in a worse situation than you were then. You have made deadly enemies in the Gifted world. And if they know you have no power, they'll crush you."

"I won't put Pat in danger," she whispered. "I'm out. I'm done. None of this is my problem anymore." She licked her lips. "We're going home to live like normal people."

"You're not a 'normal' person. According to the tradition of your House, you received your legacy directly from Jehanne d'Arc, Joan of Arc. Everyone had deserted her, except for your ancestress, the Duchesse de Bouvard. She bribed her way into Jehanne's jail cell and kept watch with her the night before her execution. She promised always to fight for justice and defend the weak. And Jehanne gave your family her sacred Gift, passed from mother to daughter, for centuries. You are the Daughter of the Flames, and you are not normal."

"According to what I've heard, we've…they've…turned our backs on the weak," she riposted. "They had a treaty with the city of New Orleans to protect the locals and tourists from the Supernaturals, as you people call them. And they didn't."

"Don't dodge the issue. They couldn't. There was a void in leadership. Your mother the *Gardienne* was in a coma for twenty-five years," he said. "There were factions vying for power, trying to claim the legacy—the Kiss of Fire. Your mother was dying, and I went to New York to look for you."

Keeping his lower body covered with the sheets, he climbed out of bed and reached for her hand. Using the chair as a barrier, she took a step backward.

"As soon as you received the Kiss, you put your life on the line to kill a vicious vampire. You did *exactly* what the Duchesse promised your patroness, despite having learned only a few weeks ago who and what you were. Jehanne meant for you to rule the Flames."

A violent shudder worked its way through her, and a tear slid down her cheek. She looked down and away—anywhere but at him. Each time he thought he was making headway with her, she erected barriers of denial.

"I still say it's insane. I don't believe it," she insisted, walking backward another two steps.

But he knew that part of her *did* believe it, or she wouldn't be here, discussing it with him. He felt another rush of pity for her…until the contamination inside him reshaped that pity into contempt.

Why do you argue with her? She's weak, foolish. But

she's also very beautiful. Have her. And be done with her. You can weave a spell of desire she will not be able to resist. You've had her before. You know how sweet she tastes.

He ignored the mocking voice, sitting back down because it was obvious he was intimidating her.

"We have both been wounded, you and I," he emphasized. "You are Gifted, but have no power, and no aura. I don't know what that means for you, but until I know for certain that you're out of harm's way, I have to keep you close by, watch over you. It's my duty."

She shook her head. "It *was* your duty. Alain explained that to me, too. When I became the Guardian of the House of the Flames, your obligation to me ended."

"My *official* obligation. My moral obligation remains."

"It really doesn't," she shot back.

"Isabelle," he ground out, "we can't continue to argue about this. We're in danger. We're endangering the life of Andre's friend every moment we stay here. We'll get to the safe house in New York and regroup. It's a magic neutral zone. Everyone's magic is less powerful there."

That caught her attention. He watched her carefully as he proceeded. "In New York, we can watch over your Ungifted relatives and family. Your father, your brother, your adoptive family. Your coworkers."

"In the neutral zone?" she said suspiciously. "If it's so safe there, why are they at risk?"

He groaned, rolled his eyes to the ceiling and ran his hands through his hair. The sheet around his middle slid past his navel, revealing his abs dusted with black hair. She averted her eyes.

"By my patron, you're infuriating! Must you argue every single point?"

Her eyes flashed. "Don't try to bully me."

Aren't you starving for her? Don't you want her? Shut her up with a kiss.

She licked her lips and smoothed down the impossibly long skirt. "You're right. I don't know why I'm arguing every single point anymore. We're done."

But she didn't leave.

The oversize boat neck of her sweater slipped, revealing her bare shoulder and the soft rise of her left breast. He was taken back in time to the night he had had sex with her, to imbue her with power; how passionate she had been as he changed the two of them into animals—dolphins, jaguars, soaring eagles—mating, coupling...

If you take her, you will reawaken her Gift.

"No," he said aloud.

Yes. You will. You know you will.

He could feel lust rising from him, encircling him; a Gifted male of his level sent out fierce emanations of desire, designed to entice an equally Gifted female. Sex between Gifted was truly magical, and transcendent in pleasure. He knew the first time he had slept with Isabelle, she had never experienced anything like it in her life. He had known how to please her, how to give her what she wanted and take her to a height of ecstasy she could never have imagined. But he had not done it only to give her pleasure; he had done it to strengthen her Gift. Just as she had had sex with him a second time, to reclaim his soul.

He had to remind himself that even with her memory intact, Isabelle still thought like an Ungifted. Sex meant something different to them. At its deepest level, it was an expression of love and commitment, manifested in the creation of life. When he had offered to sleep with her again, to further strengthen her Gift, she had refused, in order to stay loyal to Pat. He had found her refusal as charming as it was frustrating.

If you sleep with her, she will be safer.

Her chest rose and fell; beneath her sweater, her nipples were taut. Her eyes had gone soft, limpid, her lips moist and parted. The curls grazed her neck as she tipped back her head, and the sweater slipped farther off her shoulder.

She didn't move.

"Ma femme," he whispered.

He felt his body straining for her; his magical nature summoning her. The yeasty scent of lust permeated the air; his heat raised the temperature in the room. He was bewitching her with Gifted body language, and emanations. A Gifted woman would have the resources to refuse him if she so chose. An Ungifted would literally be swept off her feet. Where did she fit, in his black-and-white world of magical and mundane?

Responding, she took a step toward him. He could feel her heat, her rising desire. Man called to woman, life to life, magic to magic. She was as powerless to ignore his advances as an Ungifted, as desirable as the *Gardienne* she was.

"Jean-Marc," she whispered, *"je me sens…"* I feel… She trailed off. Her French was breathy, seductive…The words on her lips were like the softness of her mouth on his body. His sex reared against the sheets like a separate, living entity.

Take her. She wants you to.

"No," he said again, more loudly. He made a concerted effort to lift his spell off her, cool down his male heat. But she walked closer, tempting him, so close now. Too close.

Lavender warmth enveloped him. Sex with her had saved him from oblivion and worse; she had ridden him back from Le Devourer's clutches like a warrior on a stallion. If they had sex again, more miracles might spring into being.

You know you want her.

Miracles…or curses? The evil inside him wanted her, too. If they performed sex magic, it would be strengthened, too. Strengthened and unleashed…

He couldn't risk it. Couldn't do it. It would be a violation of the very obligation he had spoken of.

"Jean-Marc, *tu es magnifique, tu es beau…*"

She was speaking beautiful French. Her full-blown knowledge had frightened her before—she had never studied French, couldn't even order off a menu. He had taken it as proof of her Gifted heritage. Now her accent penetrated his defenses, created deeper intimacy, greater longing…

"Non," he said.

Mustering the full force of decades of magical training, he gathered his spell and broke it, the sensation as shocking to him as if someone had thrown him in a frozen lake. He trembled and took a ragged breath.

She blinked. Then she looked around, at the room, at her bare shoulder, and stumbled slightly. Grabbing at the fabric of the sweater, she covered her shoulder.

"What did you do to me?" she demanded hotly. "Were you going to try to…to do it *again*…" She turned around and half ran, half walked to the door. When she reached the threshold, she wheeled back around, gripping both sides of the jamb as she glared at him.

"If you do that again, I'll shoot you with that magic gun," she swore. Then she left, slamming the door behind herself.

"*Merde*," he grunted. In high dudgeon, he flopped backward onto the bed, groaning.

You should have taken her. She wanted you to.

"*Tais-toi,*" he told the darkness. "I'll be rid of you soon enough."

No. You really won't, said the voice. *Go to the door. Now. Open it.*

The darkness grabbed hold of him…had him…and he threw back the covers and got out of bed. His bare feet slapped against the cold tile. He put his hand on the brass doorknob. He couldn't fight back because he didn't want to. Steamy lust enrobed him. He looked down at the bottom of the door to find the light cut in two by a shadow. Her shadow. She was standing on the other side of the door.

Do it. She wants you.

Gritting his teeth, he opened the door.

She faced him in the dimly lit hallway, staring at him with those enormous, dark-brown eyes, as if she had changed her mind. When his arms went around her, her yielding warmth seeped into him like a balm. He pressed her length against his naked body, and lowered his head to hers. His tongue stole into her mouth and electric waves of pleasure rippled through him as she touched him back, tentatively, then gasped and crushed herself against him. She kissed him harder; he moved his hands down to her hips and ground against her.

Take her to the bed. Or take her here.

"Oh," she whispered, catching her breath, then covering his cheeks with kisses before she licked his lips. They burned him. He was starved for her. "*Oui, Jean-Marc, oui, maintenant…*"

Now.

He remembered her in bed. Joining with her, trading power with her…such that each became stronger, more delirious with ecstasy…

"Ah, *mon homme.*" She tantalized him, toying with his earlobe, smiling up at him with naked need…

….like a vampire.

He froze. "This is not you. This is not us," he said, his English thick with desire. "You have a love. And he is not I."

She rocked her pelvis and lifted up her arms, encircling his neck and urging him down to kiss her again. By the Grey King, he smelled her, felt her, wanted her.

"Isabelle, *écoutes,* you are bewitched," he said.

It took everything in him to unclasp her hands from his neck and bring them down to her sides. She moved slightly, and for one thrilling instant he thought she meant to take his penis in her hands. He grabbed both her wrists in one fist and took a step away. He was trembling.

Take her. Now.

He knew now that trying to simply negate his intense desire wouldn't work. Instead he wove a spell around them both, of calmness and tranquility. His erection ebbed; she swayed slightly, a look of shock crossing her features. After a few more heartbeats, she covered her mouth and stared at him.

He dipped his head. "It is not us," he said again.

She lowered her hands. "Thank you." Her voice wobbled; she gave her head a quick shake and cleared her throat. "I don't know what's going on, but I know you just did a nice thing." She took another breath. "A nice thing that was difficult for you."

He smiled crookedly. "Isabelle, I'm the Guardian of the House of the Shadows, not some oversexed Ungifted teenage boy." And yet, he felt like one.

"I'm sure sex with you is very nice," she said bluntly. Despite her flippant tone, she looked upset. "And given our current situation, that was a stupid thing for me to say."

"Pas stupide," he said. "Not. We are being pulled together. The darkness in me is calling to you."

"And I'm responding?" she replied. "Why? I mean, aside from the obvious." Now she managed an equally crooked grin. She reminded him of the old Isabelle, the one he'd found in New York, brassy and defiant. He felt a pang of loss, almost as if that woman had died.

"I need to tell you something," he said. "Come back in and shut the door."

He turned without looking to see if she obeyed. His bare feet slapped on the cold stone. Then he crawled back onto his bed and swathed the sheets over his private parts, more for her comfort than his own. The Gifted had a different attitude toward nudity.

"Yes?" she queried, slipping into the wooden chair beside his bed. She was much less anxious and self-conscious. That could easily be an artifact of his spell.

"There is something in me that is not me," he said. "In my soul, there's evil, and it tempts me. You're a Catholic, so I'll explain it in Catholic terms. It's a demon, or part of one."

He felt her shock; to her credit, she stayed focused. Maybe the expression of sexual desire *was* the key.

"I'm a very powerful magic user," he continued.

She kept listening.

"At the moment, I'm a powerful magic user inhabited by a small amount of demonic energy. So, if I become too dangerous, I would ask that you stop me, by whatever means necessary."

She sat back in the chair. *"What?"*

He'd moved too fast, been too blunt. His family's Gift of diplomacy had never been given to him.

"*Alors*, it seems to be our fate that I never have enough time to prepare you for the things I have to tell you."

"What do you mean, 'stop' you?"

The question hung between them. He felt a sharp chill, as if someone had just walked over his grave. He had never been afraid to die before. But if he died while he was like this…then truly there was such a place as hell.

"You know what I mean. I can feel it. I don't think Alain would be able to do the right thing. He loves me too much." He smiled faintly at her. "I have more faith in you."

"Because I don't love you?" she asked.

You do love me. You don't want to, but you do.

He shook his head. Let her make of it what she would. "Because somewhere inside you, you still know what it's like to be a leader. Alain does not. You and I, we're given the hard choices that others cannot stand to make. I can't be a danger to others. I'd rather be dead."

"But if you died with this *thing* inside your soul…"

He shrugged, as Frenchmen did. "Alain will search for a way to restore me. He's probably pacing right now, yanking on his dreadlocks and swearing because his books and arcana are back in Montreal."

"But if he can't find a way…" She moved corkscrews of hair away from her forehead. "It would be dying in a state of sin."

He leaned his back against the cold wall. It would, indeed. "That can't hold you back. You have a duty to help me."

"Why?" She raised her chin. "And what could I do, anyway? I don't have any power."

His heart sank. "Isabelle, you owe me. I was your Regent for three years. I risked my life to find you in New

York. I would rather go through eternity with half a soul than bring harm to anyone I loved."

He heard himself. He did not love Isabelle, not in the way she would think of love.

And yet, I just said it. In the world of the Gifted, words held power.

"Love? Wait a minute. This is a setup," she said angrily. "A way to get me to stay, or something. You must think I'm an idiot."

"*There's* the Isabelle I remember," he said warmly, enjoying her umbrage, her cynical New York attitude. It lifted his spirits to see her so feisty—gave him hope that not everything was lost. "Fighting me every step of the way. So exhausting and irritating."

They locked gazes. He felt the connection. Surely she did, too. "I don't even remember you," she whispered.

"You have to make this promise," he said urgently. "If I can't stop myself…"

"No." She got up. And left.

Chapter 5

After her conversation with Jean-Marc, Izzy leaned against the hallway wall, shaking and frightened. She closed her eyes and took deep breaths. A wave of vertigo forced her eyes open, and she blinked when she saw the little boy from the other van. Dressed in jeans and a faded black T-shirt, he was standing in front of her, holding the tiny kitten. He was stroking its round head, and both kitten and boy were staring up at her.

"Bijou," he said, holding it out to her. The poor little thing's hind legs pumped as they dangled in the air.

"Yes, of course," she said, pretending she remembered them both. She took the kitten from him, marveling at its featherweight softness, and brought the mewing baby under her chin. There it settled against her and kneaded her chest with its miniature claws. It yawned and began to purr.

"He loves you," the boy said. Then he took a deep, shuddering breath. "Are we going home soon?"

Back to New Orleans, he meant. He was a little homesick werewolf. A werecub. Hysterical laughter bubbled in her throat at the thought. She fought it down, petting the cat.

"I'm so sorry," she said. "There are some bad guys…"

"I know. They shot Caresse," he told her.

She stopped petting the cat. Oh God, was Caresse his mother? She couldn't ask; he'd know she had amnesia. His little face gazed up at her, so trusting, so small.

Gently she offered little Bijou back. Somberly he took him.

"We couldn't get my accordion. But Bobby said we could play video games."

"That's nice."

He nodded. "I'm sleepy."

"Then you should go to bed."

"I'm sleeping with Andre and Caresse," he informed her. "The white ladies said I could. We like to den, us."

"May I go with you?" she asked. "To see them?"

Without a moment's hesitation, he took her hand and led her down the hall. She swayed with sudden, sharp fatigue as he opened a door and ushered her in.

In a dimly lit room dominated by a plasma TV and a floor-to-ceiling entertainment system, the three *Femmes Blanches* were seated with their backs to them, preventing her view of a flowered red-and-black roll-out couch. One of them rose and turned. It was the one named Sara, the youngest of the three.

Sara curtsied to Izzy, then smiled at the boy as he petted the cat.

"Andre and Caresse are both sleeping," she said quietly as she came over to Izzy and the boy. "Beau, they said for you to brush your teeth before you come to bed. Mr. Bobby put a spare toothbrush for you in the bathroom."

Grimacing, he rolled his eyes at Izzy and shook his head like a little old man. He handed Izzy the cat again and left the room.

"How is Caresse?" Izzy asked, as the cat began to purr again. She didn't know if the *Femmes Blanches* were aware that she had shot Caresse. She had debriefed with Alain and Michel, sometimes together, sometimes separately, and she was so exhausted that her conversations were blurring together.

"She is very good," the woman reported, her expression both humble and proud at the same time. "I want to tell you, *Gardienne,* that many more of us would have come with you if there had been room in the caravan. We promised to contact the others when it's safe to meet in New York."

"That's so nice," Izzy said flatly, trying to inject some warmth in her reply. "Now is not a good time. Even to talk to them."

"I know that. 'Loose lips sink ships.' That's what they told people in World War II. The enemy has eyes and ears everywhere." Her eyes glittered. To her, this was an exciting adventure. Izzy felt old, despite the fact that she was…how old? She didn't even know that.

"Thank you," Izzy said. *"Merci."*

"De rien, Madame la Gardienne," she replied. She gestured toward the bed; now Izzy could see two forms in it: Andre and Caresse, both asleep. "If I may return to my work?"

"Please."

She curtsied again and crossed the bedroom. Izzy lingered a moment, then shut the door.

A few minutes later, she entered Bobby's home office, where a queen-size air mattress had been wedged between his computer desk and a filing cabinet. Pat lay on the mattress beneath a heavy patchwork quilt, turned to the wall, and she lay down fully clothed beside him. The *Femmes Blanches* had worked wonders on him, and he was almost back to normal—*normal* being the important word.

Blessedly normal.

"Hey," he said, rousing. He turned toward her and gathered her in his arms with a yawn. He was wearing a white cotton undershirt and he smelled of fresh laundry, sweat and leather. It was a wonderful scent. "I was wondering where you'd gotten to."

She closed her eyes and felt the soft stubble of his beard on her skin. Her cowboy, catching the first plane to New Orleans when he found out she was in trouble. Or so he had told her. She didn't remember that, either.

"I wanted to check up on people. I had to talk to Jean-Marc," she said, kissing him on the lips and settling in for more.

"About...?" As he nuzzled her neck, she caught the uncertainty in his voice.

"I told him I'm out of all this. Done. As soon as you can travel, we're leaving."

He smiled at her with his even, white teeth, smile lines forming around his deep, green eyes. He was model handsome. "I'm all for that, darlin'." He rose up on one elbow and traced the arch of her brow. "What did he say?"

"It doesn't matter. He doesn't matter. This is his battle, not mine." She gazed at him. "He didn't threaten to get in my way, if that's what you're asking." It dawned on her that, in retrospect, Jean-Marc had changed the subject...as if she weren't going anywhere.

"Iz." He nuzzled her cheek. "That's exactly the same conversation I've been having, waiting for you to get in bed. That it's high time you leave these inbreds and their shenanigans."

"Great minds think alike."

"*Our* minds think alike," he rejoined.

She kissed his forehead and laid her cheek against his. As he pulled her closer, she let herself relax against him, nestling in the crook of his arm.

"When we get back to New York, I'm going to take a leave of absence and we're going to spend some time together. Just you and me." He kissed her temple with dry, soft lips.

New York. It didn't feel like home, didn't sound like home, despite her Brooklyn accent. She thought of what Jean-Marc had said about her family and coworkers being in danger. She couldn't picture a single person she knew in New York.

I'm crazy, she thought. *This is all crazy. How did I wind up here, really?* Out of Jean-Marc's sphere of influence, she started second-guessing everything that she had experienced since she'd awakened.

He's making me crazy, she thought. *He's some kind of master manipulator. What just happened...what almost happened...it's like those guys on TV who can get you to do things by implanting suggestions...*

"Iz, honey, is this the wrong time for you?" Pat asked her gently.

Something warm stirred deeply within her, like an ember. She could never imagine Jean-Marc asking such a question. He went too far and then tried to stop. Pat was less impulsive, more calm, seasoned and reasonable. She willed away the images of the irritating man that flitted through her mind—naked, erect...and scary.

She exhaled. "It's just...we're so public here," she ventured. "I—"

He pressed his fingertips against her lips. "No need to explain," he told her. "I'm a patient man." With infinite tenderness, he kissed her forehead. "We'll have our right time, Iz. Once we get the hell out of here."

She settled gratefully against him. "All I remember from my past is you," she said huskily. "I remembered your name, and that you call me Izzy."

He chuckled. "Everyone back home calls you Izzy." He gazed down at her; he was her shelter from the storm, her safe harbor. "Your memory will come back. I've seen post-traumatic stress before. What you have is classic, and if you take it slow and talk to someone—preferably me, for the time being—you're going to be all right."

"How much did you see? How much do you believe?" she asked. "Of that world?"

From what Alain had told her, Pat had rendezvoused with him and Jean-Marc in the bayou, and they'd been captured soon after. Luc de Malchance himself had beaten Pat severely, putting him out of commission before anything magical had happened. He didn't know about the sex magic, and bringing Jean-Marc's soul back from the jaws of a demon. Alain had taken her aside and cautioned her not to discuss any of it with Pat—that he wouldn't understand.

He shook his head. "I saw way too much. Bunch of law-breaking vigilantes and cultists with a few fancy weapons. It actually makes me homesick for the homicide division." He searched her face. "I don't know how you got mixed up in it."

"Didn't I tell you, before you went to New Orleans?" she asked him. She honestly didn't know what she had and hadn't told him.

"Yeah, you did." He smoothed her hair away from her

forehead. "Magic users, a vendetta... I wasn't sure what to believe, except that you were in trouble. That's all I cared about. I only got close to the action before I was beaten to a pulp by that lunatic named Luc. For a while I thought that Jean-Marc threw me to the wolves. Used me as bait for his bungled rescue attempt."

Izzy jerked. Would Jean-Marc do such a thing?

He shook his head and sighed. "Someday I'll think harder about it. But not now. It's over, and we pulled through."

"Yes we did." She smiled at him. "And it's over."

As she gathered herself into his arms and closed her eyes, there was a loud banging on the door. *"Attends! Vite!"* It was Jean-Marc's special ops guy, Dominique. "Attack!"

The window above the computer desk shattered and a dark form shot into the room. It impacted hard against the mattress with an eerie, high-pitched shriek, skirted around Pat and launched straight at Izzy. It was like a bat, only much larger, and more human. Teeth clacking, bloodshot eyes spinning in its bone-white, ratlike face, it scrabbled over her with its taloned hands and feet while Pat brought down double fists on its head.

"Get in here!" he yelled. "We need help!"

"You will die now, murdering bitch," the creature rasped, flapping and flailing as it pressed her into the bed. Pat kicked and grabbed at its wings. *"Lilliane sends her regards."*

The bedroom door burst open and heavy footfalls thundered into the room. Izzy smelled the thing's terrible breath, felt its talons digging into her shoulders; then two sharp gouges as someone yanked it off her. Dominique gripped one leathery wing and another man, dressed in a sleeveless undershirt and a pair of camis, held the other.

Pat dove onto the bed and folded his body around Izzy like a second skin.

"Secure the area!" he bellowed.

A loud gunshot batted her eardrums. She was deaf for a few seconds as Pat, holding her Medusa, pulled her off the bed and hustled her toward the doorway. People in body armor—she saw some women among the men— poured through the doorway, aiming machine guns, revolvers and fireballs at the broken window. Jean-Marc barreled in, dressed in camis and body armor, his hair pulled back in a ponytail. Alain and Andre flanked him. Andre was transforming, and bandolier-style clips of ammo crisscrossed Alain's chest as he gripped an Uzi.

"*Bon,* get her out of here," Jean-Marc yelled at Pat, who obviously didn't need to be asked twice.

In the hallway, Pat accosted Michel, who was leading a cadre of six men down the corridor.

"Where can I take her?" he demanded.

"There's a basement," Michel replied. "Stairs are in the kitchen. Go to the left." After a glance at the two of them, he waved a hand, and Pat and Izzy both were outfitted in catsuits and body armor. An Uzi was slung around Izzy's neck.

Pat stared down at himself. "What the hell?"

"Where is Caresse?" Izzy asked Michel. "And the police officer?"

Michel looked at Izzy. "They're in their rooms. Please, madame, stay out of the way." Then he raised his hand, and he and the men stomped on down the hallway.

"We have to take them to the basement with us." Izzy yelled to be heard.

"Hell with that," Pat said. "We're not going to the basement. If this place gets overrun, it'll be a death trap."

He took her hand and threaded their way down the corridor, dodging oncoming men and women dressed in catsuits and body armor like theirs. She hadn't fully realized how many people had come with them from New Orleans. There were at least two dozen.

Pat hung a left. Their boots thundered on bright red linoleum as they crashed into a retro 1950s-style kitchen. Standing in the center, beneath a row of copper pans and skillets, their host, Bobby, was transforming into a tawny-furred werewolf. Tufts of golden hair grew along his spine as bones shifted and moved, curved and elongated.

"Jesus," Pat said, gasping.

"Get out of here, honey," the werewolf said to Izzy in a voice that was equal parts human and animal. With a hand that was forming claws, he extended one furry arm toward a square black kitchen table and four white chairs. There was a wolf's-head key chain beside a bright red vase filled with white silk roses.

He grabbed up the keys and headed for a door on the opposite side of the kitchen. Pat pushed her to one side of the doorjamb and stationed himself on the other.

"I'm going to open the door," he said. "You wait for the word."

"Got it." She raised the strap of her Uzi over her head and held it up in ready position like a soldier. She heard a voice in her head telling her how to use it: *Bam-bam-bam, rest. Any more than three bursts, you'll be shooting at the moon.*

Someone in her past had trained her in weaponry. Jean-Marc? For occasions such as this?

Just then, Bobby let out a roar, spun around and bounded toward them. His wolf features contorted into something even more wild and savage, something supernatural. Pat swiveled and aimed her Medusa at it; Izzy yelled, "Hold your fire!"

The werewolf threw itself at the door, ripping it from the hinges as both Pat and Izzy, on opposite sides, leaped out of his way. The door bowed outward, straining, and crashed to the ground beneath the creature's massive weight. Emitting an ear-splitting howl, the wolf bounded outside.

She and Pat watched as it raced up to an incredibly pale, thin figure dressed in black body armor with waist-length, stark white hair. As the werewolf approached, the white-haired hissed and bared long, fanglike teeth that flashed with jewels. Izzy gaped at him.

"*Vive* Lilliane!" he screeched.

He tried to dart away, but the werewolf took a swipe at him, sending him flying. The werewolf looked meaning-fully over its shoulder at Pat and Izzy, then threw itself forward, crashing into a second man in dark-blue body armor with a rocket launcher on his shoulder.

"Stay here. It's not safe out there," Pat shouted.

Izzy began to signal that she understood and would comply, but suddenly she *knew* somewhere deep inside herself that it was less safe for them in the house; some-thing had gotten in, and it was coming for them. For *her.* They had to leave.

"Pat, let's go!" She leaped through the doorway.

"Iz, no!" Pat bellowed, chasing after her. "I said to stay!"

She could feel his fingertips brushing her shoulder, reaching for purchase, trying to stop her. Maybe she was able to outdistance him because he was wounded and she wasn't, but a surge of energy seemed to form in her feet and push up into her legs; she shot forward despite her heavy body armor and took off, leaving him behind.

"Iz!" he bellowed.

A hail of bullets from up and behind Pat and Izzy pinged above their heads, striking targets in the darkness that roared with pain.

"Get down get down get down!" Pat roared at her. "*Damn* it, Izzy!"

This time she obeyed, shielding her head as clods of dirt smacked her shins. Figures were swarming the yard: soldiers in body armor, more werewolves and more of the things that had invaded the bedroom. The steady *pop pop pop* of weaponry buffeted her head; the night whirled with screams and shrieks and howls loud enough to wake the dead.

With a painful grip, Pat grabbed her forearm and pulled her up, propelling her along so fast her feet left the ground. He zagged to the left, to a black Lexus, and pointed Bobby's key ring at the driver's door. Maybe it clicked; she couldn't hear it. Reaching forward, he yanked it open and shoved her in.

"Gogogo!" he yelled. "Move!"

She scrambled over to the passenger's seat. Pat barreled in after. He slammed the door, jammed the key in the ignition—he got the right one the first time—and stomped his foot on the gas as the engine roared to life.

They fishtailed in the darkness. He turned on the head-lights and she screamed as he narrowly missed Michel, who was bent on one knee behind a large plastic doghouse. She looked through the car window to see hulking figures and soldiers in armor swarming over Bobby's roof, guns aimed at the troops on the ground, or shooting straight down into the ceiling.

"Oh, my God, oh, my God!" she shouted.

"You're doing great. If anything comes at us, shoot through your window. Everything's a target."

"What about friendlies?" she asked, as she caught sight of Dominique de Devereaux leaping over an evergreen bush, rolling onto his belly, firing.

"There are no friendlies," he replied grimly.

Chapter 6

The Castle of the House of the Blood
Haiti

"*They got away?*" Lilliane raged, as she showed the quivering vampire the bowl of peeled garlic cloves and swirled the holy water in the Chalice of the Blood like a fine wine. The nervous little bloodsucker backed against the slimy wall of his cell, squinting at the rectangle of sunlight that glowed around the edges of the dungeon door. He knew very well that all she had to do was open the door, and he would erupt into flames.

To her left, her favorite cauldron hissed and spit. It was boiling to the brim with the life's blood and souls of five foolhardy Malchance rebels. They'd all been brothers. Now they were all dead. Others would soon join them.

It appeared that not everyone was happy that she'd

stepped into the role of Guardian, vacated by her murdered husband. The objections were predictable: she was only half Malchance; her own sister had murdered Luc. And she was a bumbler, to boot. She'd held a Guardian's soul in her hands, and she'd lost it. She'd sent a sortie after them. Jean-Marc and Isabelle had gotten away. If anyone needed proof that she was unfit to rule…

"It was not our fault," the vampire muttered, his blood-red eyes shifting from her to the door and back again.

"It wasn't mine, either," she snapped. "I gave you backup. I gave you magic. And still you failed."

Her voodoo priests and priestesses had asked their *loa* for aid. The drums were talking, imploring the stars themselves to rain favor down upon the fairest of the fair, Lilliane de Bouvard de Malchance. She needed more magical power to back up her claim, and flesh-and-blood allies. There was certain to be rebellion. Luc's last act in life had been to start talk of war against the governing body of all the Gifted—the Grand Covenate. He had planned to open a portal to the demonic hells and bring forth an army of demons to serve as his warriors in a confrontation between the Grand Covenate and evil itself. But thanks to Isabelle, that plan lay in ashes—like that stupid vampire.

She needed Le Devourer. But he was off sulking, or wreaking havoc, or whatever it was magnificent demons did when they didn't get what they wanted. She had promised him Jean-Marc's soul, and the tidbit he'd managed to consume had whetted his appetite for the rest.

He probably wouldn't show up for her savory tribute: the stew of blood and souls bubbling in her pot. She was hoping to tempt him with home cooking. But perhaps it was as they said: Once you've had a Guardian, you can never go back.

"Jean-Marc and Isabelle escaped," she said, more calmly,

adjusting her black veil over her bare shoulders. She was dressed for torture in black lace and leather, and she was fully incapable of pity, which was good, because it would take the edge off. Torturing vampires required finesse. Go too far, and they disintegrated. Do it right, and they could last for weeks.

Vampires fascinated her. They always had. For her, sex with vampires was a fetish. Most Malchances approached sex as other Gifted did—as a means to share power and ecstasy. But Luc had been an old-fashioned man, a complete throwback to the Middle Ages, when men had treated their women like chattel. There never lived a Gifted male more possessive and jealous—and hot-tempered.

Fatally so. He'd had a wife before her, and the rumor went that he'd caught her in bed with the manager of their sugar plantation. Neither was seen again, but it was rumored he'd walled them up alive in the dungeon wall. So Lilliane had refrained from sleeping around with Gifted men, even though she really, really wanted to.

Her compensation—as she saw it—was unlimited access to vampires. Luc didn't understand her interest at all. Again, like most Gifted, he believed Supernaturals were beneath them. However, each time she slept with a vampire, she was wanton and excited for days, just *folle* in bed, and so he permitted her "eccentricity," as he had liked to call it.

Now that he was dead, she was running through Gifted Malchance men as fast as she could, taking their power, screwing them in return for their loyalty. None came close to Luc. Lilliane was certain sex with Jean-Marc would be even better than with her dead husband—better than even a king vampire.

This trembling youth would be sweet, but not worth the distraction.

"*How* did they get away?" she asked him, plucking up

a piece of garlic and letting him see it. "Were they warned of the attack? Is your sire playing me? Is she pretending to help me, when in fact, she is helping my idiotic sister?"

"Non, madame," the vampire murmured. "Madame Sange is loyal to you, and we are loyal to her."

Madame Sange was the Vampire Doyenne of New Orleans. She had been in a treaty with the House of the Flames for centuries.

Lilliane walked barefoot over the ashes of the previous inhabitant of the cell—another vampire, who had said the exact same thing, word for word. The two of them had arrived by private jet to deliver the bad news that Jean-Marc's damaged soul still glowed inside his beautiful body, and Isabelle was still alive. This vampire didn't know what had become of the other one. She'd pretended he was giving her the news of the bungled attack for the first time, to see how he would explain it.

"Madame Sange knows the House of the Flames has become divided because of Isabelle," the vampire rushed on, anxiously eyeing the door. "They're panicking, weak. She knows you're going to conquer them. She wants to be on the winning side."

"Sange is very smart." She dragged the train of the black lace robe through the ashes. The hem caught on a piece of bone. She tugged at it, swirling the Chalice, plaintively recalling the shimmering glory of Jean-Marc de Devereaux's soul.

Maybe it was just as well Isabelle was still alive. She could torture her to death for stealing it back. Meanwhile, she had other minions searching for her now. Perhaps one of them would locate Jean-Marc and Isabelle a second time, and make her, Lilliane, a happy woman.

"I'm going to send you back to Madame Sange," she told him. "I want you to make it clear that she needs to bring my enemies to me. On a plate, if at all possible. If she doesn't…" She glided toward him, waving the garlic back and forth. She plucked up another and positioned it mockingly over her canines.

"I'll tell her," the vampire promised. "I'll be your messenger."

"Mais non, mon amour," she said, giggling. She covered her mouth. She had a problem with giggling. Once she started, she could seldom stop. "No, my love. You won't be my messenger. You'll be my message."

Then she flew at him, and crammed the two pieces of garlic into his eye sockets. His screams made the stones sing.

Wrapped in a cloud of sulfur and rot, an enormous shadow threw itself against the wall.

The Jersey Shore

Izzy and Pat sat fully clothed in cheap sweat suits they had purchased at an outlet store. They wore them over their catsuits and body armor, and Izzy's ribs and back were aching from the weight. They'd been on the run all day. Night had fallen beneath a strangely red moon. They sat on the edge of a cheap, bowed bed in a pitch-black motel room. Their takeout Chinese food had long ago grown cold. The heater wheezed, dust warmth mingling with the piney smell of cheap room deodorizer. Pat ticked the Venetian blind open with the barrel of Izzy's Medusa.

"It's him, all right. He's back." Pat rubbed his forehead with his free hand while she worked the muscles in his neck. Soon after leaving Bobby's house, his head had begun to ache. It was so bad that he had lost his peripheral vision, and she'd taken over the driving.

Two stories below them, across the street, a bald man in a long black coat was smoking a cigarette and studying the next building over. They'd seen him once before, in the parking lot of the pancake house where they stopped for breakfast. As Pat drowsed, fighting the headache, Izzy watched him come and go, staring at buildings and smoking, putting out the cigarette and leaving.

Three times.

"Jean-Marc warned me," she murmured. "He said that back in New York, the Malchances sent an assassin after me. And that they'd do it again."

"He's full of crap," Pat said harshly. "He'd tell you anything to keep you from leaving."

"Then who is that outside?" she asked.

"If you'd let me call the local cops, we'd find out."

"No," she insisted. "That would only announce our location. Pat, you *saw* that thing fly into our room. And a man turned into a werewolf right in front of you."

"And we're done with it. All of it." He shifted his weight and moved slightly in front of her, creating a human shield between her and the smoking man.

"But it's not done with us," she said dejectedly. Jean-Marc had been right, damn him. She saw now that she couldn't run. "This is my fault."

He stood up and nearly fell over from the throbbing in his skull. "We're leaving."

"No," she begged him. "Pat, he's only the guy we can see. What if there are others out there?"

"Honey, we can't just sit here." He was struck by the irony of his words. Back home at Precinct Two-seven, he was known as the most laid-back cop ever born, aka

"Molasses." He was good at watching and waiting, giving bad buys enough rope for them to lasso themselves and trot into the corral.

Not this time.

Then fresh pain rocketed through his head like an electric current. Everything shimmered as he fell forward, grabbing onto the headboard to keep from crashing to the floor.

"Pat!' She sounded far away, as if he were sinking underwater.

Doggedly clutching the phone, Pat peered through the Venetian blinds as he began to dial. The bald man in the black coat ticked his attention to their building and stared straight up at their room.

In the Devereaux way of Seeing, Jean-Marc stood naked in the rocky cave beside the frigid Atlantic and cast his mind to the sky. He had bathed in the icy waters, then trekked into the cave. Together he and Alain warded it, using white sage Alain had obtained in a nearby New Age store. Then Jean-Marc poured a sacred circle of salt. The wards of a Guardian were stronger than those of lesser Gifted, and he felt relatively safe from an attack—magical or otherwise.

He Saw the twilight descending over the sea as the seagulls saw it, and for a moment he allowed himself to dip and dance as if in flight. He needed to unwind; if he didn't give himself a break, he was going to snap. Or so his fretful cousin had informed him. Repeatedly.

Isabelle, he called. He had tried to reach her so many times in the past twelve hours, while Alain attended to the more ordinary matters of handing out prepaid debit cards so everyone could buy gas and food without leaving a trail. He also transferred five hundred thousand Euros from the accounts of the House of the Shadows into Bobby's bank account, to compensate him for the damage to his home. Then he purchased a burgundy Odyssey minivan at a used car lot, paying cash. It was a ridiculous car for the leader of a family of magic users, which was exactly why he selected it.

On Jean-Marc's order, Alain also disbanded the caravan. A group presented a larger target. Most of the others were heading for New York on back roads, switching cars and switching them again. He and Jean-Marc had put glamours on a dozen volunteers; through the use of magic, six Bouvards and six Devereaux became perfect copies of Jean-Marc and Isabelle, and would fool the enemy if they were spotted. He was glad to see that despite everything, many Bouvards were still loyal enough to Isabelle to risk their lives to protect her.

As the Devereaux special ops were to him. He kept Dom and Georges with him and Alain, and seeded the others—there were nine more—among the cars and vans speeding to New York.

Isabelle, he called.

He breathed deeply in and out. He sent out images of comfort and safety, hers if only she would come back into his sphere of protection. He was trying to entice her, lure her. He would do anything to make her come back. And once he had her, he would take care that she didn't bolt again. He couldn't be angry with her, only with himself, for failing to convince her that her only hope of survival lay with him.

And yet, below the surface, anger seethed inside him. Accusations rose in his mind—that she was disloyal and deserved to die. She was a thoughtless, Giftless fool who preferred an Ungifted man to him. Put so many loyal to her at risk because she wanted to deny who and what she was. A Judas...

"This is not me," he said aloud. "I will not think like this."

He stopped listening to the thoughts, but he still could feel them. Ignoring them, he sought the freedom of the sky, with the birds. The traditional totem of his family was the dove of peace. Some said the Devereauxes never brought peace, but simply forced all conflict underground. They were called bullies and false friends, liars and spin doctors.

Once he had collected himself, he sent out his thoughts to her again, Seeing her not as a storm-tossed dove, but as a powerful falcon. It would be easier to reach her if she was sleeping; he was adept at sneaking into dreams and manipulating the unconscious. But he doubted she had slept much. He hadn't.

Isabelle. It is Jean-Marc. Let me know that you're safe.

There was no reply. He breathed deeply again, expanding his chest, making room among the chakras of his magical body for more energy to gather.

Isa—

And then he heard her.

Oh, my God, what should I do? Pat! Oh, God.

She was in trouble. He knit his forehead and stayed centered. He couldn't lose his focus, no matter how terrified she sounded. If he wanted to reach her, he must remain calm.

It is I, Jean-Marc. I am with you. Let me See what you're Seeing.

An image burst into his mind's eye—bald man, black coat, staring straight at him from across a street. His stomach clenched. It was a fabricant—a magically created assassin. The Malchances had used the same version to

hunt Izzy down back in New York. As it smoked a cigarette, the gray ocean rose and fell behind it, and the dying
sun grazed a sand dune. So it was on the coast, as he was.

A Devereaux fabricant could only last for a day or two
a most. A Bouvard creation, even less. But if this was a
Malchance fabricant—and he had every reason to assume
it was—then it would keep looking until it found her—or
was taken out by someone like him.

Tell me your location, he commanded. *Isabelle, hear my
voice and answer me. Try to think to me in your mind.*

He waited. Nothing came. He Saw the fabricant again,
pacing, turning its head and studying a row of buildings—
seaside motels, a restaurant, a gas station. So it was still
uncertain where its quarry was hiding.

Isabelle, c'est Jean-Marc. He grunted and shook his
head. In his fear for her, he was beginning to lose his
command of English. He couldn't afford the luxury of
fear. He had to stay calm, or she was lost.

The fabricant's eyes locked hard as if on a target. It
dropped its cigarette, perhaps a signal to someone else—
the person who created it, for example.

Calme-toi, he reminded himself, although he was
anything but. He could feel himself trembling, goose
bumps of icy fear rising. He tried to enter the fabricant's
rudimentary brain, cloud its single-minded directive to
find and kill its target. There wasn't anything to work with;
the thing was like a zombie, another staple in the Malchance arsenal of magic.

*Isabelle, get out of there immediately. Don't let it see
you. Don't speak. It will hear you.*

Alain's voice penetrated Jean-Marc's concentration.
"You See her, then." Jean-Marc nodded.

He's crossing the street! Her voice was shrill.

By the Patron, get out! If there's another door…go out a back window. Just get out of there!

No reply. He searched for Pat, and called to him.

Pat Kittrell. It's Jean-Marc. There's a killer outside. Run!

There was no reply.

Pushing through the haze of pain in his skull, Pat managed to lift his head. Izzy had grabbed the Medusa and stood in front of the door, legs spread wide, double-fisted, panting with fear. From his vantage point he could see the bald man climbing an exposed flight of stairs to the second story. Pat knew that was the only ingress and egress; he had scoped the place out and shown Izzy their position on the fire alarm notice on the back of the door.

It was too late to get out. Moving on automatic, he grabbed the room phone and dialed 911, stretching the cord while he crossed to Izzy. As he was connected, he gestured to her to give him the gun. She shook her head.

"You can barely stand," she said.

"This is Detective Pa…I'm Paul Allen, badge number six two fiver seven of Precinct Nineteen in New York," he said into the phone. Not his name, badge number, or precinct. Of course the call was being recorded. "I am located at two-three-one-one South Beach Boulevard, room number two-one-seven and have a subject trying to gain entry into my room. Subject is a male Caucasian known to me and is usually armed. I need backup ASAP."

He could always get another job; Iz couldn't get another life.

"Copy, that, Detective Allen. Units one-six, two-one-two and five-eight, respond. Code Three to three-one-one South Beach Boulevard, motel, room number two-one-seven for an officer assist. Caller is off-duty police officer with a subject attempting entry into his hotel room. Subject is known to him and is usually armed. Stand by for additional."

The units checked in; the dispatcher confirmed.

"Units are on their way," she told Pat.

"Dispatch, be advised, subject is on the western side of building on a second-story landing facing room two-one-seven. He is usually armed with a submachine gun and a revolver. Advise responding units I am wearing light gray workout clothes and carrying my off-duty weapon. I have with me a female Caucasian also in light gray workout clothes."

He watched the window while the dispatcher relayed the information.

"Units are on their way."

The bald creep appeared at the top of the stairs and cocked his head, as if he was listening.

Get her out of there, said a voice, muffled and distant. He could barely hear it. Was it the TV in the next room?

Get Isabelle out. Vite! Pat jumped. It was Jean-Marc de Devereaux. How the hell?

He scanned the room, his vision blurring as his head pounded harder. Then he tapped the neck area of the catsuit beneath his sweats. That bastard must have miked them! Was he in on this?

"Dispatch, please be advised I am Code Eight," he told the dispatcher. Meaning he needed the cavalry, from anywhere and everywhere now now now. Officers would drop whatever they were doing—unless they had an arrestee—and come to his assistance.

Out, get her out!

"Copy, Detective, keep on the line if you can."

"Copy, dispatch."

The bald man started walking down the open-air hallway.

His footfalls thumped as if he weighed five hundred pounds. He *did* know where they were. There were only two ways out. If they went out the door, he would see them. If they crashed through the window beside the door, he would see them. Damn it, if this was going down the way Pat figured, he was going to have to shoot him.

"Jean-Marc, come in. We can't get out," he said. "Advise." He rubbed his temples. Nausea flowed through him. His legs were rubbery. He really *was* Code Eight.

There was nothing more from Jean-Marc. Pat tapped his catsuit, but there wasn't even any static.

Izzy was shaking so badly that her bullet might go wild even if the guy was three feet away when she pulled the trigger. He didn't want her to pull the trigger at any distance. He wanted her out of the action and he wanted it now.

"Hey," he said, not using her name.

She didn't hear him. She stood transfixed. He cleared his throat and she jerked and looked over at him. She hesitated, then held out the gun. As he took it, he pulled her hard against his chest. One of the things he was really good at was crises. When all about him were losing their heads, he stayed cool and collected.

"It's going to be all right," he told her.

She looked up at him with enormous, tear-filled eyes. Her fingers dug into his sweatshirt.

"I'm sorry," she said. "I'm so sorry."

"Detective?" the dispatcher said. "Unit is nearing the scene."

"Code Three," he requested. "Respond with lights and sirens."

He handed the phone to Izzy and murmured, "Crouch down behind the bed, darlin'."

Then he doubled his fists around the gun and walked

over to the window. Pushing the throbbing in his head to the back of his consciousness, he took careful aim.

And he fired.

The window shattered; shards flew. The bald man went down on the concrete walk in a heap.

"Stay down, down, down!"

He raced for the door and dashed outside to the inert figure, and loomed over him with his gun aimed straight at his head. The man's arms were bent wrong. There was no blood. His eyes were open. His face was…strange. Slick. As if he were wearing a mask.

Pat's stomach clenched. *Oh God, if I've been set up. If this is some bullshit of that cult's…*

"He's down," Pat said into his catsuit, keeping the gun on the dirtbag. He heard a door open. Another. A shout. Great. Witnesses. The wail of a siren.

Get her out of there now! Jean-Marc's voice came in loud and clear. *But don't shoot the Medusa. Kittrell, listen to me! Don't use that gun!*

"Listen, Devereaux," Pat said, staring down at the gun in his hand. "You're a day late and a dollar short on that request. Not only did I use it, but I killed the bastard and—"

The inert figure on the cement floor changed into a mass of glittering red light. It was a mummy made out of crimson fireworks sparklers, head to toe, a perfect outline. Then just as abruptly, it vanished. There was no man, no coat, nothing.

He turned to see Izzy racing up beside him.

"Did you see that?" he blurted.

She didn't stop. She grabbed his hand and ran past him. He followed her down the stairs and across the parking lot to Bobby's car. Key in his sweatpants, gun he wasn't supposed to use in hand—good, they'd left nothing behind in their room except a mystery and dozens of fingerprints and hair fibers, if NJPD wanted to know who had carried out a very lousy hoax.

They were in the car and out of the lot maybe twenty seconds before the first NJ squad car pulled up in the lot. The officers who got out weren't looking in his direction. Pat wondered how many witnesses there had been. He wondered why he wasn't supposed to use the gun. But most of all he wondered how a man could turn into sparkles and disappear. *What the hell was that?*

"Robot," he said.

Izzy said nothing. She was leaning her head against the window, and she was crying.

"Hey, honey," he said, reaching out a hand. "Hey."

"Don't." She buried her face in her hands. "Just... don't."

Chapter 7

It was a simple thing to convince an Ungifted man parked near Jean-Marc's warded cave that he wanted to hand over the keys to his BMW to Dominique and Georges. The two Devereaux special ops screamed along the I-95, heading for the address Pat Kittrell had given the 911 dispatcher. Someone in the vicinity had to have created that fabricant and sent it after Kittrell and Isabelle, and they might still be at the scene. If they were, Dom and Georges would show the creator no mercy until that person spilled his or her guts. Jean-Marc needed to know how many of Lilliane's minions were after them, what their plans were, how to make them family. That would also include who had organized the attack on Bobby's house and how he had known where they were.

Alain drove while Jean-Marc concentrated on Seeing where Pat and Isabelle had gone. He couldn't get through to Isabelle, only Kittrell, who was driving. Through his eyes, Jean-Marc Saw a sign for a back road near Cape May.

The sun had died. The moon reigned low and red over the water, like a bubble of blood. It was not yet full; they had eight days. Vampires loved to hunt during red moons. Werewolves, too. There were a hundred things reveling in the tinted night that could take down two tired, frightened people.

"There," Jean-Marc said, pointed to taillights ahead in the distance on the lonely, two-lane road. Alain floored it, and Jean-Marc centered himself. He knew the Medusa had been reloaded during the stay at Bobby's with heart-stopping magical 9 mm cartridges. If he or Alain came within firing range, their hearts would stop, even if the cartridges didn't penetrate their body armor. The spell would be discharged when the gun was fired— and it had no safety. A panicked moment, and they were dead. It was a miracle neither Isabelle nor Kittrell had been killed.

Isabelle, Kittrell, he called. *We are in the van behind you. You can see our headlights.*

He heard no answer, but their car sped up. Alain floored the van, huffing when it continued to poke along.

"Next time, we take the BMW and give Georges and Dom the soccer-mom car," he muttered. He snapped his fingers, and the van trundled along a little faster.

Jean-Marc tried again. *Kittrell, it is Jean-Marc and Alain. We want to help.*

Go to hell, Kittrell grunted.

"He heard me," Jean-Marc announced, watching the Beemer, fully expecting it to speed up again.

But after another moment or so, Isabelle's car slowed, then pulled over to the side. Alain pulled up behind them. Both cousins checked their weapons—.357 Magnums, loaded with cartridges designed only to render the target unconscious. They had a footlocker filled with more powerful equipment in the back.

"I still say we need something stronger," Alain insisted. "If he shoots at you with the Medusa…"

Jean-Marc laid his gun on the floor. "He's NYPD," he said. "If he realizes I'm armed…"

"Just shoot him," Alain said. "It won't hurt him."

"There's no safety on the Medusa," Jean-Marc argued. "If it discharges as he goes down, it might kill Isabelle.'

"Then let me go in your place," Alain implored. "You're putting yourself at risk *again.* By the Grey King, you shouldn't do this."

"*Tais-toi.* And stay here," Jean-Marc ordered him. He allowed his aura to grow and thicken, then rendered it invisible. With a nod at his cousin, he got out of the car.

Isabelle, he sent out. *The Medusa must not go off. It will kill you.*

He walked with his hands up, slowly, sending out images of peace and security. And then, as Pat got out on the driver's side in a bulky pair of sweats, he wove a spell designed to placate and soothe him.

Kittrell was holding the Medusa. Jean-Marc moved his lips, reinforcing the spell. Kittrell hesitated, looking confused, as Jean-Marc sauntered toward him, his body language belying his apprehension.

Isabelle slid out through the same door and moved to Pat's side. Both of them were wearing oversize workout gear—over their body armor, he assumed. She was too close; if Kittrell fired the Medusa, she would die.

"Jean-Marc," Isabelle said. She looked wan and exhausted, and her eyes were swollen, as if she'd been crying. Fear rolled off her in waves. He wished he could send a calming spell her way, but he had to stay focused on Kittrell.

"Pat, put the gun down," she told her boyfriend. So she had heard him. Maybe there was a chance that they could all walk away safely from this….

"No way," Kittrell gritted, raising the gun and aiming it straight at Jean-Marc.

"You're glad to see me," Jean-Marc said aloud, "because I'm here to help you." He doubled—tripled—his magical efforts, aware that he was already sorely taxed. The attack at Bobby's house and the search for Isabelle would have drained him even if he hadn't been recently wounded and unsouled.

"I'm here to help," Jean-Marc repeated. "I'm a powerful magic user, and you're in my world now. I'm the answer to your prayers." Normally he wouldn't speak aloud, simply work in his target's mind. But he was tired, and words had power.

Kittrell frowned. The frown slipped. His face went slack.

"You are so glad to see me. Why wouldn't you be?" Jean-Marc said. The man was strong-willed, single-minded. A challenge.

Jean-Marc pushed again. Finally Pat smiled and lowered the Medusa to his side.

"Fancy meeting you here," Kittell said. "Good to see you, Devereaux."

"Likewise," Jean-Marc said, moving his attention to Isabelle. She was glaring at him.

"Leave him alone," she said angrily.

"We're here now, so we can all go in one car to New York," Jean-Marc continued, ignoring her. "That's a better idea, *non?*"

"I suppose it is," Kittrell said. He smiled at Isabelle. "I

know you're tired and my head is about to explode. We could use a break."

"Pat, he's brainwashing you."

She stepped around him and marched up to Jean-Marc. He wanted to grab her and hold her, reassure himself that she had not died. They'd had so many close calls—too many. Many high-level Gifted had died at the hands of fabricants. Stripped of her Gift as she was, it was a miracle that she stood before him now. Surely it was proof that her patroness had not deserted her.

"It's okay, Iz," Pat said. "Devereaux and I are good."

"Don't do this," she hissed at Jean-Marc. "Don't manipulate him, too."

Jean-Marc set his jaw. His fear for her metamorphosed into anger. Everything he did was to protect her. He didn't have to abandon his family in Montreal to sneak into the bayou; he didn't have to lose his soul while trying to save her. Was she so blind and so stupid that she couldn't comprehend the enormity of his sacrifices?

Merde, he wanted to throttle her. Or shoot her. *Oui,* render her unconscious and then make her beg for his forgiveness. Make her repudiate this man, this Ungifted…

…this man who had repeatedly saved her life.

"I can't release him while he's armed," Jean-Marc told her.

She blazed; there was no other word for it. Beneath the scarlet moon, she whirled on her heel, walked over to Pat and grabbed the gun out of his hand. He didn't protest, only smiled quizzically at her.

She pointed the gun toward the ground, stomped over to Jean-Marc and thrust it at him by the grip.

"Here," she said. "Take it. I never wanted it anyway. I hate guns."

Then her chin quivered and her eyes welled. "Look, I

know I have to go with you. You don't have to hypnotize me, too. But if I *ever* find out that you played us back at that motel, put the fear of God in us so we'd come with you, I swear I'll kill you myself."

"Iz," Pat protested, "He's just looking out for us." He rubbed his temples and moved his shoulders. "I'm glad we've got some backup. This flying solo is six kinds of wrong."

"Fair enough," Jean-Marc said to Izzy, ignoring Pat. He extended his arm. "If you can ever prove that I created a Malchance fabricant to hunt you down and kill you, you have my permission to kill me. Come with us in the minivan. Both of you. *Now.*"

Kittrell wrinkled his forehead. "What about Bobby's car?"

"Alain will arrange for it to be returned to him," Jean-Marc promised.

"All right. We should wipe it down for prints," Kittrell said. "That 911 call probably set an investigation in motion."

Jean-Marc waved his hand. "Done. And I have people doing cleanup on the call. It will be taken care of."

"See, Iz?" Pat said. "Everything is going to work out."

Flushing, she took Pat's hand.

"Take the spell off," she ordered Jean-Marc.

"Get in the van." He turned and walked back alone. Alain was behind the wheel with his .357 in his lap. He fastened wary eyes on Isabelle and Kittrell as he activated the door release and the panel slid back. Jean-Marc stood beside the vehicle, waiting until both Isabelle and Pat were inside. Then he shut the door, went around and climbed back in his seat.

"Allons-y," he told Alain. Let's go.

Alain turned the engine back on and angled the Odyssey onto the two-lane road. For about a minute, they rode in silence.

Then Isabelle said, "You said you'd take the spell off him."

"I'm not under a spell, darlin'," Kittrell declared.

"How's your head, Kittrell?" Jean-Marc asked pointedly. By eliminating Kittrell's combativeness, he had decreased the man's stress—and with it, his headache.

"Good. God, that was a killer migraine."

"Take it *off*." Isabelle's voice was glacial.

"No," Jean-Marc replied.

"You said—"

"I did not. I never said."

"You...*jerk*."

Alain cast a weary glance at him. "We'll be in New York soon. Everyone should try to get some rest." Then he waved his hands over the steering wheel and dropped his hands in his lap. The car was on magical autopilot now. Alain couldn't sleep, but he could take it a little easier.

"I'll check in with Georges and Dom," Jean-Marc said, pulling out his cell phone. He speed-dialed Dom.

"No sign of the creator of the fabricant," Dom told him. "There was a crowd by the time we pulled up. Over a dozen police vehicles. We assumed glamours as cops to fit in. We cleaned the room of all traces of any of you. No one will be able to collect any hair or DNA."

"Good. No voodoo dolls today, then," Jean-Marc replied. He heard a stirring in the backseat and glanced up at the rearview mirror. Isabelle's dark eyes were reflected back at him. They burned like embers.

Finally she said, "Voodoo dolls? Are you serious?"

"Yes, I am serious," he said. "It's all serious."

"Not really," Kittrell piped up.

Jean-Marc sighed. "When we get to the safe house, I'll take it off."

"I'm not thanking you," she informed him.

* * *

Silence fell; it began to rain. Thick raindrops the color of mercury pelted the windshield as they took the New Jersey Turnpike to the Holland Tunnel.

Jean-Marc watched Isabelle in the rearview mirror as she stared out the window like a tourist who had never been to the big city before. He didn't need to read her thoughts: she had lived in Brooklyn for all but three months of her life, but she didn't remember anything about New York.

Coordinating with security, they received a heavy escort through Manhattan as they neared the safe house. They blew past Rockefeller Center and the Hilton. Andre and a van full of werewolves drove on their left; two heavily warded trucks and three cars filled with Michel's loyal Bouvards and Jean-Marc's Devereaux special ops rode ahead, to the right and behind the Odyssey. Jean-Marc was on full alert, like a bloodhound. He felt the tension in the air. Anger. Fear.

They tasted delicious on his tongue.

Everyone glided into the private entrance to the building's parking garage. The penthouse occupied the entire floor of the towering skyscraper and came with a generous number of parking spaces as well as a private elevator.

Surrounded by armed Gifted, Michel joined Jean-Marc, Isabelle, Alain and Kittrell, entered the private elevator and went up. An armed Devereaux soldier stood at attention when the door slid open.

"Le Gardien et la Gardienne!" he announced. Beyond him, at least a dozen security forces in full battle regalia snapped to attention. An equal number of *Femmes Blanches* in white robes and veils knelt and lowered their heads.

"Merci bien," Jean-Marc replied.

The soldiers dropped to one knee. Michel and Alain followed suit. Only Jean-Marc, Isabelle and Kittrell remained standing. Kittrell's expression was guarded as Isabelle took his hand, signaling to everyone that they were together. Jean-Marc was certain she had no idea that the sight of their Guardian paired with an Ungifted man was extremely offensive to the assembled group who paid her homage.

He ticked his glance at Michel, who was looking up at the couple with a taut, unhappy expression. Their eyes met, and Jean-Marc realized he was going to have to tell Michel that Isabelle had lost both her memory and her Gift. She was going to make too many mistakes. Michel would have to brief her on their customs—he'd done it before, sat with her and showed her photographs of her many relatives, her allies and her enemies. A stickler for protocol, he would keep her from making more enemies through sheer ignorance of propriety.

"Madame, welcome," said Suzanne, the most senior of the *Femmes Blanches* at the safe house. She rose to her feet. Jean-Marc had ordered a group of seven *Femmes Blanches* to stay in the New York safe house, against just such an occasion as this. "It's so good to see you again."

"Thank you," Isabelle replied.

"Would Madame like to take a look around? We haven't changed a thing," she continued.

"Yes, thank you." Isabelle smiled at her.

He knew that smile cost her. He was impressed with how well she was carrying off the charade that she hadn't lost her memory. He and Alain had debated allowing the other three *Femmes Blanches*—Denise, Sara and Lucienne—to complete the journey to New York. They had either been witnesses to the revelation that Isabelle was half Malchance or knew someone who had been. But in this day and age of cell phones and e-mail, one could only assume the New York contingent had been informed and had chosen to remain as part of Izzy's retinue. Jean-Marc was grateful to them.

Pat trailed after Isabelle and the *Femmes Blanches*. Jean-Marc understood her anger; his spell had diminished Pat in her eyes. A strong woman like her needed a strong man. Pat was strong. Unfortunately he was unsuitable on so many other levels.

It would have made my life easier if the fabricant had killed him.

Such a thought was beneath him, and Jean-Marc was irritated with himself. He was in a bad spot. He felt the evil thing drilling holes in his soul and shook himself all over, like a wet dog, as if he could force it to leave.

Tense and miserable, he walked into the formal dining room off the kitchen, to find it filled with familiar faces. Alain sat at an oval, burnished cherrywood table with his most senior operatives: Dom, Lucky, Maurice, Georges and two newer arrivals—Christian and Gabriel, direct from Shadows headquarters in Montreal.

All stood and snapped to attention when he entered. He accepted their acknowledgment with a regal air and no warmth. He knew he had a reputation as a man who was tightly controlled and aloof. It had been said of him that there was a block of ice where his heart should have been. He didn't care what they thought of him; his only interest lay in using their perception to his advantage, so he could be an effective leader.

"Just what I need," he said, as he crossed to the table. Alain had opened a bottle of Armagnac, a fine French brandy. Jean-Marc assumed it was a tip of the hat to Jehanne. She had fought on the Armagnac side of the war.

A shimmering lead crystal goblet etched with the Bouvard logo of a trio of flames sat before each man. Jean-Marc had personally selected everything in the coop himself, to introduce Isabelle to the family she had been chosen by fate to lead.

At the head of the table, an empty glass awaited him. It was customary not to serve food or drink to a Devereaux Guardian until he was present, to make poisoning less likely. As his men remained standing, Alain filled Jean-Marc's goblet.

"To Jehanne d'Arc, patroness of the Flames, and to our Grey King," Jean-Marc intoned, raising his glass. "And to my brave Shadows."

"To the patrons, and to Jean-Marc, our *Gardien*," Dominique replied. The others raised their glasses as well, although Christian looked down, uncomfortably. His dark hair was gelled, and a dove tattoo graced the back of his hand. His lips were pursed and tight. Jean-Marc knew that something was very wrong. He could feel it. Everyone else at the table could, too. Faces were tense; backs were up.

Each took a sip, ritualistically savoring the bouquet. Then Jean-Marc set his glass on the table, and everyone sat. Soon he'd unpeel this damnable armor and take a shower. He was fortunate; he'd washed off layers of magical residue when he'd dipped himself in the Atlantic. He doubted that the others had had such an opportunity, and they would be suffering depression and anxiety due to that lack.

I must remind Isabelle to take a shower, he thought, then wondered if she had any magical residue to wash off. She certainly hadn't cast any spells recently.

Except on me. She holds me in thrall. By the Grey King, when I saw her alive and well…

"Let's debrief," he said. "*La situation.* Christian."

Christian lifted his glass of Armagnac off the table and studied the ring of condensation on the wood.

So the news was to be of the worst kind.

So be it.

"Monsieur, you have been deposed," he said simply. "Declared a traitor."

Roars of anger ringed the table; Jean-Marc held up a hand to quell them. It was nothing less than what he expected. He wasn't regretful—he would have done anything to save Isabelle from Luc de Malchance—but it was a blow. Until Isabelle, he had always put the family first. It was what he had been trained to do.

"Go on," he ordered his man.

Christian took another sip of Armagnac, as if for courage. Oranges and roses wafted around the table—the men were attempting to maintain some semblance of calm—and Christian raised his chin.

"It was declared that the *Gardien* had abandoned his family to rescue Madame de Bouvard. Then it was learned that Madame is half Malchance, which would not normally have posed a problem, as we Devereauxes declare ourselves neutral in the dealings with both the House of the Flames and the Blood."

"These are not normal times," Jean-Marc said flatly.

"*Non,*" Christian replied, gazing back down at the table. "They are not."

Gabriel took up the thread. "When Luc de Malchance invaded the House of the Flames, he thumbed his nose at all the Houses and clans who are members of the Grand Covenate—that would include us, of course, as well as the House of the Flames. He promised to destroy us with demons and dark arts. All around the world, evil is manifesting—demons from the Dark Side are rampaging in the night; vampires are emboldened. Werewolf howls were heard last night within the Montreal city limits."

"These things can be taken care of," Jean-Marc said.

"The Malchances are being blamed," Christian said.

"Isabelle conjured a demon, and that demon killed Luc de Malchance," Jean-Marc countered. "Proving that she is loyal to the House of the Flames."

"With all due respect, you have no proof that she did any such thing," Christian put in. "We have no reliable Devereaux witnesses to corroborate that story. You were unsouled at the time. And Alain had been beaten unconscious. There were no other Devereauxes there."

"It has been claimed," Gabriel said delicately, "that by remaining in the United States with Madame Isabelle instead of returning to Montreal, you've sided with the Malchances."

"*C'est fou*. That's ridiculous," Jean-Marc scoffed. "Who came up with this convoluted nonsense to defame me? It was my idiot brother, François, *non?*"

Their long faces were his answer. His younger brother, François, had coveted the crown of the House of the Shadows his entire life.

Idiot. Traitor. Order his death. Make it slow.

Jean-Marc tamped down his fury and silenced the demonic voice in his head. He wondered what Callia thought of all this. They weren't formally engaged, but the expectation was there.

"Last night, the council approved François's request to be named as Regent," Christian explained. "Then he convinced them to take a public stand against the Malchances. The House of the Shadows has formally declared them our enemies."

"Putain de merde," Georges groaned.

"We never declare anyone an enemy. We gain nothing by such grandstanding," Jean-Marc insisted, exasperated. "Neutrality has always served us well."

"You weren't there to argue that point," Christian said coldly.

Why didn't you speak on my behalf?

Why didn't you murder my enemies?

Jean-Marc took a sip of Armagnac and pondered what to say. The men were scrutinizing him, waiting to see how he would react. Jean-Marc was not a man who reacted; he acted.

"So be it, Christian," he said. "I will assume that you're here as a messenger, and you may safely return to Montreal in the morning." He looked at the rest of his men. "I offer the same to all of you. Whoever stays here will be branded with the same iron as me."

Most shook their heads. Christian stared at his glass. Then Dom pushed back his chair and stood.

"You're still my *Gardien,* monsieur. My commander-in-chief. We'll fix this."

"I appreciate your loyalty," Jean-Marc replied, "but things aren't that simple. I can't go back right now."

"Madame Isabelle is not your concern," Gabriel asserted.

"Monsieur has sustained some terrible magical injuries and can't travel," Alain said. "But I have hopes of restoring him before the next full moon."

"The next full moon?" Gabriel cried. "We need you *now!*"

"We can plan. Once monsieur is better, we'll kick François's ass," Dom declared, plopping down in his chair and pouring himself more Armagnac.

"But your brother is going to thrust us into a war,"

Gabriel said. "The Houses are going to fight the Mal-chances and their dark allies. And François is committing us to join in."

"That's not our way," Maurice insisted. "Our posture is always neutrality. Once more Devereauxes realize what's happening, they'll welcome you back with a thousand apologies."

"And a terrible accident will land your brother in the crypt," Georges added.

"François *là-bas!*" the men chorused, raising their glasses. *"Vive Jean-Marc!"* They drank, except for Christian, who only brushed his lips to the rim of his glass.

Jean-Marc would not be placated. "While you're in this safe house in the neutral territory of New York, I request that you conduct yourselves as peaceful, neutral Shadows. But even among us, our neutrality has been compromised. If you need to go back to Montreal to support my brother, leave now."

Christian and Gabriel slid back their chairs.

"With your permission," Christian said tightly.

Jean-Marc inclined his head, and the two left the room. Georges, Maurice, Lucky and Dominique remained at the table.

"This is a sad day, and I'll never forget it all my long life," Dom said, shaking his shaggy head. Then he flashed his trademark quirky grin and lifted his glass. "To Jean-Marc, then, *Gardien* in exile."

"À Jean-Marc!" the four chorused.

While Jean-Marc conferred with his men, Izzy surveyed the large, elegant apartment with Pat and the famed healers of the Bouvard family. The place was decorated in dark woods and tints of white—cream, ivory, alabaster. The icons of triple flames and Joan of Arc's face were every-where, woven into a large rug in an octagonally shaped library, on the dinner plates, the boxes of tissue, the guest towels in the bathrooms.

Now she and Pat stood alone in the center of her bedroom in the coop. She had gleaned that Jean-Marc had decorated the dark, forbidding room of heavy stone and dark wood to match her bedroom back in New Orleans. Her canopy bed was hung with white pennants and banners with the triple-flames icon, and there was a painting of Joan of Arc's face on the headboard with a matching mosaic on the floor.

"This is the work of a disturbed mind," Pat drawled.

Izzy put her arms around him and held him. True to his word, Jean-Marc had lifted his spell on Pat as soon as the three of them were alone in the penthouse. Then he had stood still and took the hard right Pat delivered to his jaw. His head had snapped back, but his feet stayed planted to the floor.

"I deserved that," was all he'd said.

A disturbed mind, she thought.

"And speaking of disturbing," Jean-Marc said from the door. He had taken a shower; his hair hung in damp ringlets over his shoulders. He was wearing a beautifully cut black suit with a white shirt and a charcoal-gray tie, and he looked like a high-priced lawyer.

"Get out of my head," she snapped. "Stop reading my mind."

"You need to take a shower," he said. "Gifted slough off magical residue. If it accumulates on your body, it can cause mood swings and depression. It's debilitating."

'I don't have any magical residue," she reminded him.

"Perhaps." He smiled at her. She had seen him smile so seldom that she was surprised his face didn't crack. "But

at any rate, a shower would be good, given how many
people are crammed into the coop."

*What exactly is he trying to say? That I have an odor
problem?*

"Perhaps." His smile faded. "I'm serious about the need
to cleanse yourself. There are towels, plenty for both of
you." He turned to go, wheeled back around. "There's a
two-person hot tub in there, too."

Then he closed the door behind himself.

Pat watched him go. "I used to be jealous of that guy."

She rolled her eyes. "Of Count Dracula? Please."

"Some women think Count Dracula is pretty sexy. "

"Yeah, and as we both know, some women think serial
killers are pretty sexy," she said, working overtime not to
blush. Jean-Marc obviously assumed they were going to
shower and soak together…and make love. She just
couldn't do that, not with Jean-Marc around. Whether or
not it meant something, she had slept with him. She had
to get clear of him before she could give herself fully to
Pat.

"So, the shower…" she began.

Understanding, he smiled. "It's all yours, honey. Take
your time."

How much time? she wondered. When *would* she be
clear of Jean-Marc?

Chapter 8

In a small antechamber decorated in blue and gray stonework, Jean-Marc and Alain put on their spangled, dark blue robes, picked up their jeweled ritual knives and lit long blue tapers. Alain carried a sacred book of spells from the coop's well-stocked octagonal library. Then they entered the altar room of the safe house, Jean-Marc first. The others had been alerted to leave them alone to do their magical work.

The walls were bare except for two medieval tapestries. One depicted a black-haired woman wearing a halo being burned at the stake. Joan of Arc. The other showed the by-now familiar icon of House Devereaux: a castle turret surrounded by clouds, and a white bird flying out of the gray arched window. And as before, the gauntlet—freeing the bird, or trying to grab it?

The only other object was a pitted, worn stone altar in the center of the room. Jean-Marc had brought the revered relic, an anchor of Devereaux vibration in a dwelling dedicated to Jehanne, from Montreal. On the left side of the ancient stone table, a blocky granite figure, the oldest known image of their patron, the Grey King, rested behind a simple stone bowl of water surrounded by blue candles.

On the right, a likeness of Jehanne d'Arc held her sword and pennant before a vase of lilies—her flower—and a single white taper. Symbols of the lily-white Bouvards. The Malchances didn't mind their reputation as an evil family; the Devereaux enjoyed their status as neutral observers. But the Bouvards toiled to present a façade of purity and goodness to the world.

It was ironic that the House of the Flames had been reduced to a persecuting mob by a *scandale*—a forbidden passion resulting in two mixed children.

Jean-Marc wondered about that. Marianne de Bouvard, Isabelle's mother; and Etienne de Malchance, her father, had defied the laws of both Houses to bring the twins into the world. Gifted were able to magically prevent conception; no one had children by accident. Perhaps they had done it in some insane scheme to merge their Houses.

Or more likely, Etienne de Malchance had deceived Marianne, *Gardienne* of the House of the Flames, into thinking that was the plan. More likely, he had schemed from the beginning to control her Gift and her family. Promised her love and planned for her death. They both had much to answer for and, if after death he crossed paths with either of them, Jean-Marc would get those answers.

He lay the matter aside and focused on the task at hand. There was much to do to prepare the altar room. He and Alain were here to strengthen its protective fields. It was already the most heavily warded space in the coop—probably in all of New York City. Magic use was forbidden in New York. That had never prevented it, but Jean-Marc had no interest in advertising where he and Isabelle were. But during tomorrow night's rituals, the rafters themselves would shake with magic before he and his cousin were through.

They bowed to the symbols of both patrons and placed their candles and knives on the altar. Alain reverently laid the book in a central spot between the two figurines.

Then both knelt in prayer. Within seconds, sweat beaded Jean-Marc's forehead as the evil inside him raged against being forced inside a sacred space to pay reverence to anyone.

Get out of here, get out get out. Pat Kittrell is circling around her, confusing her. That low-born Ungifted; he will convince her to leave and everything you have sacrificed will be wasted.

"Jean-Marc?" Alain ventured. "What is it?"

Opening his eyes, Jean-Marc looked down at his hands. He had dug his fingernails into his palms, and his blood was dripping onto the altar.

"You know what it is," he said shortly. "Let's continue."

"Perhaps I should do this on my own," Alain suggested. "Or ask someone else to help me."

"Don't be an idiot. I'm your Guardian," Jean-Marc snapped. Then a wave of angry despair washed over him. "You're right, *mon cousin*. I can't help you. I shouldn't even be here."

He got to his feet. Alain did the same. Alain's face was clouded with sadness and caution. He reached out and touched the place where Jean-Marc had been wounded. It burned as his magical energy penetrated the newly forming scar tissue.

"You're not in the best of shape," he observed.

"It's not my physical wound. It's my own little piece of

hell. Inside me." He allowed his aura to become visible. The streaks of black undulated seductively within the shimmering blue.

Alain watched. "It will be gone soon. I promise you," he said.

"Sooner would be better than later. I can feel evil coming into the world. It's as Christian said—the fabric between our world and the next is thinning. My own loyalties are torn. Thanks to the thing inside me."

"We'll get rid of it," Alain underscored.

Jean-Marc picked up his jeweled knife, also called an athame, its intricate gold and silver pattern of inlaid sapphires and blue diamonds as unique as the whorls of his fingerprints. He and Alain had made their knives together decades ago, under the tutelage of Jean-Marc's father.

Alone, he walked toward the door.

"I've been giving the ritual some thought," Alain said behind him. "It requires sex magic, Jean-Marc. And it seems to me that you and Isabelle must be together, as you were when this terrible thing happened to you both."

Do it, the voice whispered. *He's right. You know you want to. To have her a third time...it would be the charm.*

He kept his back to his cousin. "No. I won't risk it. I'm tainted. If we give this thing more power, it may overcome me."

"But from my reading, I believe it's necessary. Otherwise—"

"Non."

"Then someone else. Someone very strong. A partner for each of you. Dom for her, perhaps. Suzanne, for you."

Jean-Marc knitted his brows as he studied the flickering flame of his taper. He thought of Isabelle with the lusty Dominique.

"She would never do it," he said flatly. "She doesn't remember our ways."

"We can make her do it," Alain countered. "We can cast a spell on her."

Jean-Marc remained silent. Alain spread his arms wide, then breathed in slowly and shook his head, his dreadlocks gently bobbing.

"How did this happen to you, this possessive, limited love? We were raised in the same House, trained in the ways of Gifted men. You know what the act of sex is, and what it's not. But ever since you found her, you've changed."

Jean-Marc frowned. "No. You're wrong. I have not changed. Or if I have, it's because Le Devourer has polluted me."

"Non," Alain insisted, as blue energy thickened around him, then, sparkled through the air, washing the simple white walls with magic. "Your detractors are correct. You did abandon your post to rescue her. You got us into this mess. We, the House of the Shadows, who have stayed out of all the quarrels and battles among Gifted and Ungifted alike, for centuries. Our traditions are smashed. Because of a woman."

"François smashed them. Our neutrality is our most sacred tradition."

"Non. Isabelle was the open door. Or as she was once known, Isabella De Marco, of Brooklyn. Everything began to fall apart when you found her."

"And would things be better now if the Malchances had found her first? I had a duty to her," Jean-Marc protested, examining the blood on his hands.

The blood on his hands.

"Accent on 'had' a duty, *mon vieux.* Once she had

received the Kiss, it was up to her to sink or swim," Alain replied. "Your duty was to lead the Devereaux family and look out for *us*."

"*Et tu*, Alain?" Jean-Marc said sourly, crossing his arms over his chest and cocking his head.

Alain didn't back down. "Jean-Marc, you know that I love you like a brother. Because of that, I'm speaking frankly. I will conduct the ritual we are planning for the purpose of healing *you*. I hope that it will help her as well, because I, too, care deeply for her."

"*Merci*," Jean-Marc grunted.

"But if this works for you only, and you're restored and she is not, then we must move on, at least for the time being. It is unfortunate that this happened to her, but you have to make peace with the House of the Shadows *now*."

"*Non*," Jean-Marc snapped.

"*Oui*." Alain's features hardened. "You're indispensable, Jean-Marc. You are the Son of the Shadows. If you don't step up and assert your claim, François will destroy us."

"I'm sure a dozen plots are being hatched to get rid of him," Jean-Marc said.

Alain huffed, exasperated. "And if you're not there when it happens, another unfit Devereaux will take his place. You were chosen in our most ancient and revered ritual, and you accepted your charge. You have to let her go. Be the doggedly pragmatic Jean-Marc I know…and respect." He let the last word hang in the air.

Jean-Marc chewed the inside of his cheek to keep from lashing out. The demon inside him urged him to be wild, ungovernable, vindictive. To deny everything Alain had just said, and punish him for his audacity.

Except…Alain was right.

Jean-Marc remembered his prayer in the bayou clearing when he'd been hurt. He had prayed not to die, so that he could protect Isabelle. There had been Devereaux special ops in the bayou, fighting her battle. His men, in place because he was there, and he had ordered them to protect her. And yet, he had prayed to his patron for *her* life, *her* safety…but he hadn't prayed for his Devereaux soldiers. And some of them had died that day. They shouldn't have been there in the first place.

He was not his own man, not some maverick warrior who could pick his own battles. He was the leader of a family, and his family was in trouble.

"There are no divided loyalties here," Alain underscored. "Your duty is clear." He exhaled and clasped his hands around the back of his neck, looking weary and perturbed. "In the past, we wouldn't even be having this discussion. You were the most levelheaded man I knew."

"I'm still that man," he argued. "I can't lead my House in this condition. And as you yourself said, she may be key to my healing."

Alain sighed and wordlessly nodded. Silence hung between them.

Kill him. Take your athame and run him through. He's from the old days.

I'm the new days.

"Perhaps Dominique can help me with the warding," Alain said. "He's definitely on our side."

We must make this ritual work, Jean-Marc thought. *I must bring her back with me from the depths. I know that in my soul. I can't abandon her.*

The thing inside him moved and shifted. *I really think you should,* it whispered. *In fact, I think you should kill her. And you will, sooner or later. I'll see to it.*

The Castle of the House of the Blood
Haiti

"No, no, enough, you're so messy," Lilliane huffed, as she pulled Baron Noir's ritual knife out of the forehead of her prisoner, Richard de Malchance. Realizing she had just ruined its magical charge, she shrugged and handed it back to the baron, formerly her chief voodoo *bokor,* now her High Priest of Darkest Magicks. No more voodoo for the select inner circle of Malchance Gifted. Thanks to her, they were tapped into a far more powerful magic system. They were already seeing results, all over the globe.

Baron Noir accepted his useless knife with a great deal more resentment than a man in his position ought to display. Petulant lackey; he could make another one. In his other hand, he held the Chalice of the Blood. Three souls fluttered inside it. They would soon be joined by a fourth.

Wearing domino masks and standing inside a freshly drawn pentagram in the dungeon, her former *voudon* priests and priestesses looked on, stiff-shouldered and sulky.

She had taken away their old voodoo regalia—the black and green robes and claw-foot charms—and outfitted them according to the demands of the new rites and rituals. Everyone was draped from head to toe in black veils sewn with the bones of demons. The fragments clacked like wind chimes as they dipped and swayed, chanting in a tongue more ancient even than the Old Language.

Their cheeks were tattooed with the runic symbol for Chaos, and they'd all lost their pinkie fingers. She'd sliced them off herself with her athame and burned them on the desecrated altar. She would have done the same to herself, had the new rites and rituals required such a sacrifice from the Great High Priestess. Luckily it had not.

The bleeding man chained to the floor tugged wildly at his handcuffs and ankle restraints. Lilliane frowned at him, placing her hands on either side of his head on the wet, slimy dungeon floor. No need to tell the assembled priests and priestesses that shortly before their arrival, she had straddled the prisoner and taken him sexually, draining him of as much power as possible.

Now she leaned over him and put her face close to his. What would happen if she bit off his nose?

She started giggling. She'd done a bit of research on inappropriate laughter. To some, it was an indication of insanity. And insanity was an indication of communion with the gods. Close enough. She giggled some more, lifting her right hand off the dank dungeon floor, covering her mouth and clearing her throat. Enough was enough. This should be a dignified ritual.

"You might as well stop struggling. It's going to happen, Richard," she taunted him. "And you did it to yourself. The minute you and your stupid woman tried to sneak out of here, your fate was sealed." She smiled over her shoulder at his mindless, unsouled wife and two small sons, barely toddlers, as they drooled and muttered incoherently. Locked in eternal torment, they served as proof of Richard de Malchance's treachery. It was their three souls inside her chalice.

"Hiding behind your wife and children," she chided. "Claiming you wanted to get them to 'safety.'" She rose up on her knees, making air quotes. When what you really wanted to do was find *her* so she could destroy me."

He shook his head. "Mmm, mmf," he protested behind his gag.

"There is nothing unsafe here!" she shrieked at him. "This is House Malchance! We are invincible! Isn't that right, my patron?"

She leaned back on one hand and traced the huge silhouette shifting and moving on the dungeon floor. Images of steam and smoke rolled off the great horns and massive head of Le Devourer. He turned in profile and opened his enormous mouth. Black strings of drool roped his razor-sharp fangs as he clacked them at the man on the floor.

"C'est vrai," Le Devourer whispered in her mind. You're right.

He had returned to her; not only returned, but brought with him such incredible magic—the blackest, most world-changing magic she had ever heard of. On the night of the full moon, she would conduct a ritual of the darkest, vilest magic imaginable. Then he would blast into being in this very world and take her as his consort. By then, her world would be very different. It was already happening. They'd destroy the other Gifted families. Get rid of all the Ungifted lowlifes. And as for Isabelle…*the one my mother protected, her favorite…*

She stiffened. She would tear apart heaven to find her mother and make her suffer for abandoning *her* and not that moron, Isabelle. That ugly slut, that useless *bitch.*

She jerked, aware that she'd gotten distracted. The man on the floor had stopped writhing. Maybe he actually hoped that he would be spared.

Oh, my God, she thought, *how did such a stupid person live so long?*

She smiled at the shadow of her patron. He was still physically locked in his own dimension. He couldn't manifest in her world, not yet. The last ritual must be conducted on the full moon, when the tides of magic were strongest. She had six more nights until the world was remade. She couldn't wait!

"Set the Chalice of the Blood down beside me," she

ordered Baron Noir. "I've spent way too much time on this. There are a million things to do to get ready for the full moon."

She bobbed her head imperiously as he stepped forward and put the Chalice next to her knee. The metal clanked on stone.

"Now, watch. You make it far too difficult, Baron. No cutting of the victim is required. I let you disfigure the others, but it's so amateurish. Plunge and grab, that's all there is to it." She extended her hands toward the bleeding forehead of her captive.

"Barbaras est magnus," she chanted.

Red light blazed around her body.

"Cason magnus dux."

Her hands glowed bright crimson, even her French manicure. She leaned forward and plunged them into Richard's skull. Rearing back on her knees, she yanked out his soul. His eyeballs turned white. He went into convulsions. The pulsing mass was warm and tickled her skin. The long, golden cord that anchored the soul to the body gleamed and pulse.

She pulled up her dress and slid her athame from the black leather sheath tied to her bare thigh.

Lilliane giggled under her breath as she deftly wrapped the cord around the knifepoint and jerked upward, slicing through it like black velvet.

She blew it a kiss, knowing that even that tiny pressure would cause Richard raging agony. Let him twist.

"This is how all my enemies will suffer," she told the priests and priestesses. "Spread the word to your congregation. I won't tolerate betrayal. If anyone so much as *thinks* about leaving, or helping my sister, this is their inevitable conclusion."

Everyone had thought she was too stupid to use words like that; they had assumed she was Luc's plaything, his strange half-breed, his little Bouvard whore. No matter that they had married according to all the rites and rituals of the House of the Blood. Little Lilliane wasn't good enough, would never be good enough.

Fine, then. She would be *powerful* enough. Luc's patron had died with Luc, and House Malchance needed someone new. No one had expected his widow to attract a patron like Le Devourer. All those times Luc and his inner circle discussed the care and feeding of demonic allies, she'd listened. Reading Luc's books one by one, sliding them under the bed when he came to take his pleasure, assert his dominance…

She dropped Richard's soul in with those of his family and stirred them with her athame. The air around the Chalice vibrated with their soundless screams. There, everything was ready. She raised a tired brow and mouthed a yawn. All this soul-stealing and ritual-preparing was wearing her out.

But so very much worth it. Let them see what crazy Lilliane had in store for them.

"You may all leave now," she informed the group, gesturing with her head toward the dungeon door. "*Allez. Vite.* I must commune alone with my patron."

Baron Noir opened his mouth as if to speak. Behind his black half mask, his eyes darted left, right, at his brother and sister priests. The atmosphere shifted again. They were nervous. Tense.

Are they going to attack me? Here? Now? For the love of all that's unholy, they couldn't possibly be so stupid, could they? Am I completely surrounded by idiots?

"*What?*" she demanded.

"Nothing, Madame," the man said, dipping his head.

"Nothing, *what?*" Her voice rose shrilly. She tapped the ball of her bare foot against the floor.

"Nothing, *Madame la Gardienne,*" he grumbled.

Someday soon, I am going to torture him to death, she thought, giggling. *I am, I am, I am. I deserve a treat.*

"Baron, you're wasting my time," she chided him playfully. He didn't smile. "Now, off with you. All of you. Scoot!"

She waved them away. As they uneasily bowed and curtsied, glancing at each other, she decided to ask Le Devourer to butcher all of them after he appeared on earth. Baron Noir would be last. Or maybe first, in case he had a few tricks up his magical sleeve. Allies, such as her slut sister.

Note to self: increase surveillance on the baron.

They took forever to leave. She pointedly tapped her foot and hummed to herself, swirling the souls in the Chalice. The four unsouled traitors chattered like monkeys. Flashing with irritation, she kicked Richard in the head. Of course it did no good. Maybe she should just slit his throat. But then, the horror of his agony would no longer serve as a deterrent to the others.

"By my blood, there's so much to keep track of," she groaned. Then she doused all the torches in the dungeon except one. Lovely, lovely darkness. She swirled in a circle, ripping off all her clothes as she spun, tossing them to the floor.

Naked, she lay on her back inside the pentagram. *Ooh, chilly! We'll have to talk about a wrap. Something soft, like rabbit. Or bristly, like werewolf.*

She parted her legs slightly and closed her eyes, reciting the chant Le Devourer had taught her. She couldn't speak his ancient language; she had learned the syllables phonetically. Her mind glazed over as goose bumps raised along her skin and her nipples grew taut. Over and over she chanted, losing more and more of herself, striving to become a conduit for Le Devourer—his devouring mouth, here on earth. His mouth *piece*. She giggled.

"Lilli, stop it," she ordered herself. "Don't be naughty."

It took her a long time to get back in the mood. Maybe she should have screwed a vampire after she'd ravished Richard. That would have charged her up.

"Brachilili sizhsal," she intoned, spreading her arms wide, as if she were making snow angels. Not that she had ever made snow angels. She lived in Haiti, not the North Pole. And she certainly had no love for angels. *"Dhililu, shamash."*

Her aura flared like flames, brilliant scarlet, pure and bold. The syllables washed over her; the sounds had power. She began to sweat and roll from side to side, losing sense of herself. Losing track…she was the words, and she was his vessel…she was his mouth….

She raised herself up on one elbow and grabbed the Chalice at her side. She whispered, giggled, drifted. The stone walls blazed with her, as if the dungeon was on fire. She quivered and shook. Red magic danced along her skin, singeing her.

"Brachilili, Le Devourer," she grunted. Then she tipped back her head, put the Chalice to her lips and drank down the four souls of her betrayers.

It was like drinking acid. She screamed. Spasms of pain racked her bones as she jerked and stiffened, jerked and stiffened. Her body mimicked the chewing of his huge, fanged mouth, gobbling up the souls, sucking the marrow of their Gifts. Shredding them, and spitting out the residue, which formed as a crust at the corners of her mouth.

She jerked, stiffened, jerked, stiffened, while she screamed.

The profile on the stone beneath her darkened. A huge hand cradled her as she rocked and whimpered, stretched and contracted. The pain made her delirious.

The pain was delicious.

More, Le Devourer demanded, once she had quieted. *I'm starving.*

"Oh," she said languidly, letting her legs splay open and flopping her arms above her head. "You're insatiable."

She giggled.

Chapter 9

The safe house, New York City

Izzy and Pat each took a shower; then, at Pat's insistence, Izzy soaked in the hot tub. She was aware of him through the door; aware, too, that Jean-Marc was nearby. It shouldn't matter. But it did. She felt self-conscious as she unwound her tense body, her hair caught up in a messy bun and her head draped back. She was exhausted and on edge. Lovemaking would have helped with that.

She sighed and emerged from the bubbling, scented water.

Two bathrobes had been hanging neatly from the bathroom door, one for her and one for Pat. She toweled off and slipped into the buttery soft robe.

When she came out, feeling fresh and rosy, she found Pat wearing his robe, gazing thoughtfully into the fire blazing in the stone fireplace. She wondered if he'd built the fire himself. The room was warm and inviting.

He looked over, joyful at the sight of her.

"Looks like that did you a world of good," he said. "Feel better?"

She nodded. "I'm hungry."

"It's time to check in with Svengali, too. See if he's made any progress on getting you out of his witness protection program."

She detected the tension underlying his flippancy. He was scared. So was she.

"Okay," she murmured.

Izzy crossed to the armoire beside the fireplace. Beautiful white cashmere sweaters, wool pants and floor-length skirts hung from cedar hangers. They were in her sizes. So were shoes—flats, heels, snow boots.

There was a beautiful long-sleeved white satin gown with the trio of flames embroidered on the bodice, and ivory satin high heels with the same embroidery.

Pat whistled. "Interesting fashion. Yours?"

"I guess so," she said. She wondered if they were thinking the same thing—that it looked like a bridal dress, House of the Flames style. Uneasily she moved on.

Drawers revealed beautiful jewels—rose quartz necklaces and loops of what appeared to be enormous white diamonds.

"Well, we know who to call for a donation for the benevolent fund," Pat quipped. But his delivery was off.

She opened another drawer and discovered clothes for a man: black boxer shorts and socks; a black turtleneck sweater, black wool trousers and boots. There was a white card lying on top of the sweater: a thick cream business card embossed with the by-now familiar turret-clouds-dove logo. The initials "J.M." stood alone on a line. There was a New York phone number beneath it.

"Nice," Pat said, setting it back down. "Real French-Canadian hospitality." He examined the trousers. "No size tag. I think these were custom made." He looked skeptical. "Not sure they will fit."

Because Jean-Marc was six-two or so and long-limbed, while Pat was muscular and just cleared six feet, she translated. Still, she had a feeling that Jean-Marc would make sure everything did fit—he was scrupulous that way, detail-oriented. A tightass.

Pat gathered up his clothes and took them into the bathroom to change. The pants fit as if they had been made for him. Ditto everything else.

Then it was her turn.

In a white turtleneck and a long white wool skirt, Izzy slipped on matching leather boots. Then she found a vast array of high-end makeup products in the bathroom and did her face. When she returned, Pat looked surprised.

"You never used to wear makeup," he said. "Or girlie clothes."

"Oh." She felt so odd, not knowing that.

"But you looked good, in your all-business outfits," he added, reaching for her hand, squeezing it as he swept her gently from side to side, admiring her. "You look good now."

"You do, too," she said.

They smiled and held hands as they walked back across the room. Gazing at her in unabashed rapture, Pat pushed open the bedroom door.

They strolled down the hall into the foyer and came to a dead stop.

Jean-Marc stood with Andre, Michel and a tall, pale woman dressed in a black sleeveless satin gown. Ringlets of shiny white hair brushed her hips. Her eyes were blood-red, and her long teeth were studded with jewels. Her posture was impeccable, elegant. Izzy knew she was a vampire, and a thrill of fear jittered up her spine.

"Isabelle," the woman said. Her voice was sensual, hypnotic, and Izzy found herself taking a step toward her.

"Madame Sange just arrived from New Orleans," Michel informed her. "And the werewolves have shown up as well." His lip curled as he barely looked at Andre.

"Andre, how's Caresse?" she asked.

"She's much better. Jean-Marc's offered to let us rest here. Hope dat's okay." He smiled broadly at her.

"It's more than okay," she said warmly. "You're very welcome."

"Well, no one is welcome in New Orleans anymore," Sange informed her haughtily. "It's completely out of control. The voodoo drums are talking. The veil between this world and 'the places of evil' is thinning. Someone is practicing black magic on a scale no one has ever seen before."

"Malchance," Andre grumbled.

"How is the family?" Michel asked Sange.

"I assume you mean *your* family, and not mine. Frankly they're wondering where you and their Guardian are. They have no one to lead them, and they're scattering to the winds in a panic."

She smoothed her long, white hair. "By the way, your mansion burned to the ground. The Ungifted fire department tried to save it, but you know how they are."

Michel sagged. In the space of three seconds, he seemed to age thirty years.

"Merde," he grunted, shaking his head. "Unbelievable."

"As you say. I'm very sorry. It was a fine old mansion. I remember when it was built back in the late 1700s."

Beside Izzy, Pat caught his breath. "Was this where you were living?" he asked her.

She had no idea.

"Of course it was," Jean-Marc said.

"Until that assassination attempt, anyway," Sange added. "Listen, Madame, my sirelings are in danger. Everyone's in danger. Now that you're back in charge, you've got to do something quickly."

"Madame has something of a situation of her own," Michel said. "Perhaps you've heard about her, ah, unusual bloodline?"

"Interesting choice of words, Michel." Sange tapped her jeweled canine as her gaze swept down Isabelle's body, then up again. She lingered at Isabelle's neck. "*Oui,* I have heard that Isabelle is half Malchance." She clucked her long teeth. "If the Malchances are doing this, perhaps you can ask them to make sure your allies are safe."

"We were attacked two days ago," Jean-Marc declared, his face unreadable, his tone neutral. "The sortie included vampire minions and vampires."

Sange didn't miss a beat. "If I attacked you, would I be here asking you for help?"

She sauntered toward Izzy, and Pat took a protective step in front of her. A pained expression crossed Michel's face. *Now what?* Izzy wondered.

Sange smiled brilliantly at Pat, her jeweled teeth glinting in the soft recessed light.

"You're the Ungifted lover, are you not? I've lost an enormous wager because of you." She turned and smiled slyly at Jean-Marc. "Defeat in romance becomes you, *Gardien.*"

Oh, my God, shut up, Izzy thought, as Pat glanced quizzically at her.

Impassive and unruffled, Jean-Marc looked at the vampire. "It seems odd that you would bait the people whose help you seek."

"Humans fascinate me," she replied. "I've lived practically forever, and I still don't understand them. We have a treaty. I expect you to honor it. I shouldn't have to cajole you into doing what you've already sworn to do."

Her ringlets gleamed as she looked at Michel, her beautiful profile accentuated by the jewels on her teeth. "I understand there's to be a ritual tonight. Something about strengthening the two Guardians after all their trials."

"Oui," Michel said. "We are making some preparations."

"Oh?" Izzy looked at Jean-Marc. No one had said anything about it to her. They probably hadn't had a chance, yet. She wondered what it would be like.

"I'd love to observe it," Sange continued.

"Sange, you know quite well that that sort of ceremony is for Gifted only," Michel said. *"Only."* He glared at the werewolves with undisguised disgust.

"Andre and his clan won't be at the ceremony, either," Jean-Marc said, each word brittle as an ice chip. "It is as you say, for Gifted only."

Sange considered. "Which means that the lover will also not be permitted to attend. That will probably make the sex magic go better for Isabelle. As she was raised among Ungifted, I'm sure that part's still a little strange for her."

"What?" Pat said, sliding his arm possessively around Izzy's waist. "The sex *what?*"

The room fell silent. Izzy felt dizzy. The one thing she didn't want Pat to know about…one of the only things she knew about herself, her, out in the open: she had had ritualistic sex with Jean-Marc to reclaim his soul, and it was the reason she had amnesia.

"Oh, dear." Sange looked from face to face. "I seem to have committed a faux pas."

"Michel, please show Madame Sange to the door," Jean-Marc bit off, the light moving across the angles of his face as he glowered at her. "Madame, we'll contact you when we have something to say. I have your cell number."

Sange lifted the hem of her gown in one long, white hand. "One would do well not to bait *me,* either, Jean-Marc. I, too, have friends."

"Then ask them for help," Jean-Marc flung at her. His eyes flared. He stood lightly on the balls of his feet, as if he was forcing himself not to rush at her. Michel pursed his lips in tight disapproval and walked up to the vampire.

He took both her hands in his.

"Madame Sange, you know that we have always valued our treaty with you. We'll do everything in our power to protect you and your sirelings."

"That's better," she said pointedly. She looked hard at Jean-Marc, raising her brows when he remained silent.

Finally he ground out, "Michel speaks for all of us, of course. We would never leave an ally out to dry."

She narrowed her crimson eyes at him. "You're different," she observed. "You're usually the cool customer spouting the party line. No emotion, just what will advance your cause most efficiently. I've never seen you this…petulant before."

Her jewels danced and sparkled as she smiled at him. "I like you better this way. Less ambassador, more warrior."

"I'm no different," he said. "Just a little tired, and for that I apologize."

"I accept your apology." She leaned toward him, almost as if she were about to kiss him. Instead she inclined her head regally and walked toward the elevator door. "*Bon soir,* Isabelle. I do hope it goes well. Detective Kittrell."

Gliding past Andre, she put her fingers to her nose and sniffed, but otherwise ignored him as if he weren't there. Michel accompanied her to the elevator; he waved his hand and the elevator door opened. Inside, a cluster of young white-haired men and women dressed in long black peacoats and boots brightened at the sight of her. The two closest to her, a young man and a woman, slid their arms around the vampire queen, making a sandwich. The slender woman nuzzled Sange's neck while the pale, red-eyed man laid his cheek against the back of Sange's head. They gazed back at the assembly in the foyer.

"Two Guardians," the young male vampire cooed.

"And an Ungifted man. *Maman* Sange, he's so hot," the woman whispered loudly. "Yum."

"I'm certain of that," Sange replied. "Don't call me *Maman.* It's gauche. I'm your sire, not your mother. We ate your mother."

"Yum," the girl whispered.

Sange took the young man's hand and laid it over her breast. *"Adieu,"* she said, as the elevator door closed.

Pat turned to Jean-Marc. "What was that all about?" he asked carefully. "A ritual? Sex magic?"

Jean-Marc's expression didn't waiver. He looked composed as he said, "Let's go into my office."

Izzy watched in dismay as Jean-Marc and Pat squared off in the foyer of the coop. She felt like a possession they both were fighting over—or a female animal in the wild.

She didn't like it.

Jean-Marc led the way out of the foyer and through the octagonal library. Izzy followed after, and Pat took up the rear. The shelves were crammed with beautiful books in leather bindings—with titles like *Danced Spells* and *Une Histoire des Sorcières 1300–1500*. He touched a black leather book with ornate blue lettering that Izzy couldn't read, and the entire shelf disappeared.

He entered a corridor as dark and oppressive as her bedroom…except that at the far end of it, a two-story waterfall tumbled into a churning pool ringed with chunks of crystal. A stone statue of a man wearing a medieval-style crown and a cloak rose from the center of the water. Jean-Marc bent his knee and lowered his head, then straightened and turned, waiting for Izzy and Pat.

Neither of them bowed to the statue.

Our minds think alike.

Then a wispy blue mist swirled around their feet, filling Izzy's nose with the by-now familiar scent of oranges and roses. Pat grabbed her hand and backed her out of it.

"It's all right," Jean-Marc said over his shoulder. "It's normal. It simply means that you're entering my territory."

The mist curled around their knees. "Turn it off, Devereaux," Pat said, "or we're stopping here."

At once the mist vanished. They stood in front of a door beautifully carved with the same design that Izzy had seen on the patches of the Devereaux soldiers: a castle tower with a dove flying out a window, an arm in a gauntlet, reaching for it.

Or maybe letting it go.

The door opened by itself, and Jean-Marc stood aside, revealing a small office dominated by a gilded dark wood desk and chair, a wafer-thin laptop…and Bijou, the little kitten, curled up on top of a dark blue athletic gear bag. Bijou popped up his head, blinked at the trio and yawned.

"After you," Jean-Marc invited Izzy.

"No, you first, " Pat insisted.

Jean-Marc ignored him. Izzy felt caught in the middle again. She said to Jean-Marc, "Please, go in."

"As you wish."

As he walked into the room, a couch upholstered in dark blue leather and two large overstuffed chairs appeared. Next came a table, and three glasses filled with burgundy liquid.

Jean-Marc remained standing until Izzy sat on the couch. Pat sat beside her. He didn't take her hand. She licked her lips and slowly filled her lungs. Her heart was pounding.

Jean-Marc walked over to Bijou and picked him up. Then he sat in the chair facing Izzy and Pat, settling the kitten on his lap. Bijou began to knead his thigh and purr.

"I'm not sure what you know," Jean-Marc began, addressing Pat, but looking directly at Izzy.

"I'm guessing I'm missing a few data points," Pat replied.

"You've had a lot to absorb in a short time," Jean-Marc said, petting the cat. Then he gathered the kitten in his large hands and held him out to Izzy.

"He's your cat," he said.

Thinking of the serious little werewolf boy, she reached for him, and their fingers brushed each other.

I have no desire to come between you. She heard his voice in her head. *I'll help you explain to him.*

She gazed hard at him. And as she petted the purring kitten, something came back...an image of him on a moonlit night, his hair held back in a ponytail, running through the bayou surrounded by howling wolves. Voodoo drums pounded in the background, shaking the balcony she stood on...the balcony to the miniature mansion he built her in the swamp, after the attempt on her life...he looked savage, unreal.

I want you. Every cell in her body stretched toward him as if he were the sun, and she a bud beneath the snow. *Jean-Marc, it is you...*

You're responding to my sexual emanations. I'm not trying to manipulate you, but I can't turn them off. Try to pay attention to my words. I am not like an Ungifted man. This is not fairy-tale love at first sight. It is sexual attraction.

"What's going on?" Pat said.

Jean-Marc held Izzy's gaze and licked his lips. He gave her a slow nod.

"Kittrell," he began. "Let me try to explain."

"What are you doing to her?" Pat got to his feet and took a menacing step toward Jean-Marc. Izzy took Pat's hand and eased him back down.

I'll help you explain. It was only sex. You're still his, as an Ungifted would think of it. Jean-Marc picked up his wine and took a sip.

"Pat." She touched his face. "I'm so sorry. I'm sorry." She lowered her head and caught her breath in a long, shuddering sigh. She tipped up her chin. "Don't do anything. Don't say anything," she flung at Jean-Marc. "Let me do this my way."

Both men remained silent. Jean-Marc moved his hand, and tissues appeared on the table, beside her glass of wine. The white box was monogrammed with a gold B inside a trio of flames. She realized her eyes were welling with tears.

"Izzy, you were in New Orleans alone," Pat said. "Practically a prisoner, from what I gather. Sometimes people do things in situations like that that they wouldn't do otherwise."

She shook her head as she took a tissue and dabbed away her tears. Tears would change the subject. She had to be as honest with him as she could. On her lap, Bijou raised on his hind legs and batted at a black ringlet of her hair.

"People under stress look for strength. They reach out." Pat cupped her chin and made her look at him. She could see the hurt in his eyes, but the steadiness, too.

"You have done hostage negotiations, in your work," Jean-Marc said. "So you do know how it can be."

"I do." Pat smoothed her hair away from her forehead. "Maybe they've mixed you up, gotten you involved in something you didn't want to do."

You see? He will forgive you. We can find another way to perform the ritual, Jean-Marc said. *I'll find a partner among the White Women. Their magic is very strong.*

He'd sleep with someone else if it got him what he wanted. Sex didn't equal love. He had been her teacher in the ways of the Gifted. She didn't remember it, but she knew it. He was teaching her now—to stay away from him, and not to pin romantic hopes on him.

It is not either-or for you, he underscored. *Either Pat or me. There is no me. No…us.*

She heard the briefest hesitation in the voice in her head. She glanced up through her lashes at him and, for an instant, before he realized she was looking at him, his face was filled with undisguised longing. It sharpened the angles of his face, cut his features as if out of stone. When Pat had wanted to make love with her, his face had gone smooth, and gentle, and loving.

Jean-Marc was none of that. None of that.

None of that.

Jean-Marc rose. He picked up his wine and walked to the door. Without saying a word, he left the office.

Pat tried again. "Iz, it's okay. Whatever it is, we'll figure it out."

"You know," she said, wadding up the tissue and turning to face him. "You do know. That I…that I've been with him."

Pat went completely neutral, and she knew he was putting on the mask he had cultivated for his work as an NYPD cop. Putting distance between himself and her, so he could process her confession.

"It was to make me stronger, magically. The first time." She heard herself. She sounded like some kind of deranged cult groupie. Only this was real. This was happening. This was her life.

"We only started dating just before you left," he ventured, and she knew the terrible cost to his ego, especially in front of Jean-Marc. "We didn't make any promises."

"You can't pretend. It *does* matter. It happened. I did it a second time to strengthen him. And…and I don't know about tonight. I didn't know about tonight."

"You're not a slave here. You can leave."

"I can't." She searched his face. "I have to get put back together or I'm going to take you down with me. And everybody else."

He opened his mouth but she held up a finger, steeling herself to go on.

Don't do it, Jean-Marc said inside her head. *Don't tell him that you have feelings for me. That can go nowhere, Isabelle. I am not available for you.*

"Get out of my head!" she shouted.

Startled, Pat took her hands in his and held on tight. "You're under a lot of strain."

Her face was pressed against his chest. "Pat. With everything you've seen, why can't you see that *I'm* part of it?"

You're not part of it. You're all of it, Jean-Marc said. His voice was lower, huskier. It sent ripples through her lower abdomen.

Unaware, Pat took a breath, held it, let it out. Then he

lowered his head. "I'm struggling here, Iz. I'm a man." He gazed at her and squeezed her hands. "We hardly got to know each other before you left, but—"

Mon amour, ma femme, ma vie. Jean-Marc's throaty whisper caressed her. She felt as if his fingers were trailing down the center of her throat, to her collarbone. *I surrender, Isabelle, to my feelings. I want you. I want to take you, and lie you down, and cover you, and we'll mate like lions. Tonight.*

And then she was in the grip of it, needing him as badly. Wanting him as much. Disoriented, losing track of where she was, she exhaled. *"Je te desire. J'ai envie de toi,"* she murmured beneath her breath, her eyes half closing. "Ah, Jean-Marc, *alors…"* The dark, sexual undercurrent washed through her, over her.

"What are you doing to her?" Pat said loudly.

His voice called her back to herself. Humiliated, bewildered, she got to her feet, holding the kitten against her chest as she stumbled out of the room. Bijou yowled and leaped out of her arms, skittering back into the office.

Jean-Marc stood in the hallway. His eyes were flinty and hard. He took her by the shoulders and pushed her firmly against the wall. Then he bent down his head and kissed her. She groaned deep in her throat and wrapped an arm around his neck, pulling him close, rising to meet him as he slipped his tongue into her mouth. He tasted like honey.

"I taste like you," he said. "I know how you like it. I know things about your body that you don't even know. When I get inside you the magic will happen. You will go somewhere you never even dreamed of. Over and over again."

"This isn't you. This is that *thing* inside you…" she said, gasping.

"And what is the thing inside you that responds?" he

whispered, grinding his pelvis against her. He was rock-hard. "What wants me so badly you'd fall down on the floor right here, and—"

"It's not me. You're doing this. You told me so." She unslung her arm from around his neck and flattened her palm against his chest. His suit shirt was damp.

She edged past him and ran down the hall.

He let her go.

"*Putain de merde,*" he swore, as the sensation subsided. His body was finely trembling. To be that close to her, and not have her…

"You bastard." Pat stood in the doorway. His face was purple with fury as he rushed Jean-Marc. "You asshole."

He launched an assault on Jean-Marc; the man knew Krav Maga, the street fighting style of the Israeli Defense Forces. Jean-Marc let him land some brutal punches, then pushed back, landing Pat on his ass in the center of the hallway. He took a step backward, giving Kittrell the chance to get back up. He didn't send out a spell to calm him down, although he thought about it. Kittrell didn't have a lot left right then; Jean-Marc didn't want to take the rest of his dignity and his pride.

"I swear I am going to kill you." Kittrell's sides were heaving. Blood dripped from his nose.

"Kittrell," Jean-Marc began, "this is why the ritual must be performed. I'm not myself, and I need to be restored. If there were some other way, I would do it."

"Restored." Kittrell advanced on him again, crouched in a battle stance, ready to take him on. "Is that what you call it?"

Jean-Marc assumed a defensive posture, but he knew he wasn't going to fight anymore. *I will not hurt him. She loves him.*

Kill him, the darkness urged. *He's in the way. He's confusing her.*

"This is what I suggest you do," Jean-Marc said. "Leave." He held up a hand before Pat could protest. "Leave, and let us help her. She can't do what she has to if you're here. When she's restored, she can send for you."

Pat balled his fist. "You're incredible. I'm surprised I haven't met you down the road from the precinct house, beating up your underage hookers while you try to score some blow."

Jean-Marc took that, too. "It's a bizarre world to you. The moral code you live by is not our code. That's why we walk among you without revealing ourselves."

"Well, I've seen it all," Kittrell sneered.

"*Oui.* In other Houses, you would be killed for what you've learned. All I can do now is ask you for your silence."

That took a bit of the wind out of Kittrell, as if he hadn't considered before that he himself might be in danger. His thoughts had been of Isabelle's safety. They had a lot in common. Despite their current predicament, Jean-Marc liked him very much. Isabelle had good taste in men.

"My silence," Kittrell said slowly. "And my consent."

Jean-Marc shook his head. "*Non,* not your consent. Isabelle doesn't need your permission to do anything. She is her own woman. And she needs our help."

"She doesn't need a thing from you. You've messed with her, brainwashed her and given her amnesia—"

Jean-Marc cocked his head. "I remember when I first met her. She pushed me to prove every claim I made about the Gifted. All she talked about was you. She worried about you, dreamed about you."

"Don't patronize me. You're the last person in the world I want to discuss Izzy with."

"I'm the person closest to her in the world of the Gifted. I was her mentor. It was my responsibility to show her how to use her Gift. The world of the Gift can be a deadly place. As you know."

"I don't know squat," Kittrell flung back. "And I'm sure not going to take your word for it."

Jean-Marc jumped ahead. Kittrell was calming down and talking to him. He sensed this might be his only chance to get through to him.

"I've been with her twice, and it was not out of desire, or a bid to move in on her. I performed sex magic with her because she needed power. She was in danger. The jackals were circling. It worked. It probably saved her life.

"So I offered myself to her again, and she refused, because she wanted to be loyal to you."

Kittrell's face worked. Jean-Marc could see how badly he wanted to believe him. But he cast no spells to make him believe. This was between two equals, even though one of them was Ungifted.

"I was afraid she was going to die because she was too weak. I told her that. She knew sleeping with me would make her stronger. But she sent me away."

"How noble of you. What a champ." Kittrell's voice was like acid.

"In the bayou, Luc de Malchance ripped my soul from my body. After he died, his minions spirited it to Haiti. Isabelle performed sex magic with my physical body to try to get it back. I was not present during the act of inter-course, until it was over."

"You raped her," Kittrell spat.

Jean-Marc jerked, privately shocked that Kittrell would rather think that, than accept the truth he had just heard with his own ears. The love of the Ungifted *was* possessive and limited. He and Callia had compared notes, chuckled over their various *amours,* even suggested partners for each other to give and receive magical power—which they could then share with each other. No one was harmed; many benefited.

And Callia has seldom crossed my mind, since Isabelle came into my life.

"Understand me," Jean-Marc said. "She needs help. I will do everything in my power to bring your old Izzy back to you. But as she is now, she is frightened and miserable."

"I'm going to get her and take her out of here." Kittrell turned his back and began to walk away.

"You two were lucky today," Jean-Marc called to his retreating back. "But Lilliane is still after her."

Kittrell didn't answer. His footfalls rang on the stone.

Kill him now. No one will know. No one will care. He's alone here.

Chapter 10

After Kittrell slammed out of his office, Jean-Marc told his men not to interfere with the detective or Isabelle. Hours after vowing not to let her out of his sight, Jean-Marc was relinquishing all control. If she wanted to leave with that deluded Ungifted, let her. He'd been a fool to assume anyone could tell her what to do. Especially him.

Glum, he doggedly went through paperwork, approving the payment of bills associated with the upkeep of the coop; reading through a report on advances in body armor. As he has suspected: the Malchances had equipped themselves with something out of Switzerland. Kevlar was *passé*. He ordered twenty sets to outfit everyone in the safe house.

Decades of focus kept him at his desk and his mind out of Isabelle's business. He conjured a felt mouse for Bijou and listened absently as the playful kitten batted it across the wooden floor. He made himself a cup of tea and an open-faced shrimp sandwich. He sipped the tea and left the sandwich untouched.

A short time later, Michel came to inform him that Kittrell had just left, alone. Jean-Marc refrained from asking how Isabelle was taking it.

"I created a scrying stone linked to his apartment," Michel said, showing Jean-Marc the rough-hewn rectangle of crystal. Jean-Marc gazed into it and saw an apartment decorated with washed Southwestern furnishings and a stack of mail on a granite breakfast bar. There was a framed commendation on the wall beside a *Maxim* calendar. "And we put guards on him, as you requested. He's walking the streets, in a temper."

"Do you think he'll talk?" Jean-Marc asked, as he put the stone on his desk. "Tell the Ungifted about us?"

"I don't know," Michel replied honestly. "In the old days, he wouldn't have left here alive. Some of your own men are talking about going after him. If he tells *anyone* where we are…."

"He wouldn't be so stupid. He loves her."

"He's Ungifted."

"But he's not a fool," Jean-Marc countered.

"He's a cop," Michel shot back. "He is good, we are evil. The way he sees it, we've brainwashed his lover and taken her hostage. It's time for the cavalry. He might even ask them to surround the building. Then there will be news trucks. Helicopters."

"*Merde,*" Jean-Marc grunted. "They're all crazy, those Ungifted."

"One would have to be, to live in the world as it is and be as helpless as they are."

"I thought about killing Gabriel and Christian and those five others when they left," Michel added.

"Me, too," Jean-Marc said. "I spoke rashly when I promised them safe passage. François's had an earful by now."

"He already knew about the safe house location, I trust."

"My men knew. They're not my men anymore," Jean-Marc replied. "What's the saying? 'Three men can keep a secret if two of them are dead.' It's well warded, but if he comes after us…"

"Neutral territory," Michel reminded him. He sounded bitter. "I supposed most of the rules have gone out the window."

"Leaping to their deaths as we speak."

They regarded each other, two world-weary soldiers. As much as he disliked Michel, at least the man knew how things worked. He couldn't deny that Michel had toiled long and hard to hold the House of the Flames together. There was still hope.

"I'm going to ask Alain to delay the ritual," Jean-Marc announced. "It's too much for her now. She needs a little time. And we should transfer as much money as possible out of the Flames' accounts before someone back in New Orleans remembers to freeze access. I have a personal fortune, but we have a lot of mouths to feed and we might have to tap into my money later."

Michel looked as if he were about to argue, but he clamped his mouth shut and nodded. Resentment came off him in waves. Jean-Marc felt for him. Nothing was as it should be, and Michel had no way to set things to rights.

As if he had heard his thoughts, Michel gestured for Jean-Marc to move out of the way of the computer keyboard. Jean-Marc complied, and Michel typed in the protocol to access the vast wealth of the House of the Flames.

"I'll take twenty percent," Michel muttered. "And put it into my private account."

"That's the best place for it," Jean-Marc said.

"My assistant will howl when she realizes what I've done. So now I've cast my lot in with you," Michel said, pressing the send key. "Not my best day."

"But your best move," Jean-Marc reiterated.

"My only move," Michel retorted. "I'm practically a hostage here."

We all are, Jean-Marc thought.

Michel left Jean-Marc's office under a cloud of high emotion. Then Jean-Marc summoned Alain to his office and revealed his decision to delay the ritual.

"That's a terrible idea." Bijou batted his felt mouse around Alain's shoe. Irritably Alain, snapped his fingers and the mouse vanished. The little black cat looked bewildered.

"You're fragmented and wounded. You promised me you'd put our House ahead of your personal feelings. And hers."

Jean-Marc pinched the bridge of his nose. Heavy hung the head that wore a crown, indeed.

"Now about Kittrell," Alain said. "There's a lot of concern that he'll reveal our location."

"I know."

"There's only one way to guarantee that he doesn't. And if we kill him, we should destroy his body. All evidence tracing—"

"Non." Jean-Marc glowered at his cousin. "I won't have him killed. That's a direct order. It'll go very hard for anyone who disobeys it."

"You see how it is with you?" Alain said through his teeth. "All these chances you're taking…"

"They are mine to take," Jean-Marc said, reaching for his PDA, dismissing him.

Alain turned his back and left, slamming the door. Bijou jerked, startled.

Jean-Marc sighed heavily. He laid down the PDA and examined the scrying stone. Kittrell had not returned to his apartment. He was standing at a crosswalk, hands in the pockets of the peacoat he, Jean-Marc, had purchased for him. It was raining hard. It would be so easy to make him think the light had changed and no cars were coming. Isabelle might even be fooled. Misfortunes occurred all the time to the Ungifted.

Non.

Reconjuring Bijou's toy, he pushed back from his desk and walked through the penthouse, acknowledging each Devereaux who snapped to attention and each Bouvard who did the same, though perhaps with a little less gusto.

Kittrell is a loose end.

He went into the kitchen. Dominique sat at a white wood table decorated in the center with the face of Jehanne. The operative was dressed in a navy-blue turtleneck sweater and a pair of jeans. He was drinking Armagnac and reading a book from the library. iPod buds hung from his ears.

When he saw Jean-Marc, he leaped to his feet and pulled out his ear buds. *"Gardien,"* he said jovially, "come and have a drink."

Jean-Marc cocked his head. "What do you think of the situation we're in?"

"That it's temporary," Dominique replied, with a saucy toss of his hair.

Thank you, my patron, for a man who is loyal and optimistic, he thought. He walked to the sideboard, where the crystal goblets gleamed in tidy rows, and filled one of them with the brandy. He hoisted it; Dominique did the same.

"What are you reading?" Jean-Marc asked him.

"Rereading. *The Prince*. Machiavelli."

Jean-Marc grunted. The book his grandmother's lover had written was required reading for every Devereaux.

"About Kittrell," he said.

Dom tapped the cover of the book. "Permission to speak freely?"

"*Bien sûr*. I'd appreciate your honesty."

"There are Ungifted all over the world who know about us. There always have been, but it's getting worse, with all their technology—spy cams, the Internet…" He scratched his face. "All the same, I would have killed him. But you're the Guardian, not me."

"And since I've given the order that he's to remain unharmed…"

"I'll obey it."

"If you find out someone's planning something…"

Dom made a face. "Monsieur, please don't ask me to spy. I'm no Machiavelli."

"Fair enough. Forget I asked," Jean-Marc said, taking another sip of Armagnac. "Please, return to your book."

"*Merci beaucoup*," Dom replied, putting his ear buds back in his ears.

Loyal to a point then. Even Dominique.

Jean-Marc wheeled out of the kitchen with the goblet, nodding at a Devereaux guard on duty. He retrieved his athame from his bedroom and headed for the altar room. A few minutes later, he pushed open the door and went inside.

The candles still glowed before Jehanne and the Grey King. The thing inside him hissed in protest, and he ignored it.

He drank down the wine and set the empty goblet on the floor. He took off his clothes and folded them beside the goblet. He stood naked before the altar. Then he bowed deeply to both patrons and showed them his left palm. He sliced it open with the athame and pumped it, forcing drops of blood onto the altar.

"I give you my life, patrons of the Gifted families," he murmured in Old French. "Help me. Tell me what to do. I'm losing track. Abracadabra, abracadabra, seven, three, one."

His blood dripped steadily onto the ancient stone. Then it began to smoke, and he bowed his head in gratitude for the assurance that his patron was present. He knelt on the icy stone with his hand draped on the stone, bleeding, and chanted in French, Latin and the Old Language. He entreated his demon patron to come to him and guide him.

I will pay the price for answers, he pledged. *Don't let my family suffer.*

His heart hitched and lost beats as Isabelle's image blossomed in his mind.

Don't make her pay my debt. It's mine. Don't take it from me. I am your son, forged by magic, strengthened by trials. I can bear whatever you ask of me.

His knees ached; his back throbbed. He could have disposed of the pain but he kept it, to honor Pat Kittrell, who was in pain tonight. Pain like that was why Gifted and Ungifted should never mix. Their worlds were too different.

Demon, come, Father Patron, mon Rois Gris, show me what to do, and I will do it. I give you my life.

The candles flickered as the door to the room opened.

He looked up, and caught his breath.

Isabelle stood in the doorway, and she was magnificent. She had put on her white satin gown embroidered with the trio of flames, her rose quartz necklace and her white satin shoes. Her hair was wild around her shoulders, and her eyes were tearstained, haunted. So many tears from Isabelle.

When she saw that he was naked, she looked away.

"What are you doing here?" he asked her.

"I heard someone calling me," she replied. "Telling me to put on this dress and come in here." She lifted her head toward the ceiling, and the candles gleamed against her cheek. He could almost imagine her missing aura cloaking her in its brilliance. "It wasn't you?"

"*Non.* This is your altar room, created for you. Perhaps Jehanne is able to make contact with you here."

"Created…?"

"Yes, by me."

At that, she turned to him with her deep-set, haunted eyes. Her face changed. He felt the air in the room shift. Something was happening.

Then she walked to the altar and stared at his hand as it dripped blood on the altar. She reached for his athame, then drew back her hand before she touched it. Maybe she remembered that coming in contact with another Gifted's ritual knife would make it useless.

After she glanced around the room, she saw his neat stack of clothes. She walked over to it, picked up his goblet and crashed it against the altar as if she were christening a ship. Crystal flew everywhere. Then she took a shard and sliced it across her right palm.

He said nothing, only let the magic unfold. Was her patron telling her what to do?

She knelt beside him and raised her hand over the altar, as he had. Her body heat permeated his icy flesh. She smelled like lilies, and smoke—like the martyred Catholic saint who favored her line.

"I don't know what to do next," she said. "This is all I

know." She lowered her voice. "It's all I remember," she said wonderingly. "Jean-Marc, I remember this."

"I'll show you. Repeat what I say. *Ma patronesse, je vous en prie.*" Although it wasn't entirely accurate, he began to recite the traditional Catholic Novena Prayer in honor of St. Joan, hoping to connect her old memories to her present quest for power. Catholic supplicants, of course, didn't cut their palms and bleed on their altars. But they did pray to Jehanne.

"O Joan, holy liberator of France…" His English was heavily accented. It would have been easier for him to pray in French, but he stuck with it.

She whispered along with him, tenderly, emotionally, and he dared to hope that she was beginning to remember who and what she was.

"…transmit your talent to inspire your soldiers to accomplish great deeds of valor…"

They prayed for courage, and wisdom. Jean-Marc knew these things were inside Isabelle; she just needed to find them again.

"Amen," he concluded.

"Oh, my lady," she whispered, gazing at the statue of Jehanne. She choked out a sob. "I will do anything, oh, please…"

She was grieving for the loss of her lover, bargaining for his return. Jean-Marc wanted to say, *I, too. I will do anything, to bring your soldier happiness, and peace.*

But he couldn't. That could not be his prayer. Her happiness and peace were not his concern.

How can that be?

Mists swirled from the floor, white and blue, rising from the frigid stones and curling around his thighs, his ass, his penis. It was warm, and soothing. His aches and pains ebbed.

"I'm afraid," she whispered. "I'm alone now."

"Never," he promised her, although he knew what she meant. He wasn't her love.

"Always. We are always alone, you and I," she replied.

With a breath, she turned to him and held up her bleeding palm. He did the same; they pressed their hands together. The mist rose above their heads, and he thought they might be floating toward the ceiling. He felt weightless, and bodiless. He couldn't see her through the thickening ether, but he felt her blood pumping into his wound, and his into hers.

"You must pull away," he ordered her. "Our blood will mingle, and I am diseased."

"And I'm half Malchance," she replied.

He swayed. He could no sooner lift his hand from hers than grab his knife from the altar and stab her through the heart. And yet, hadn't he promised the Grey King that he would do anything he was asked, to protect House Devereaux? Was this a test, to see if he was capable of it?

Guide me, show me, my patron.

Words swirled around his ears, in French:

You must go to Haiti, my son. You must face Lilliane, and defeat her. If you don't stop her, the consequences for all of humanity will be horrible. The Ungifted will perish from the earth. The Gifted will be locked in perpetual war against the Supernaturals. Do you hear my words?

"Oui, mon pére," Jean-Marc murmured. "I hear your words. But they make no sense to me. Haiti is the last place we should go, *non?* We're in hiding from Lillianne. If she captures my soul, it will go worse for us, will it not? She has promised it to Le Devourer."

Lilliane and Le Devourer have been plotting. Dark magicks are tearing the fabric of this world apart, and evil such as lurks in your soul is pouring into its wounds. If you don't stop them, hell will reign on earth.

Isabelle is key to stopping her twin. She must go with you.

He shook his head as his heart picked up speed. A terrible fear of what was to come rattled his spine, yanked the hair at the back of his neck.

"I can't take her there. Not to that madwoman…"

You swore to pay the price when I saved your life in the bayou. Know this, then: Death waits for one of you. A bad death.

"Even if we succeed?"

Even if you succeed.

"Let it be my death," he prayed. "Father demon, let Le Devourer eat my soul, and spare her."

That is not for you to say. Nor in my power to accomplish.

"Take the power, King of the Shadows—"

Do not plead with me. It doesn't become you. Jehanne summons you, Gardien. *Answer her call.*

Jean-Marc gazed down and saw a vast, green field of rolling hills and brilliant, glowing suits of armor on a thousand foot soldiers. Pennants flapped in a stiff breeze.

At the head of the thundering army sat the Maid of Orleans—Jehanne d'Arc, with her cropped hair, as she was depicted in the safe house. She carried her banner of an angel holding a lily. She was very young, maybe seventeen, and a hooded pure white peregrine falcon rested on her gauntleted arm.

"Jean-Marc," the wind whispered. Jehanne looked skyward and saw him floating on the clouds. Then she lifted the hood off the falcon and lofted it upward. It took flight, fluttering up into the brilliant sunshine.

"Catch my little one," she called to him in medieval French. *"Take her under your wing!"*

He stared at the sight of the falcon rising above her gauntlet. The image was the exact likeness of the armored hand and dove of peace of his House. As he watched, he remembered flying among the seagulls, looking for her; he had Seen her as a falcon then. So was this the image upon which his House had been founded—the patroness of the House of the Flames, sending forth Isabelle of the Flames, to his protection?

"Fool, save her!" Jehanne commanded him.

An arrow shot from the army on the field of green. Whining through the air, it hit the falcon directly in the breast. The impact flung it upward toward the sun; it held for a moment as if still in flight, then plummeted toward the ground. Billows of gray clouds rolled in from the north, swallowing it, cloaking Jehanne and her followers. He heard the whinny of horses, the clank of armor and Jehanne.

"Don't let that happen to my nestling," she exhorted him. *"You take the arrow. You die for her."*

"I will," he told her, as smoke and fog surrounded him. He heard low laughter; a hiss.

Jean-Marc, I search for you, my handsome one. Where are you? Come back to me, and give me the rest of your soul. We need it.

It was Lilliane. He set his jaw and narrowed his eyes. Le Devourer would never have the rest of his soul, ever.

Izzy heard herself speaking in perfect French.

"Jehanne, *ma patronesse, je vous en prie.*" Joan, my patron, I entreat you.

And suddenly she was floating in a tunnel of white

light. Sweet soprano voices raised in song, surrounding her as she floated past glowing beams and gentle waves of light. She looked down at her hands. Dressed in her white satin gown, she was solid flesh and bone. Ringlets of her hair bobbed in front of her eyes. She moved them away from her face, blinking as a sphere of light more dazzling than the sun blazed at the opposite end of the tunnel.

She tried to look away, but she couldn't close her eyes. She was mesmerized. The sphere separated into two smaller spheres. They became human-shaped—woman-shaped—and the one on the right opened her arms, as if in welcome. The taller one, on the left, did not.

"Isabella Celestina De Marco, I summon thee," said the tall one.

"Jehanne," she whispered, wondering how she knew.

"Oui. I am your patron. Or rather, I was." The figure became clearer; it was the young woman whose face was featured all over the safe house. Unsmiling, angry, she wore chain mail over her head, and light glinted off her armor. Gloves of chain mail covered her hands. A sword appeared in her right hand. She raised it toward Isabelle.

"I withdrew my patronage from you because you conjured a demon. I forbade you, but you continued. You defied me."

Izzy took a breath. *"I don't remember that. But if I did it, I must have had a good reason."*

Jehanne's mouth dropped open. *"How dare you speak to me so. You were to be a general in my army, but in my army, not yours."*

She raised the sword over her head, as if to cut Izzy down. *"You pray to me, and beg me to forgive you, and then you insult me and argue with me?"*

Izzy ticked her attention from the furious woman to the

less distinguishable figure at her side. Hidden by light, it took a step toward her. The light dimmed, and Izzy saw her own face, slightly younger, staring back at her. It was her dead mother.

She felt as if someone had just thrown her off a cliff. She panicked for a moment, mentally grasping at anything that would break the fall. The ground, the world, rushed up toward her, to flatten her.

And then, she floated.

"Ma fille," her mother whispered, reaching out a hand. *"I'm here, my sweet. I'm here."*

Her mother turned to Jehanne. *"My patron, will you kill my daughter in front of me? Where was your mother, when you burned at the stake? My ancestress watched with you, prayed with you. She risked her life to comfort you. Though she could have been arrested for treason, she stood witness when you died. Where was your mother?"*

Jehanne blinked hard. She looked from mother to daughter and exhaled heavily. The sword disappeared from her hand.

Izzy's mother held out her arms, and Izzy moved into them. Her mother was warm and solid, and as Izzy sank against her, she wrapped her arms around Izzy and cradled her against her breast. Izzy heard her heartbeat. She smelled her skin.

"Oh, my poor darling," her mother whispered. *"It has gone so hard for you. My fault, all of it."*

"She has free will, the same as you," Jehanne said impatiently.

"Tell me who I am," Izzy whispered. *"I can't remember."*

"You've been told the truth. You're my daughter, the child of Marianne de Bouvard, Guardian of the House of the Flames, and of Etienne de Malchance, Guardian of the

House of the Blood. I was such an idiot. I was as blind-sided by passion as any Ungifted, and I called it love."

"*Maybe it* was *love*," Izzy murmured, holding her close. She had roots; she had a history. She was not just a pawn in a game she didn't know how to play.

"*It was far from love,*" her mother said. "*Limited, possessive, manipulative. When I realized it for the mistake it was, I tried to run away, to protect you both. He was coming for you. He wanted to raise both of you in the House of the Blood.*

"*After your birth, I wove spells around you, Isabelle, and my nurse took you to safety. I was exhausted. I had nothing left for your sister, Lilliane. My nurse came back for her, but Etienne found them both. He killed the nurse and took Lilliane. And she grew up in that evil, demented family.*

"*Then I began to die, and blood called to blood. Your Gift began to manifest, and the Malchances became aware of your existence. They wanted both of Etienne's daughters.*"

Jehanne took up the thread. "*Luc de Malchance was your cousin. He invaded your House and took you prisoner. He stole the soul of Jean-Marc, and that was when you called forth the demon. And I turned my back on you. At that precise moment, I took back the Gift I gave you.*"

She narrowed her eyes as she continued. "*But when you risked your life to save Jean-Marc, you were able to save him. You didn't do it with Bouvard magic.*"

Izzy took that in. "*I'm half Malchance. I must have used Malchance power.*"

"*Impossible. Malchance magic couldn't be used against itself,*" Jehanne replied. "*I don't know how you did it. In any case, your mother begged me to reconsider my withdrawal of patronage. And so I have attempted several times to give it back to you. And I have failed."*

So I'm off the hook, Isabelle thought.

Jehanne smiled grimly at her. *"I can't tell you how many times I, too, hoped that I was 'off the hook.' I was nineteen years old when I was burned at the stake."*

"She didn't mean any disrespect, ma patronesse," Izzy's mother said quickly. *"She was raised among Ungifted. She doesn't know our ways."*

"Rest easy, Marianne. I know that," Jehanne said gently. *"I was able to overlook your indiscretions, was I not? And bring you to me after your death?"*

"Am I dead?" Izzy asked anxiously.

"Non," Jehanne replied. *"Miraculously, you are still alive. The Malchances have come at you hard, but here you are."*

"And where is that? Is this heaven?"

"Not even close," Jehanne said. *"But it is a place where we may speak to you."*

"But is there a heaven?" she pressed.

Jehanne held up her hand. *"These are questions for another time.* Attends-moi, ma fille. *Listen well, my child. I believe it lies within you to accept your Gift again. But first, you must rise above your Malchance nature, and I can't help you with that. I have no influence over that side of you. And I believe it is preventing my helping you."*

Her mother stepped forward. *"Your sister has conjured a terrible demon."*

"Le Devourer," Izzy murmured. *"He took part of Jean-Marc's soul."*

"Oui. And they are feeding him the souls of others to strengthen him and bring him into this world. If they

succeed, this world will pay a terrible price. You have to stop them." Jehanne looked hard at her. "*You. The Daughter of the Flames and of the Blood. With Jean-Marc de Devereaux.*"

"*The Son of the Shadows,*" Izzy murmured.

"*So he is called.*"

"*But why not take her power away and make her like me?*"

"*She has never used Bouvard power in her life,*" Jehanne said. "*Everything she has done has been as a Malchance.*"

"*Then why don't I have Malchance power?*"

"*Perhaps you do. There are many things I don't know, Isabelle. I'm only a saint, not God Himself.*"

"*Is that what you are?*" Isabelle asked fervently. "*And is there a God?*"

"*Many claim so. But you must put those questions aside. You're not off the hook. You're a Guardian, and you don't get to quit.*"

"*I don't want this,*" Izzy murmured. "*I want to be a normal person. My boyfriend…I can't even have that.*"

"*Je sais,*" Jehanne replied gently. "*And though I grieve your loss, I envy you the experience. I died never knowing the love of a man.*"

The sword reappeared in Jehanne's hand. Izzy could see it clearly now—it was steel-colored, inlaid with flames of silver and a string of words in Gothic script bordering the blade. The only word she recognized was *Jehanne.* The hilt was golden, corded with silver.

"*Kneel.*"

As her mother looked on, Izzy sank to her knees. Jehanne lowered the flat of the blade onto Izzy's shoulder. It was unbelievably heavy. It felt like the weight of the world.

"*I send you on a dangerous journey to Haiti,*" Jehanne

said. *"There's no one else I can send. But the enemy is your own sister, and it is our responsibility to stop her."*

Jehanne raised the sword and placed it on Izzy's other shoulder. Her spine bowed.

She trembled.

"You are my knight. My warrior," Jehanne intoned. *"Will you go?"*

Izzy shuddered, as if the hand of death, and not a sword, lay across her shoulder. She didn't want to say yes. But she knew there really was no choice.

"I'll go," she said in a whisper. Something shot through her—a burst of energy, a quickening pulse—was it her Gift?

Her mother gazed at her with tender pride…and great fear. She reached out a hand and touched Izzy's cheek. She closed her eyes and felt the soft sweetness, so long denied.

"I am so sorry," her mother said. *"And yet, I can't regret that I brought you into this world. You are my life."*

An image of Jean-Marc blazed into her mind—damaged and fragmented because of the actions of the women of her family. She couldn't let those actions stand. He must be healed, and her family redeemed.

He is my life.

"A warning," Jehanne said. *"This quest may kill you."*

Izzy said, *"Then I will die."*

Chapter 11

"Then I will die," Isabelle murmured.

Jean-Marc jerked out of his reverie. The mists were gone; she was still kneeling beside him with her eyes closed, her hand pressed to his.

The blood from their hands dripped onto the bodice of her white satin dress, soaking into the fine fabric. He saw the magical evidence of her Malchance heritage—the deep, nearly black blood. The sight must have appalled the Bouvards. As a Devereaux, he didn't have such a visceral reaction. Bouvard, Malchance—they both were not Devereaux, and that was all that mattered.

He murmured a few words and the stains disappeared. She hadn't seen them, didn't know they had been there, as she opened her eyes.

"St. Joan of Arc spoke to me," Izzy said, dazed. "She actually spoke to me. And my mother was there."

"And she said?" Jean-Marc prompted her. *Something about your dying?*

She looked down at their hands and pulled hers away. She caught her breath as she traced the cut across her palm. "I…how did this happen?" She didn't remember slicing her flesh with the shard of glass.

"What did your patron saint say to you?" he pressed.

She examined the wound, as if the answer lay there.

"I'm supposed to go with you to Haiti, where my sister is," she said, not looking up at him. "And stop her and Le Devourer from destroying the world."

He molded his hand around hers and willed healing energy into it. He wasn't very Gifted at such things, but when she opened her hand, the cut had at least closed.

"That's what I was told, too," Jean-Marc said. *And that death would go with us. Did your patron tell you that you would die? Did you see a falcon with an arrow through its heart?*

"I don't have my Gift back," she added. He was terribly disappointed. "Jehanne said she wouldn't be able to help me in Haiti. The Malchance influence is too strong there."

"My patron said the same, of me. " He took a breath. "I'll go alone."

"I can't let you do that," she said.

"You're weak."

"You're wrong. She knighted me. She said I had to go for her. For my family." Her voice shook.

"You're afraid."

"Of course I am." She studied his face. "Aren't you?"

He took her hand. Flesh on flesh. Desire and tenderness rushed through him, accompanied by a thoroughly masculine need to shelter and protect her. He had told her his heart wasn't available, and he had to keep it that way. But every part of him wanted her. He felt like the sun, blazing through a thousand midnights.

How can what I'm feeling be seen as limited?

He didn't understand his passion for her, his...love. He didn't want to understand it. He didn't have time or room for it. He had a family to save, and possibly, a world.

But I can't let her die.

"I want to show you something," he said harshly.

He snapped his fingers. Instantly his clothes appeared on his body. Then he walked her to the opposite side of the altar room, away from the door. He moved his hand and mist drifted down from the ceiling, eddying and thickening. Jean-Marc inhaled the calming scent of lavender and sent out thoughts of serenity to Isabelle.

The mist thinned, revealing the entrance to a tunnel cut from living rock. Of course she was startled; she didn't remember that her bedroom back in New Orleans had contained such a tunnel. It had led to the bayou. This one led to part of the penthouse not permitted for public viewing.

He went in first, easing her behind him. Creating a ball of light, he allowed it to drift above his head, showing the way. After a minute, they came to a door marked with protective runes in gold and silver. In the center was a rectangular-shaped box. Jean-Marc spread his fingers and pushed his hand against it. The box glowed blue.

As the door slid open sideways, he pointed to the thin sliver of blue light across the threshold.

"That's a very powerful ward," he said. "Your lack of Gift might trigger it. It's very painful. So if I may, once again..."

He scooped her into his arms. She said nothing, only looked down at the azure glow as he walked through it. He kept walking, savoring the sensation of her body against his, trying to force the images of her and Pat out of his mind. Their passion had nothing to do with him.

They faced a second door, then one made of reinforced steel. There was a card reader beside it. He pulled a magnetic card from his trouser pocket and swiped it through. The door *thwummed* open and he carried her across that warded threshold, too.

He felt her tense at what they saw.

Six fully veiled White Women sat like specters on backless marble benches on either side of a hospital bed. The walls of the room were painted soft green, and lilies and roses were arranged in waist-high alabaster vases shaped like flames, rising up behind the benches.

In the bed, the unsouled policeman twitched and shivered beneath a white satin quilt stitched with flames and ornate *B*s for Bouvard. Speech had been taken from him so that the *Femmes Blanches* could concentrate on their work. Otherwise, he would have gibbered and groaned incessantly, in the throes of perdition.

On either side of the man, a *Femme Blanche* held his hand. The next *Femme Blanche* on the bench held both her hand and the hand of the woman next to her. The two on the ends laid their loose hand in their laps.

"Oh, my God," Isabelle whispered, instinctively clinging to him.

"This is what I was like after my soul was taken. Just like this. You performed sex magic with this. If your soul is ripped away, this is what you will look like. He is dying without a soul."

If there's a choice, feed her to Le Devourer. Let her die soulless, rather than you. Better yet, use her as bait. Lilliane will want to destroy her for revenge, if nothing else. Let it happen.

"Ouch," Isabelle protested. "You're hurting me."

"*Pardon,*" he murmured, easing his grip. "You had to see this before you agree to go. You have to know what you'll be getting into."

It was wrong of him. The Grey King had told him she must go. Why was he doing this to her? To make her careful.

"That won't happen to either of us." Her voice was hoarse. She pulled herself out of his arms. He set her down and she took the hand of the *Femme Blanche* nearest her.

"Thank you for helping him," she said. "Please don't give up. He's suffering."

The woman gently lowered her head. Isabelle jerked as if in response. Her lips parted, and she looked from the woman to Jean-Marc and back again.

"I'm going to call a meeting to discuss the op," Jean-Marc said. "The best thing you can do is get a lot of sleep."

"I want to help, too," she insisted. "I'll come to the meeting."

"You'd just be in the way," he said. "You don't remember your training and I have a lot to deal with."

"Then I'll stay here." She gestured to the woman whose hand she held. "She just told me that I'm welcome."

The heads of the veiled women shifted slightly. He was pleased to know Isabelle had been able to hear the woman's telepathic words. That was progress, indeed. And of course they would welcome her presence—she was their Guardian.

But he didn't want her lack of healing Gift to be paraded before them. And besides, she must attend to her own preparations for war. Maybe deep down inside, she knew that another test waited for her even as she stood here with him. A test he had devised, in order to save a life.

He allowed himself a moment of pity for her, then steeled himself. He would be waiting for her on the other side. But it wasn't his place to walk her through it. In this, she was alone.

Not alone. Just, not with me.

"Go to your bedroom," he said firmly.

"I'm feeling dismissed," she said, then she flushed and shrugged her shoulders. "And you don't care."

"I don't have time to care," he informed her. He studied her face, the classic oval, the high cheekbones. She was beautiful. A pang of sympathy prompted him to add, "I can make a potion for you that will put you to sleep, if you find you're having trouble…later."

"I'm fine," she retorted.

He inclined his head. "Remember that, Isabelle. You're fine."

Izzy didn't know what he was getting at but she was too tired to pull it out of him. Being around him was a lot of work. Frustrated, she picked up the skirt of her long satin dress and made her way back to her room. There were guards posted everywhere, both Devereaux and Bouvard; each snapped to attention as she walked by. It made her feel awkward and strange.

Suzanne was seated in a white brocade chair outside her door. When she saw Izzy, she got to her feet and bowed.

"I hope it was all right," she said, twisting her hands. "The *Gardien* assured me it would be…"

Puzzled, Izzy opened the door.

Pat sat in a chair facing the fire. He turned when he heard her come in, got to his feet and faced her. His hair was wet, as if he had been walking bareheaded through the rain.

"Oh," she breathed, and she started to go to him. She wanted to throw her arms around him and hold him. She wanted to thank him for coming back, and tell him that she would never stop loving him. Instead she stood rooted to the floor and waited for him to speak.

"I've been walking for hours. Never made it back to my place." He looked down at her dress. "Is that for your... ritual?"

"We haven't. We didn't..."

And then she realized that she and Jean-Marc had done something more intimate than have sex. They had shared a vision. She had merged with him at a deep and profound level, and she wouldn't be able to explain it to Pat, ever. And she wouldn't try. It would hurt him too much.

No. Please, no. I want Pat. I need him.

Her world shifted. The room tilted. She heard her heartbeat roaring in her veins. It was too fast. Her life was hurtling by like a comet.

It was all too fast.

In the flickering firelight, they regarded each other. His sweater clung to his muscular shoulders. He slung his thumbs in his front pockets like the cowboy he was. She kept looking, drinking in the sight of him. Loving him. Wanting him.

But knowing that, this time, it was she who had to walk away.

Pat was a seasoned detective, skilled at reading people. After a few seconds, he sighed and dropped his gaze to the floor.

"You have to give me some slack here," he said. "I'm just a guy, Iz. I didn't grow up worshipping Stonehenge or whatever it is these people are into." He smiled dully. "Remember when your father asked me if I was Catholic? Sorry, of course you don't."

He pressed his fingertips against his forehead. His hand was shaking.

"So say I'm this basic Texan, a fuzzy United Methodist if that, and a guy with a French accent who looks like an eighties' rock star tells me he's going to have sex with my girlfriend. Only it's nothing personal because she has to get her kundalini on and he's got the once and future mojo that she needs."

"Pat—"

"I interviewed a subject once, told me he had to kill hookers because then his mom would go back in time and he would never be born. He's doing life in more ways than one." He looked at her with raw need. "Damn it, Iz. *Please.*"

She covered her mouth with her hands. It hurt too much.

Please, she wailed inside her head. *No, I want him, oh please.*

Je suis là, Jean-Marc said inside her head. *You're not alone. I swear it.*

Jean-Marc was lying. She had never felt more alone in her life.

Je suis là. *I won't abandon you.*

But he would never love her, never sit with her in a hot tub and nuzzle her...

No, I won't. I won't lie to you, Isabelle. That's not why you're letting him go. Don't draw it out. This is torture for him.

As if he cared.

"Iz," Pat whispered, "let me get you out of here."

Goodbye. It could have been so wonderful. You and me, a normal life...

She flooded with numbness. She wasn't even sure where the floor was. All she saw was the desperate love on his face.

"I'm part of this now, Pat. All this craziness and chaos

and…and you aren't, honey." Her voice cracked. "You never will be."

"Wrong answer," he said. "This isn't you. You're mixed up."

She remained silent. She had the right, the need, to remain silent. She was mixed up, but she had to sort it out. *She* had to.

He ran his hands through his hair and dropped them to his sides. He was at a loss. How could she tell him that he hadn't lost her? She wasn't his to have. She didn't know who she was.

I have nothing to give him.

And suddenly, despite her intense pain, she felt a strange lightness. She was doing the right thing, and she knew it. That pain, at least, was cut with a dull knife.

Are you doing that? she asked Jean-Marc in her mind.

Non. *You are.*

The silence stretched between them: a chasm. She thought of his becoming like that unsouled police officer. She could never, ever let that happen to him.

"It's kind of…awful," she said aloud. Her voice cracked as if she hadn't spoken in a month. "I know I had a million dreams that starred you, but I can't remember them. I can't remember any dreams at all."

He tried to clear his throat; he sounded as if he were strangling. "You told me some of those dreams. I can lie beside you in the night and tell you what they were."

"I don't think there's any room in my life for dreaming." Tears welled. Her throat was so tight she could hardly make a sound.

"Pat, I have to go…someplace with Jean-Marc. We have to do something. I can't take you with me. And…and things may have to happen…."

"You're going up against Lilliane," he said. She wondered how he knew. She said nothing.

He narrowed his eyes. "This whole thing is driving me batshit. Half the time I believe it, half the time I think it's mass hysteria."

"I know the feeling." Her lower lip was trembling. "I hate this," she confessed, knowing it was the wrong thing to say. It would give him hope.

There was another long silence. The fire hissed and spit. Her heart pounded.

"Okay," he said at last, lowering his head. "Okay."

No. No, don't listen to me!

"Thank you," she said, as calmly as she could.

"But I'm not leaving. My world's changed, too, Iz. I've been to Stonehenge, and…" He shrugged, silently and mournfully laughed. "I'm a bulldog. Once I'm in, I'm in. I can help you."

She gaped at him. "I just said—"

His voice was soft, his face, kind. "Iz, I know you don't remember, but we had barely begun to date. You had me over for dinner. We went to the movies. And we went to bed exactly once. Afterward, I found all these little satin bags around my house. Those were magical charms, weren't they? And you performed sex magic to protect me from the bad guys, right?"

"I don't know. I don't remember."

Maybe she wasn't supposed to remember. She was riveted by the thought. Maybe she had to forget her past altogether, to face her future. Her amnesia might be a form of protection, to keep her focused on what she had to do.

"We're going to Haiti to face down my sister and a demon she's in league with, and you can't come with," she said in a rush. "There's nothing you can do there."

"I've got street smarts. I'm hell in a firefight."

"I'll worry about you. I'll be distracted by you."

Pat looked stricken. "He can't love you if he's willing to put you in danger."

"He doesn't," she said. "That's not why we're going together. We're going because we have to."

"That's crazy. I don't believe a word of this."

"You don't have to," she reminded him gently. She wanted to break down sobbing, but her intuition guided her on. She had to do this. "You're not watching my back anymore, Pat. I'm on my own."

"God." He wiped his face with his hands and sat back in his chair. He watched the fire for a long time. Her heart beat like a ticking clock.

The flames crackled. Shadows moved across the mosaic of Jehanne on the floor. Izzy felt the heaviness of her sword on her shoulders.

She opened her mouth to speak, but Pat beat her to it. Scooting back his chair, he stood and faced her again. She saw the fight go completely out of him.

"Okay, I told you I can do it, and I will. You have some serious tactical problems. Your people are stretched thin and they need someone who can move around in the city." He raised his chin. "That's me. Damn it."

I don't deserve you.

"Thank you, Pat," she said feelingly. "If you're sure you can do it—"

"I'm sure."

"Then I thank you as well," Jean-Marc said, walking into the room. Pat stiffened, and Jean-Marc extended his hand. "Pardon my eavesdropping. Sometimes I can't prevent it."

Pat grunted.

"I take no joy in this, Kittrell. But you're right. We need you. Badly."

Pat hesitated, then reached out his hand. The two men shook. Izzy understood what they were doing—burying the hatchet, putting aside their differences—but she was angry. No one had asked how *she* would feel if Pat stuck around and helped them.

"I'll escort you to the war room," Jean-Marc said. "We'll outline a role for you. My first thought is that you can run some local recon, see if you can locate any more of Lilliane's minions. If you're agreeable, I'll give you a couple of men. Georges and Maurice. They're excellent."

"That sounds good," Pat said. "We should check out that vampire. Sange. I don't trust her."

"Moi non plus," Jean-Marc said. "Me, neither. I know you don't trust me, either. That's fine." He gestured to the door. "Shall we make our plans?"

Pat hesitated. Izzy knew that once he stepped across the threshold with Jean-Marc, he was fully committed.

Jean-Marc said, "You need to know that there were people in this safe house who argued for your death, Kittrell. As I said, the world of the Gifted is kept secret from the Ungifted. Especially under the current circumstances."

"Oh, my God," Izzy gasped, covering her mouth.

"Understood," Pat replied. "Looks like I bought myself some time."

"Looks like you did," Jean-Marc said with a thin smile.

Pat stepped across the threshold. Jean-Marc followed.

As the two men left the room, Izzy sank down on her bed in a morass of emotion—sorrow, relief, desperation. They'd talked about killing Pat. How could she live among people like that?

Then Jean-Marc's thoughts came to her:

How you feel is unimportant. The same for him. It's time to move on.

"That's easy for you to say," she said aloud.

No, he replied. *It really isn't.*

Chapter 12

The next forty-eight hours raced by in a blur. The safe house went on red alert as Jean-Marc, Michel, Kittrell and the Bouvard and Malchance security forces planned their operation. Kittrell located Sange in an old forgotten graveyard near the Cloisters medieval art museum. She'd moved her nest into an old crypt.

Without the vampire queen's knowledge, Kittrell attached some tiny button mics to the walls of the crypt she had moved into and listened in on all her conversations. She received several delegations of vampires offering her a new place to live—in Washington, D.C.; Salem; Paris; and even Portland, Oregon—but if and only if she agreed to merge her nest with theirs.

"Jean-Marc and Isabelle are really the only game in town. Isn't that sad?" she asked one of her sirelings, as they fed off a gasping, willing human donor. Word had spread on the net that there was a sexy new vamp nest in town, and vampire wannabes were lining up in droves to offer their living blood. Sange was trying very hard not to kill any of them. That would certainly dry up the supply.

"Merci," Jean-Marc told him, as he listened. Sange spent most of her time rutting and feeding. He wondered what the Ungifted man thought of that.

He made no mention to Kittrell that he had already known where Sange's lair was, and that in his office, he had a scrying stone that showed the interior of the crypt. He hadn't told Isabelle, either. Kittrell needed to keep busy and he needed to produce results. That would improve morale among those who wanted him dead.

He would never tell anyone that he had visited Kittrell's subconscious mind when the man was lurching through the rain. He Saw the oncoming headlights through the rain, smelled the wet wool of the other pedestrians. He clouded Kittrell's mind, giving him the illusion that there were no moving cars; the Walk sign shone green and bright.

Cool as a blue mist, he urged Kittrell to move to the curb. Not to hear the blare of horns and protests of his fellow pedestrians as they became aware that he was getting ready to take a step, just one step...

And Jean-Marc couldn't do it. A man who had grown up among poisoners and psychic manipulators, who had watched uncles murder nephews and mothers plot with sons...

He couldn't do it. He sent out new thoughts:

Stop.

Stay on the curb.

Turn around.

Come back here.

And so here Kittrell had come. Why? Because things

would have been far more complicated if someone else had violated the Guardian's direct orders and killed Pat Kittrell. Bringing him back killed the need to make an end run against the resident Guardian for the good of the group.

And only because of that.

Keep your friends close, and your enemies closer. Machiavelli would have been proud.

He fed Kittrell a small measure of ease against the romantic pain in his heart. He also made it possible for the Ungifted man to garner some respect as he maintained his op on Sange and ran covert surveillance on the streets surrounding the safe house. It turned out that Kittrell played a mean game of poker, and some of the Gifted voluntarily played blind with him, shielding Kittrell's thoughts about his cards from themselves. The NYPD cop wiped them out.

Jean-Marc turned down all offers to play. He didn't need to bond with Isabelle's ex-boyfriend. He had to put his Haiti team together. Dom would go, of course. And Lucky. Georges, and Maurice.

Five of his special ops had returned to Montreal with Christian and Gabriel. It was actually a good thing that Jean-Marc and Isabelle had to leave New York. François was sure to take a shot at him, in some devious, Devereaux way. A moving target was harder to hit.

"All right, tell us what you saw," he told Kittrell, as he, Jean-Marc and Alain met in his office. Kittrell had just returned from patrol, and he had bad news.

"It was a vampire minion," the detective said, taking a hefty swallow of beer. Pretzels appeared in a bowl at his elbow. He jerked, startled, but helped himself to a handful. "I was in Battery Park just as twilight fell. It leaped from behind a warehouse and attacked a woman. I fought it off and it flew away."

"Did it say anything?" Jean-Marc asked. "Do you think it recognized you?"

"Negative on both counts," Kittrell replied.

"You didn't discharge your weapon," Alain said warily. Kittrell shook his head. "There would have been so many questions. Especially since you're a cop."

Kittrell ate a pretzel. "No, and I'm a cop who's about to be declared AWOL. All my leave's been chewed up. It would be bad if someone started looking for me."

"I'll take care of it," Alain assured him. "Make some calls, plant some suggestions." He looked hard at Jean-Marc. "I'll do it before *we* leave for Haiti."

"For the last time, *you're* not going. Neither one of you."

Alain huffed. "I'm not a baby-sitter. Or a nursemaid."

"You're my trusted lieutenant," Jean-Marc replied. "This penthouse is our way back. Our retreat. If it's compromised, we'll have no place to rest and regroup."

Alain's dreadlocks bounced as he shook his head. "I won't let you go into battle without me."

"You have no choice," Jean-Marc said. He turned to Kittrell. "Tonight, patrol in Brooklyn, where Isabelle used to live. See if anyone is trying to track her down."

"I'm going to Haiti, too," Kittrell replied.

Jean-Marc gestured to both his cousin and the detective. "You two and Michel will oversee the safe house and patrol the city."

"Michel. I don't like that guy," Kittrell grumped.

"We don't like Michel, either." Jean-Marc snapped his fingers and another round of beer appeared on the table. "But the Bouvards who are here are loyal to him, and he can advise you and Alain on Bouvard customs. He'll cast his runes and say his spells of protection and tell you which fork to use." He smiled sourly. "In all seriousness, if François drags us into a war, I want as many Flames as possible to think of us as friends."

"Haiti," Kittrell insisted.

"Haiti," Alain added.

"New York," Jean-Marc replied.

Jean-Marc was worried. The operation was moving forward, but he had no clear-cut plan to take down Lilliane and Le Devourer. So far, he had brute force in the form of Ungifted weapons and magic spells and a well-trained elite ops team, but he had no actual mission.

We can't just land on the island, guns blazing, and kill them.

He went deep within himself, searching for answers. Nothing came. He danced spells, meditated and prayed. After belittling Michel to Alain and Kittrell, he humbled himself and asked him to cast the runes. Michel had no answers for him, either.

He moved on to basic archival research. He walked the stacks of the library with his hand extended, remaining open to the call of the right volume.

He started with a biography of Joan of Arc. There was an eyewitness account that stated that on the night before her execution: "Ye Moone was blotted out by Daemon's wings."

Maybe Jehanne herself had been tempted to call forth a demon to save her life. But a quick check of facts revealed that the blotting out of the moon was in fact a lunar eclipse. He was intrigued. Gifted drew their power from the moon. If there had been an eclipse, she would have been weaker than normal. Add to that that she'd been tortured, starved and malnourished, and she'd have been at her lowest point.

But that was the same night she transferred her power to Antigone, Duchesse de Bouvard, creating a legacy of power that moved from Bouvard mother to Bouvard daughter down through the centuries, until it had deserted Isabelle. How had Jehanne managed such a monumental magical feat, if she was in a weakened condition?

Setting aside the book, he rose from his chair and walked the perimeter of the octagonal room again. His hand extended, he demanded that any volume that would be helpful to him make itself known.

There.

It was a thin book, one he didn't recognize—yet he had stocked the library himself. It was bound in bleached animal hide, and there was no writing on the outside. But when he flipped it open, he caught his breath.

Une Histoire de la Maison des Flammes, he read. *A History of the House of the Flames.* The author was Antigone de Bouvard—the duchess who had received power from Jehanne before she died.

He couldn't believe it. The actual account of the founding of the House of the Flames?

The hair on the back of his neck rose. He had seen wonders and horrors in his day, but to find this book…it would be the same as an Ungifted discovering evidence of his own beginnings—Adam and Eve's birth certificates, the first Torah…

How could I not know this was here? he thought suspiciously. He flipped the pages, trying to detect a fraud. Then he carried it into the altar room. He lit the white candle on the altar and bowed to the statue of Jehanne.

"Mademoiselle la Patronesse," he began, holding out the book. "If by your magic this book has arrived to help us…"

There was no response. He lit the blue candle of his patron.

"I entreat you. If you can tell me about this book…"
Nothing.

He sat down on the floor and read the medieval French as easily as if it were current French. All Devereauxes could read several dozen forms of their native language.

It was this way, as I sat with Jehanne in her cell. She told me that her voices had given her the power to fight for the cause of justice, and that as she was now about to die, she had no need of it.

"Would that I had it!" I cried. "I would seek justice for all in your name!"

At those words, her face glowed, and she dropped to her knees and prayed.

"So be it," she said to me. "If you swear to be true to those in need, my voices will accomplish it."

Like many of our family, I originally believed that she had been touched by God Himself to save France from the English. But as she had now been captured, and faced death, I had to admit that my faith wavered. I had dared the wrath of my husband, the Duc de Bouvard, to sit with the poor maid until her death. No one was allowed to see her, but I had bribed her jailers. I vowed to keep vigil. Not because I believed any longer that she had been touched by the divine, but because she was alone, and friendless.

"I swear to seek justice in your name," I promised her. For there was no lie in what I said.

Her joy was boundless! She laughed and clapped her hands together, and showered me with kisses. Then she showed me a cross she had hidden among her clothes. It was a lady's cross, delicately fashioned of gold. I was astonished that her greedy jailers had not stolen it.

Then she cracked it open—I was horrified, thinking it a blasphemous act to break the symbol of our Lord! I well

*remembered she had been convicted of heresy, and I im-
mediately became frightened for my own soul.*

*But from inside the cross, something fell into her hand.
There were several white grains—at first I took them to be
bits of stone—and she sprinkled them over me. I smelled
lavender. Then she began to recite words to me.*

*She prayed for what seemed like hours. I wrote down
the prayer as she spoke it.*

Jean-Marc stopped reading and riffled the pages,
skimming in search of the prayer. There was nothing.
Maybe it was encoded in the writing itself. He went back
to reading where he'd left off.

*Outside the window, as the dawn approached, they
prepared her funeral pyre. They piled log upon log until the
stack nearly touched heaven. The Duc de Malchance
arrived, bringing brandy for the workers, laughing and
boasting about the rich reward he had been given for her
capture.*

*Jehanne stopped praying. Her fists, clenched together,
grew bloodless. She raised her face and I saw the most
terrible expression of hatred blazing across her features.
She was in a fury, and it was as if the fires of hell itself
burned in her eyes.*

*"My betrayer," she murmured. "Damn him for his evil
deeds. Punish him."*

*"God surely will," I told her, alarmed at the change in
her. She seemed possessed, and I was afraid.*

*"I call upon thee, my voices," she murmured. "I call you
to drag that filthy soul down to hell!"*

*Outside the window, the moon winked out. That is the only
way I can describe it. I smelled the stench of death, or worse;
I heard men screaming. And though I wanted to look away,
I hurried to the barred window and gazed out. Beneath icy*

starlight, something enormous hulked beside the funeral pyre. It was as huge as a catapult, and covered with shiny, leathery skin like a snake. Its eyes glowed pure red, and it had a snout like a bat. Horns rose from the sides of its head and smoke ushered from rows of fangs in its mouth.

It lowered its head over the Duc de Malchance, resplendent in his ermine furs. The duke fell to his knees, screaming.

"Take him!" Jehanne whispered fiercely. "Demon, I charge thee to eat his soul!"

"Non," you cannot wish that," I abjured her. "You are a saintly maid, a daughter of God and of the church! Jehanne, do not do this!"

I grabbed at her and clung to her, falling to my knees, begging her not to damn herself before God and her Savior in this way.

"Would you have him burn me instead?" she demanded, gripping the bars as the huge mouth opened to devour Malchance. "Would your rather I writhe in agony, burning in the fire, as punishment for sins I did not commit?"

"Oui!" I cried. "For the sake of your soul! I would! Oh, blessed Daughter of the Flames, deny it! Send it away!"

"Oh, my God, my God," she whispered, shaking and weeping, "then take this cup from me. Never tempt me thus again!"

In an instant, the demon disappeared in a cloud of foul odor. The Duc de Malchance swooned and the servants of the church, who had hidden, emerged and revived him.

"She did it!" he shrieked, and pointed to the window, shouting that sure this was proof that Jehanne was the Devil's own and must be burnt at once!

And so they came for her, in a mob, and in that short

moment before they took her away, I received the Kiss of Fire."

He heard the door open.

Isabelle was wearing the warm white cashmere robe he had purchased for her. The matching slippers were on her feet.

"Oh, hello," she said.

His body warmed at the sight of her. Her hair was tousled over her shoulders. The robe caressed her slender curves.

"Did a voice bring you here?" he asked.

She shook her head. "I couldn't sleep. What are you reading?"

He held the book out to her, waiting to see if she could read the French. She glanced at it, then shook her head. Her command of French came and went. He wasn't surprised, given her scrambled memory.

"This was written by the first Daughter of the Flames," he said. "She speaks of a prayer Jehanne recited the night before she died. Then she received the Kiss of Fire, and her Gift."

Isabelle gazed at the book. He handed it to her, and she turned it over in her hands. She trembled. Her knees buckled and he shot out a hand to steady her. She acknowledged his gesture with a nod, her attention riveted by the book.

"Where did you find this?" she asked him, running her hand along the cover. Then she flipped it open, her eyes searching the page. "Why didn't you tell me about it before?"

"It wasn't here before."

"Jehanne," she whispered, sinking to her knees in front of the altar "Please tell us about this book."

"Tell us about the prayer," Jean-Marc added, sinking down beside her. He took her hand in his and lowered his head. "If you can speak the prayer, Patroness, and return Isabelle's power to her, I beg you to do it."

They waited. The candles flickered. After a time, they burned down, casting the pair in darkness.

Lavender-scented white mist rose from the floor.

The grains in the cross smelled like lavender, Jean-Marc recalled. Was it some concentrated form of mist?

"Ask her to come to you," Jean-Marc urged Isabelle.

"Jehanne, je vous en prie," she began. "Please, please help us. Tell me the words of the prayer."

He joined her. *"Jehanne, Patronesse, je vous en prie."*

They knelt side by side, waiting. Isabelle's nearness distracted him, tantalized him. In any other circumstance, he and his fellow supplicant would disrobe and perform sex magic. They needed that boost right now. They were on the verge of discovery; they needed an edge, a secret weapon. He hadn't found this book by accident.

"Isabelle," he began. "We must…"

Don't ask her. Force her. Show her who is the master here.

The darkness surged and rolled inside him. He felt it, icy, burning, freezing, boiling. His blood rose; his penis stiffened. He was in this fix because of her. The world was falling apart because of her. And he thought he had to *grovel* like some underling so as not to offend her ignorant, narrow-minded prudery?

She ought to be grateful you even want to screw her. She has no idea how to reciprocate and give you any pleasure at all! It's always that way with her—take, argue, risk your life, argue some more…look how she emasculated that Ungifted man. Threw him out of her bed like a bothersome cat.

He balled his fists. A hand over her mouth, then a takedown. He was a skilled martial artist. He could subdue her in five seconds. And once it was done, and they had some results, she would understand why it was necessary. No doubt she would thank him for it.

Just do it. Who cares if she understands? She'll love it. Sex with a Guardian. How many Gifted Devereaux women would give years of their lives to get in bed with you?

She sighed beside him, her warm breath caressing the back of his hand. His penis strained against his black trousers. Her robe gaped open; he saw the swell of her round breasts, her nipples tautening. It would be a simple thing, to slide his hand into her robe and fill that hand with her softness…seduce her, mesmerize her.

They were dealing with life and death. If a little forced seduction got him what they needed…why hesitate?

Forget all that. Just take her. Rape her. Have her now.

No. The word echoed through his head, his rib cage, his bones. His nerve endings said no. The air in his lungs.

Do not.

He shuddered as if someone had thrown him naked in an icy river. He saw himself having sex with her, and she was burning, on fire, set ablaze by his touch. Screaming. Her face melting.

Stay away.

Every fiber of his being told him what he must not do. He mustn't have sex with her. It would be the exact *wrong* thing…

She opened her eyes and gazed up at him. He lost himself, fell into her frightened-doe expression. Waves of instinctual protectiveness washed over him, around him. He couldn't breathe.

"I need to work alone," he said. "Since nothing's happening, I'll try another tack."

"Or maybe I should pray in here by myself," she murmured. She sounded almost disappointed.

"That's a good idea." Shaking, he got to his feet and reached for the book, but she gently picked it up.

By the moon, how I want you, he thought, as he left the room.

He bypassed the library and went straight to his quarters, where he took a long, cold shower. He pressed his body against the chilly tile and breathed in slowly, breathed out.

If we had moved forward with the ritual, who knows what would have happened? Thank the Grey King for Kittrell, breaking the chain of events.

He crawled into bed naked, grunting when he lay on something hard. Assuming it was one of Bijou's toys, he reached behind himself and plucked it off the mattress.

It was a battered piece of copper-tinted gold shaped into a crosshatch.

Or the fragment of a broken gold cross, he thought excitedly. He tipped it upside down.

A voice flowed out of it.

"Go to Haiti," it said. *"Don't delay. I will give you a weapon."*

He closed his fist over the cross and brought it against his chest.

"Oui, j'irai avec elle," he vowed. I will go with her.

He climbed back out of bed to show Isabelle. He drew on a dark blue robe, placing the cross in his pocket. Then white mist surrounded him, enveloped him; his eyes started to close. His strength ebbed, and he sank slowly to the lush bedroom carpet.

He dreamed. There was blood in the center of her chest, spreading like a red rose over her white gown; there was blood and she was dying; and it was exactly what had to happen. She must die a martyr's death. Like her saint.

She must die.

* * *

In the morning, he jerked awake on the floor. He tried to remember his dream, and couldn't. There was no cross in his pocket. He searched the carpet, and the bedclothes, stripping the bed, casting spells. He looked hard at Bijou.

"Did you take it?" he asked the kitten. In answer, Bijou mewed and licked a paw.

He rushed to the altar room. The candles were out, and in the darkness, Isabelle was asleep on the floor. Her back was to him, and her black hair fanned out behind her like a war pennant.

"Isabelle?" he whispered. He created a sphere of light and took a step closer. Something glinted beside her on the floor.

His heart skipped beats. He stopped breathing.

She was curled around a medieval broadsword. Words in Latin were etched around the edge of the blade.

Let it be the answer, he thought, as he gently shook her awake.

"Isabelle," he whispered, touching her shoulder.

She jerked awake and gazed up at his face. Then she looked down at the sword and caught her breath. She grabbed it up by the hilt and tried to lift it, then slid her other hand around it and managed to raise it a couple of inches off the floor.

He supported it with a hand beneath the flat of the blade and brought it closer to their faces. He increased the intensity of the ball of light and made out the words.

"Who holds this sword is beloved," he translated into English.

Isabelle gazed from the sword to him and back again. "The beloved of Jehanne?" she asked him. "Her name isn't on the blade. When I saw it in my vision, *Jehanne* ran right down the middle."

"It's not there now," he confirmed, disquieted.

"Is there more? Is the prayer on there?"

"Maybe that is the prayer," he replied. Just in case, he spoke it aloud in Latin and several variants of French. He kept contact with his fingers, then slid his forefinger along the razor-sharp blade, in case the spell required a sacrifice to work. All magic cost something. The price varied. But nothing happened as the droplets tapped rhythmically onto the steel.

"You know the story of the Trojan horse," he said. "The Greeks wanted into Troy. They built a huge wooden horse and offered it to the Trojans as a gift. But it was filled with Greek warriors, who slaughtered the Trojans as soon as it was wheeled into the city.

"But it looks like her sword," Isabelle argued.

"Where is her name?" Jean-Marc persisted.

"Maybe it's not her sword anymore," she replied. "Maybe it's mine."

Chapter 13

They were leaving for Haiti. The elevator doors opened and closed as Jean-Marc's men carried supplies into the parking garage: Ammunition. New body armor—dark blue for the House of the Shadows, and black for the House of the Flames. Food and money. Crystals, herbs, athames and spell books. Antigone's book, and the sword.

She had on a black sweater and olive parachute pants, and a new kind of body armor. Since she didn't remember wearing body armor before, Jean-Marc's careful explanation about how it was different from Kevlar was lost on her.

A shoulder holster held her Medusa, loaded with the same magical 9 mm rounds that could stop hearts. A foot-locker in the back of the Hummer carried additional caliber ammo loaded with spells to create dampening fields, cause explosions and stop hearts.

At her request, Alain escorted Izzy to visit the unsouled police officer one more time. She was horrified by the change in him. Lesions had formed on his skin, and his face was skeletal. He was small and shrunken, like an Egyptian mummy. They had forced his eyelids shut with magic, and his eyeballs jittered endlessly behind the crepey flaps.

"He doesn't have much time left," Alain said gently, placing a hand on her shoulder.

"Take care of him," Izzy asked the veiled women. "We'll try to get his soul back. I promise."

"You are the true Guardian of the Flames," one of the women murmured beneath her veil. "We believe in you, Madame."

"Thank you," Izzy said feelingly.

Denise and Sara, two *Femmes Blanches* proficient in field medicine, rose to leave with her and Alain. The rest were staying behind. Pat wanted more personnel to go with the team; Jean-Marc argued that they had to travel light, or they might be detected.

Casting one more glance at the officer, she, Sara and Denise left with Alain.

Jean-Marc was waiting for them beside the elevator. The door was open, and Dominique, Lucky, Georges and Maurice were crammed inside.

"We're ready," Jean-Marc announced, as he flipped his cell phone shut and he escorted Izzy toward the private elevator. They were wedged in with Dominique, Lucky, Georges and Maurice. "We'll pick up Sange and her sirel-ings."

Izzy didn't understand why Jean-Marc had agreed to Sange's request to go with them. He said it was to keep an eye on her, but how did he know she wouldn't signal Lilliane as to their whereabouts and hand them over?

"Because," Jean-Marc began. Then he looked past Izzy's shoulder. "Kittrell."

Izzy turned and exited the elevator. He was wearing all black, almost as if he were in mourning. His green eyes were hooded. There was a lot of tension across his shoulders. The little boy—Beau—stood beside him, holding Pat's hand. Bijou was cradled against his chest. The kitten stared up at Isabelle with enormous, innocent eyes.

"Don't die, lady," Beau pleaded.

"I won't," she said, kneeling down and gathering him in her arms. His little body seemed too thin. Life was so fragile.

"We're going down to the garage," Jean-Marc told Izzy. "I'll send the elevator back up for you."

The door closed. Beau stepped away. Then Pat put his arms around Izzy, one across her shoulders, the other slung low across the small of her back. He pressed her against the length of his body and kissed her long and hard. She let him. It might be the last time they saw each other in this world and the thought made her want to weep sick, frightened tears.

"This is wrong in so many ways," he ground out. "Damn it, Iz, don't go."

And that was why she couldn't take him with her.

She pulled gently out of his embrace and cupped his face with her hands. He was clean and smooth-shaven; he was strong and worried. He loved her.

"Goodbye," she said. "I'll be back soon." She molded her fingertips into the hollows in his cheeks. "I will."

He turned his head and kissed her thumb. "If he does anything, I'll come after him and shoot him like a dog. I swear it, Iz."

"I know." She almost kissed him again, but she had already let him go. She couldn't confuse him. It wouldn't be fair. She said, "Don't wait for me, Pat."

"I won't." She knew he was lying.

The elevator arrived again. The door opened and she stepped inside, waving goodbye to Beau as the door closed. He held Bijou's paw and made the kitten wave back.

Then she descended to the parking garage. Jean-Marc waited on the other side, walking with Dominique.

"We have a dozen men patrolling the coast," Dominique reported. "So far, all's clear."

"Good." Jean-Marc briskly walked Izzy to an armored Hummer. Two panel vans idled beside the exit. Andre was in the back of the Hummer, looking like a different person in battle gear over a khaki-and-olive camouflage shirt and black parachute pants.

"I still can't believe you're going," she said by way of greeting as she climbed inside.

"You're pack," he told her.

"I almost killed your mate," she reminded him.

"It wasn't you." He tapped the side of his head. "It was bad *juju*. We'll go kill it together, us. Then we'll have a *fais-dodo* on its grave."

We're not talking about an "it." We're talking about my sister, she thought.

"Here's your sword," Jean-Marc said, handing her a leather sword case. "You have your Medusa?"

She showed him the weapon, lodged in her shoulder holster, then set the sword case carefully on the floor. Both of them had prayed to their patrons last night and at dawn. Neither Jehanne nor the Grey King had responded. They were alone.

The drive out of New York was a combination of tedium and high anxiety, as Dom drove their armored, warded car through a circuitous route designed to evade a tail. It was night, making it possible for Sange and her sirelings to join the convoy, climbing into a HumVee with tinted windows.

They drove for hours and hours. Izzy smelled oranges and roses; Jean-Marc was keeping her calm. Her head bounced against his shoulder as she dozed.

She jerked awake when the vehicle rolled to a stop. She gazed out her window to see three private jets idling on a narrow runway. Each one was surrounded by at least half a dozen Devereaux and Bouvard special ops, Uzis slung around their necks. They hadn't been staying at the safe house; she wondered when Jean-Marc had called them in. They looked battle-tough and competent. They looked like it would be easy for them to kill lunatics and demons.

She was grateful to her soul that they were there. Their camouflage pants bulged with weapons—grenades, something called *sploders,* clips of ammo. Plastic crosses that glowed in the dark and vials of holy water.

She had all the same equipment. She just didn't know how to use most of it.

The running lights led directly to the shore. Stars glittered in Jean-Marc's raven-black curls as he hustled her onto the tarmac. As they jogged to the nearest jet, she felt the corded muscles in his wrist and forearm. Her sword was in a leather case in his other hand.

He's got my back, she thought, and she began to shake. She didn't know what she was doing. She didn't have any magical powers and she didn't know how to defend herself.

He gripped her hand. The turbulence from the engine caught his wild hair and blew it around his head like a nimbus of black light. His eyes blazed with star shine. He was wound tight as a spring, and the air itself vibrated with energy.

"You won't die," he said. "I swear you won't."

Don't you die, either, she thought.

He smiled at her, said nothing.

They boarded several small private jets and shot into the night sky without delay. It happened so fast Izzy couldn't keep track of how many aircraft they had. Jean-Marc piloted the small but luxuriously appointed craft; Dom served as his copilot. She was the only passenger. That seemed wasteful and dangerous, but there must be a reason.

Jean-Marc urged her to lean her head back against the velvety reclining seat and rest. He gave her a thick blanket and a pillow.

How can I? she thought, but again she dozed. She dreamed of the man somewhere in New York who was her adoptive father. She hadn't called him. She didn't know what to say to him.

I took care of it, Jean-Marc told her. *He thinks you're visiting some friends in New Orleans.*

I'm asleep, she said. *Am I dreaming this conversation?*

I am giving you the dream of a conversation. Now, sleep.

Now, sleep, and lie helpless because I am coming for you. I am going to take you, Isabelle, hard; I am going to push you onto your back and hold your hands above your head and you'll lose that tiny little flicker of yourself forever. You'll never remember anything but what it was like to make love to a damned man.

"*Oui,*" she whispered. "*Je suis prête.*" *I am ready for you, my love, my damned man…*

I am not your love. But I will take you. Tell me you'll submit.

* * *

She jerked awake in her airplane seat to find Jean-Marc crouched over her, studying her, the way a jaguar watches its prey. When he saw that her eyes were open, a slow, wide smile spread across his face. He traced his finger down the center of her face, from her forehead, down her nose, over her lips, to her jaw, to her neck, to her collarbone.

"Stop it," she said huskily.

His answer was a low, rumble of laughter.

"Jean-Marc?" called a voice. It was Dom.

Jean-Marc blinked and cleared his throat. Twin spots of color rose on his cheeks and he straightened as if he was afraid of her. His aura flared, revealing black streaks. Were they thicker?

"Come," he said, gesturing to her fastened seat belt. "We've landed on a small island near the main island of Haiti. We have transport waiting."

Okay, what just happened? Her question was a lie: She knew what had happened, because it had happened before. The demonic force inside him had just called to her Malchance blood.

He deplaned, boots clanging on roll-up metal steps, thudding against packed earth. She unbuckled her seat belt, got to her feet and stuck her head out the door. The air was moist and hot; she immediately began to perspire. Surf from the nearby beach crashed in counterpoint to her footfalls on the metal.

Approximately two dozen men jogged toward the water, a few carrying footlockers of equipment. Some of them faced outward, Uzis pressed up against their shoulders. Their orders were to shoot to kill.

"I hate flying," Sange murmured, coming up beside Izzy. She and her six sirelings were dressed in fatigues and sleeveless olive T-shirts. "If the plane crashes, and the sun comes up…" She shivered.

Jac put his arms around his sire and hugged her. Louisette nuzzled her cheek. They were like cats…or snakes.

"Let's go," Jean-Marc said, leading the way to the beach. He had slung an Uzi over his shoulders, and he carried her sword case in his right fist as easily as someone else might carry a piece of fruit.

Contrasting with the field of white sand, five gray, rigid inflatable boats bobbed in the water, moored to wooden posts driven deeply into the sand.

"Zodiacs," Jean-Marc explained, as he placed the sword case in the bottom of the nearest boat. One foot on the round, rubbery side of the vessel, he nodded at Dom and Lucky, who were hefting a strongbox of supplies into the craft. Andre followed, carrying a matte metal case on his own.

"We're an hour away from the Haitian beachhead," Jean-Marc announced, straightening. "We'll take all the Zodiacs. Sange, you and your sirelings are with Andre and Georges. Isabelle, you and I—"

"You grouped all the Supernaturals in one boat," Sange objected, fixing her red eyes on him. "Why is that?"

Her six sirelings raised their heads, too.

Jean-Marc froze. He crossed his arms over his chest and stared at the vampire queen. Tension crackled between the vampires and him, and Izzy took a cautious step out of the line of fire. She remembered his terrible temper in the bayou. The fireballs, the fury.

Beneath the moon, Andre's face elongated an inch or two. His eyes darkened. A low growl rumbled in his chest.

"Don't question me," Jean-Marc said. His voice was icy, furious. "I am in command of this operation. You will do as I say. There is no room for discussion. Are we clear?"

"I came here as a favor." Sange's lip curled back slightly, revealing her jeweled fangs. "Not to die."

"You came here because we have a treaty," he retorted. "I expect you to honor it."

Jac hissed softly. Without looking at her sireling, Sange gave him a pat. *"Calme-toi, mon amour,"* she soothed.

"I still don't understand why we came." Louisette pouted.

"And *you* are not to question *me*, Louisette," Sange replied. She moved her shoulders, very French. "Very well, Jean-Marc. We'll get in the boat with the werewolf."

Izzy realized then that her objection was to sharing a Zodiac with Andre. There seemed to be a universal prejudice against werewolves. Michel had been most unhappy about letting them stay in the penthouse, despite the fact that they had risked their lives to protect Jean-Marc and her.

"I got crosses, me," Andre said to her, patting his black pants. "And holy water."

Sange rolled her red eyes. "As if I would ever bite *you*."

Soon the boats were loaded with the equipment from the jets. Jean-Marc's men covered the aircraft with palm fronds and netting, securing the ends against the building wind. Then they moved their hands over the boats, chanting spells. The engines silently engaged, and the two Zodiacs idled without making a sound.

"Nicely done," Sange allowed, holding out an olive branch.

"Put this on," Jean-Marc told Izzy. He handed her a life vest and strapped one on himself. He unmoored their Zodiac; Georges did the same on the other one.

Then he handed her the sword case. She took it with

both hands, nearly dropping it. It was too heavy for her. It couldn't possibly be her sword.

They silently sped away from shore. The open water was choppy; after a few minutes, it was less so. The stars glittered. Moonlight glowed beneath banks of clouds. A storm was coming.

Jean-Marc snapped his fingers and a sphere popped into being, hovering above his left palm. It was a map.

He saw her looking at it and smiled. "It's a GPS," he said. "Gifted magic meets Ungifted technology."

"Why do you do some things the normal way?" she asked. "And for others, you use magic?"

"The normal way." He grunted. "You asked me that a few months ago. I'll give you the same answer: magic costs us. It takes effort, and energy." He smiled at her. "Would you rather walk five miles to the grocery store, or take the subway?"

"I'd rather get on my broomstick and avoid the crowds."

He guffawed. It was the first time she could remember hearing him laugh, and it startled her.

She shifted gears. "Besides Sange, I'm the only woman here. Aren't there any Bouvard or Devereaux female special ops?"

"Many. But I handpicked these men. I know them best."

She considered. He watched her as they bounced through the darkness, beneath a filling moon. She gazed up at it.

"This is the third night since we had the visions. In four nights, the moon will be full," she said nervously, fiddling with the strap on her life vest.

"Four nights is a long time," he said. He cocked his head. "What do you really want to know?"

"How it will turn out."

"Not even the patrons can tell." He cricked his neck and

moved his shoulders. His body was sculpted and sinewy, long-limbed like a runner. Pat was more compact—

"Don't compare us," he said. "There is no either or."

Then, as if to belie his words, he reached out and adjusted a life vest strap himself. "It's tangled in your hair," he said hoarsely.

Her body flooded with desire. She looked down, away. Her hands trembled.

"I feel it, too," he told her. "We're getting closer to Malchance home base. You're half Malchance. Maybe your Blood Gift will manifest."

"I've thought about that," she said. "My Malchance wickedness freed, with no Bouvard magic to counter it. I could wind up like Lilliane."

"She grew up as a Malchance. You didn't."

"I thought of that, too." She took a breath. "I'm so scared."

"I'm here." He gazed at her. "I will do anything to protect you. I told both our patrons that, and I meant it."

"I know." Her voice cracked. "Thank you."

"You've already sacrificed so much," he said. "Lost your Gift, given up on love…"

"It wasn't love," she said, locking gazes with him. "I wanted it to be. I like him so much. Admire him." She was mortified to be telling him that. But he probably already knew it anyway.

"You loved him," he said. "In a different way than what you think love is."

He looked like he was going to say something then. The boat rocked as she waited. She saw his hands dangling between his knees. Imagined them on her. She tried not to think. She didn't want him to know that she was hanging on to the silence, holding out for him to change and admit that he did have feelings for her.

Love her.

The moment passed. She felt the crushing weight of Jehanne's sword on her shoulder.

Take it from me, she begged. *Let someone else be your warrior.*

That moment passed, too.

"They're probably getting ready for us," she said. "They must have spies. We're heading straight for them."

"We don't know that," he reminded her.

"All we have is us."

He quirked a brow, smiled at her. "I think that'll be enough."

"More than enough," she replied, fighting hard to smile back.

"Et voilà," he said. "Izzy De Marco, daughter of Brooklyn."

"Don't mess with New York."

And there, that was their moment.

"You made me a promise," he said. "You'll take me out before I hurt anybody."

"I never did. I said no." Queasiness rushed over her. "I'm getting seasick."

He moved his hand in a circle, and the nausea subsided. "You're not seasick. You're scared."

"We should have brought more people."

"We have to slip under her radar." A beat. "You promised your patroness you would pay any price."

"I promised *her.* I didn't promise *you.*" A chilly spray of salt water slapped her cheeks and forehead. Her chest tightened painfully. Her throat closed up.

"This whole thing's a trap," she croaked. "We've been tricked. Those weren't our patrons telling us to come here. This is insane. We should turn back."

"They were our patrons." The boat rocked and he grabbed her shoulder, steadying her. She knew he could have done it with magic. Did physically touching her cost him less effort?

"In your faith tradition, your saints require much of you, *oui?*"

"Mostly, to have faith," she said. "At least, I think so. I don't remember my faith formation lessons."

"Micah 6:8, of your Bible," he said. "'And what does the Lord require of you, but to do justice, and to love kindness. And to walk humbly with your God.'"

"I don't see anything in that about storming the gates and stopping my crazy twin from taking over the world. Or is that the justice part?"

He smiled sadly at her and nodded. His body language changed; the boat rocked again. At the bow, Dom glanced at him. He steadied her again. She had the feeling he had made it rock himself, so he could justify touching her.

"Back in Montreal, there was an understanding between a woman named Callia and me," he said. "We were to marry."

Izzy shut her eyes, mortified. "Will you *please* stay out of my head?"

"We slept with others, for power as well as pleasure. Sensual delight replenishes everyone. Even you."

"Jean-Marc, we have been over this and over this," she said flatly. "You're not the dreamy high school quarterback, okay? I'm not the moony unpopular girl. It's okay. I'm all grown up and I know the score."

"You were brought up with different values," he said. "I don't want to see you hurt."

"I *am* hurt." She tugged herself away from him. "I'm hurt, I'm scared, I hate this, I want to go home."

He nodded. "*Moi aussi.* I want the simple life. I should be home quietly poisoning my enemies and preparing for the arrival of my firstborn."

"Your…?" She licked her lips. Dreamy quarterback or not, it was still startling news. "Is Callia pregnant?"

"I doubt she and I will have children together," he replied without inflection. "Our lives have taken decidedly different paths."

"But once this is over…"

"Once this is over," he echoed. His words were overlaid with layers of complicated meaning. She decided not to try to decipher any of them.

"Kittrell's a straight shooter," Jean-Marc said. "He sees no point in subterfuge, where his emotions are concerned. But he's Ungifted."

She pursed her lips. "You were brought up with different values."

"*Touché.*" He quirked a half smile. "I've missed sparring with you."

"I haven't missed it at all." *I don't even remember it.*

He frowned slightly, listening. Then he nodded, gazing past her to Dom. "*C'est bon,*" he said aloud. "Isabelle, the time has come for my men and me to ward each member of the team. We have to shield our minds from one another. We'll perform other spells to render all of us as invisible as possible."

"Not literally," she said, alarmed.

"*Non.* Although I wish we had that magic."

"Wait." She gestured for him to come close. She smelled salt and spice on his cheek and neck as he pressed his ear toward her lips. The boat rocked again, and he grabbed her clenched fists with his left hand. "What about Sange?" she whispered.

He reached into his pants and pulled out a rough-edged, rectangular stone approximately one inch on each side. It softly glowed. She gazed into it and saw Sange, Jac and Louisette chatting among themselves on the other boat.

"When this is over, we'll have a masked ball," Sange proclaimed. "We'll invite some tasty Ungifted and drink them dry."

Izzy raised her brows and looked up at Jean-Marc as he put the stone away.

"So I'll be able to watch her," he said. "One false move and…" He mimicked slitting his own throat.

"Isn't this keeping your enemies a little *too* close?" she asked.

"It's a tricky game," he agreed. "If it makes you feel any better, this is what Montreal is always like."

"I can see why you miss it."

He patted a pocket on her thigh, bulging with glow-in-the-dark crosses and vials of holy water. "These are effective defensive weapons against vampires. If things get scary, stick with Dom, Lucky and Andre. Any of them would give his life for you."

"I nearly killed Caresse."

"You didn't. That makes all the difference. Andre's hardwired for pack loyalty. I'm the only Gifted who has ever protected his people. He loves me for that. Back when I was your Regent, he promised always to look out for you."

"Then why don't you ask *him* to…to deal with you if you go out of control?"

His face was impassive. "I did. He said yes."

"Then…*oh*." She wasn't stupid. He'd need more than one person to kill him, just in case—she could change her mind…or die…

"You won't die," he said. But the pulse in his throat added cold comfort to his words.

"Stop it," she ordered him. "Go away."

"We have to start working on the shields," he said. "In about twenty minutes, I'll be completely out of your head."

Unlike my heart, she thought.

Chapter 14

Just before he shut down all telepathic contact, Jean-Marc felt Alain attempting to communicate with him. They had not traded scrying stones; to work at such a distance, their emanations would be too easy to trace. So he closed his eyes and listened.

Things have gone from bad to worse, Alain informed him. *Our family has declared you an outlaw. I'm sure François bought them off.*

Perhaps we should take him out now, Jean-Marc said. *The resulting chaos would disrupt the damage he's causing.*

It might not matter for too much longer. Reports are flooding in from our spies all over the world. Hell is breaking loose. Perhaps literally.

Explain, Jean-Marc ordered.

Gifted families are quarreling. Vendettas are forming— there's even talk of civil wars. Supernaturals are attack-

ing Ungifted with more stealth and aggression than they have shown in centuries. The Ungifted are retaliating. A mob in Barcelona attacked Juliana Escobedo, the daughter of the Spanish Guardian. She barely got away. It's like the Middle Ages.

The lines of battle are being drawn again, Jean-Marc said wearily. *Just like in France nearly six hundred years ago, when our three Houses battled the English and each other.*

The Flames, the Shadows, the Blood, Alain agreed. *Some say we originally sprang from the same roots.*

When that was believed, we didn't know that there were Gifted all over the planet. Now we do.

Jean-Marc ticked his glance to Isabelle, who was staring at him. She couldn't hear a word he said. At the bow, Dom and Lucky wore night vision goggles and fanned the dark water with their Uzis. He knew the two could feel his telepathic communication with Alain, although they couldn't listen in without his or Alain's consent. That was why they had to go completely silent. All communications carried footprints, emanations. Just as an enemy could pick up cell phone signals and radiophone chatter, a Gifted could detect the use of magic. The scrying stone was risky, but he had to maintain surveillance on Sange.

Tell me how Kittrell is doing.

Magnifique. He's committed himself to the cause. And I think, Jean-Marc, that perhaps he has a little bit of a Gift. Most of the time, he's one step ahead of me. Finishes my tactical analysis and my sentences. And he has a good sense of whom to trust.

And he doesn't trust me, Jean-Marc thought.

Maybe someone in his family tree screwed a Gifted, Jean-Marc ventured. He heard himself coarsening his speech. It was an act of male aggression, pure and simple, and it embarrassed him. *Alain, we're going on silent running now. We're nearing Haiti, and the Malchances.*

I'll pray to the Grey King for your safe return.

Jean-Marc gazed at Izzy. *For everyone's.*

I'm not praying for that vampire.

She, you can skip. Tell Caresse that Andre is well.

Ah. There was a pause.

And in that instant, Jean-Marc knew. He *knew.*

Sickened, he closed his eyes. Absorbed the shock. He carefully did not look at Isabelle. She would see it. She would know that Caresse was dead.

What happened? Tell me, Jean-Marc ordered him.

There was magical residue in the chamber of the Medusa, Alain said. *When Isabelle shot Caresse with it, there was enough to cast a spell, but it took a long time to work. The Femmes Blanches couldn't intervene.* Je regret, *but her heart stopped two hours ago.*

Jean-Marc remained silent.

Don't tell Andre. Don't tell anyone, Alain begged him. *Stick to the mission.*

Done, Jean-Marc said evenly. *Of course I won't tell them. Is there anything else?*

Non. *I am so sorry.*

Then I'm cutting off communication. In three…

No one there is worth more than you, Jean-Marc. We are depending on you.

Jean-Marc shut him down. Broke their bond. Stared out to sea. Anger and despair warred in him. Sweet Caresse. She liked to feed him beignets, fuss over him, tell him that he should have been born a werewolf instead of a stuffy Gifted. They adopted him into their pack; he ran with them, howling…

Izzy was watching him closely. He steadfastly turned his head away. She reached out and cupped his chin, eased his face back toward her.

"Is it something you can share?" she asked. "Did something happen to—"

"No. Pat is fine."

"I wasn't thinking of Pat," she replied. "I was thinking of Beau."

She was too close to the truth. He looked out at the water and shook his head. Poor little cub.

"Beau is fine," he lied.

Lilliane fed Le Devourer a dozen fragrant souls for dinner. She was very disappointed to learn that a lot of Malchances were displeased with the way she was running their House. Things were out of whack; a crew of zombies working in a cane field shuffled after the overseer and beat him to death with their hoes. The voodoo *loa* complained that demonic forces were interfering. And the vampires were spooked and skittish. They had heard that several nests had been wiped out by hostile Ungifted who had suddenly turned very aggressive—like dogs with rabies.

The *loa* were right. Demonic energy was pouring into their world. That was the *point*.

She had originally planned to let everyone in on the plan to bring Le Devourer through, by conducting the ritual in the castle square on the night of the full moon. But the last public ritual hadn't gone very well; Jean-Marc's soul had been snatched away in the middle of it. Besides, she was beginning to think that very few Malchances had any sort of imagination, or vision about the future. Mostly they just wanted to overthrow her.

So she had a young and ambitious vampire brought to

her room for a little bit—*no pun intended*—of cheering up.
The bloodsucker was adorable, virile, and after they were
done making love and drinking each other's blood, she
stretched across her fur-covered marriage bed, smiled at
him and played with his long, white hair. She braided it,
unbraided it.

"I have a job for you," she told him.

"Your wish, my only command," he replied. He had a
tattoo of a skull by his left temple.

"I know you have big plans to kill your sire and take
over his nest," she began. At the rictus of horror on his face,
she giggled—*stop all this giggling at once!*—and chomped
his earlobe. She tasted his blood. Vampire blood was so
heady, musty.

"Don't worry. I have no plans to tell him...*if* you do
your job well. *Oui, oui, oui,*" she said impatiently, to cut
off his inevitable, boring assurances. "I want you to get
some friends and fan out over the island. I have had my
own sentries in place, of course, ever since my beloved
husband died. My situation here is so precarious..."

A tear welled in the corner of her eye and slipped down
her cheek. To his credit, he lapped it up like a kitten with
cream. It was a very romantic gesture.

"I need someone I can trust. Take Stefan with you,
Claude. He's very trustworthy."

"Is something happening?" he asked as neutrally as he
could.

"Something's always happening," she replied. "Stay
alert, and report anything suspicious."

She didn't want the countdown to her ceremony interrupted. For all she knew, some idiot had sent out an SOS,
and some greater idiot was en route to answer it. To com-
plicate matters, she hadn't heard from Sange in a few days.

She'd never trusted that vampire. She acted too much like a Devereaux, shifting with the wind.

He lifted her hand and kissed it. "I won't fail you."

"I know," she said silkily.

"I'll go now." He rose naked from her bed. As he picked up his clothes, he smiled at her. "You *didn't* know about my plan to kill my sire. You were just fishing."

She mimicked sticking a fishhook in her mouth and yanking. When he didn't respond, only stepped into his black silk trousers and pulled them up, she fell back onto her wrists and arched her back.

"You *didn't* have a plan to kill your sire. Then why did you let me blackmail you?"

"If the Guardian of the House says a thing, it might as well be true." Then he bowed and left.

I have that much power? she thought delightedly. She bounced a little on the bed. *Nice to know! Soon I'll have more.*

Izzy's Zodiac surfed the breakers and headed for shore. Stepping into the foam, Dom and Lucky unloaded the large footlocker while Jean-Marc finished dabbing black paint on Izzy's cheeks, chin and forehead. His dark eyes gazed back through his own camouflage. No glamours for them now; there would be no magic use until Jean-Marc ordered it.

Edgy, she fidgeted as the two Devereauxes carried the footlocker out of the moonlight and into the shadows of an overhanging cliff. She didn't like landing near a cliff. She couldn't get rid of the sense of being watched.

Dear God, let us be victorious, she thought. *Let this be over soon.*

Jean-Marc climbed out with the grace of an athlete and held out his hand to steady her. He held the sword case in

his other hand. He was troubled, worried. She wished he
was confident and breezy.

By prior arrangement, the other Zodiacs had landed at
scattered locations. Everyone would rendezvous with
Jean-Marc and Izzy in four hours.

Once Izzy's boots hit the sand, Jean-Marc bent down
and picked up a handful of shells. He handed them to
her.

Curious, she took them. He lifted a brow, and she
shrugged and gave them back.

"You used to have the Gift of psychometry," he said.
"You would have visions when you touched things."

"You're kidding."

He shook his head. "I also think you could time-travel.
We believe the Borgias's disappearance from New York is
the result of time-travel experiments gone wrong. So
perhaps residue from their spells built up in New York,
where you lived all those years without realizing who you
are. Residue can cause a time delay...a spell can take
effect much later than when it's cast..."

He trailed off, clenching his jaw. A muscle jumped
there. In his black paint, he looked like an otherworldly
being as his face hardened and his eyes narrowed. He
looked away from her, his body tensed and rigid.

"What's wrong?" she demanded. "Something's happened."

"There's a cave up ahead," Dom announced, his boots
crunching softly in the shell field as he walked up to them.
He, too, wore black face paint. "Perhaps Madame would
like to rest."

She studied Jean-Marc, who kept his gaze averted. She
wanted to say that she wasn't tired. No one else seemed to
be. But the truth was, she was exhausted. And maybe with

a little privacy, Jean-Marc would tell her what he was so angry about.

"Bon," Jean-Marc said. "I'll escort Madame there. Distribute the weapons."

Dom nodded and loped away. Izzy watched him hail a Bouvard operative and the two joined Lucky and Georges, who were passing out Uzis.

"Nothing like warfare to bring people together," Izzy muttered.

"This is not warfare," Jean-Marc said. "This is a commando raid designed to prevent a war."

"Do you always have to argue every point?" she snapped. "Jeez."

"You *must* be tired," he continued smoothly, pointing toward the cave.

Tired of you. Tired of this.

The cave was dark until Jean-Marc created a ball of light to illuminate it. She saw what appeared to be a canopy bed of rock columns surrounding a large mattress and piles of fluffy pillows, dressed in white satin sheets.

"You have to be kidding," she blurted.

"Why?" He shrugged and led her to the bed. With a snap of his fingers, her battle gear vanished; and in its place, she wore a long, white satin nightgown with a dipping front that grazed her nipples.

"What are you doing?" she demanded, covering herself.

"You prefer nightgowns when you sleep," he said. The barest hint of a mischievous smile played on his lips. "And I prefer them low cut."

"What a letch." She tried to keep her voice even, but currents eddied between them. The tension between them rose; she was aware of his body heat, and his scent.

"I'm a man. Gifted men are highly sexed, as a rule."

"And Gifted women?"

He moved his shoulders in a Gallic shrug. "We're not here to have sex. We're here so you can rest." He held out her sword case. "Do you know the story of Tristan and Isolde? They were in love, but she was married to someone else. So they slept with Tristan's sword between them."

"Are you saying you're going to sleep with me?" She was alarmed at the way her body instantly flooded with moist heat. She wanted him to sleep with her. Wanted to feel his nearness, his body. Smell his skin and feel his lips on her.

It didn't take any sort of magic ability to know that he felt the same. Desire flared in his eyes and his lips parted slightly. Then he frowned as if in anger, and shook his head.

"While this *thing* is inside me, I can't," he said. He crossed his arms over his chest. "And as long as you equate the sex act with a profession of romantic love, we shouldn't."

She flooded with embarrassment. He was hell on her ego. *I had a guy who thought the world of me. And this, jerk...*

"You can't read my mind, right?" she asked hotly as she wrapped an arm around the stone column at the head of the bed. "I'll bet you know what I'm thinking anyway."

He started to say something, then closed his mouth and looked down. His face paint vanished. Twin spots of color rose on his cheeks. He shifted his weight and ran his free hand through his hair. The ball of light hung in the air like a candle, casting shadows on his cheekbones.

Implacably he walked toward her. She took a step backward, coming up against an outcropping of rock.

"Stop there," she whispered.

He kept coming. He took her wrist and guided her to

the bed, pushing her to a seated position. The sheets vanished, then reappeared beneath her arms.

He laid the sword on the bed and climbed up, forcing her to lie back. He nudged her legs open with his knee and leaned over her.

As his mouth dipped toward hers, his clothes disappeared. He was magnificently naked; she saw the rounded sinew of his shoulder and bicep, the length of his neck; the cut of his jaw with its five-o'clock shadow. The sprinkling of dark chest hair and the white scar; the whorls along his abdomen, the tantalizing dark thatch.

"Ma femme," he whispered, and she couldn't imagine that any darkness was in the words. They were spoken with heartbreaking tenderness.

With love.

No matter what he wanted to call it, or deny it, she heard it.

"Ma femme de ma vie, mon âme. My soul. Isabelle, you are my soul."

"And you're my Gift," she whispered, as he rested his chest against her breasts.

"You don't remember what it was like. It was glorious," he said, running his lips along the side of her face, his tongue trailing after. He cupped her shoulders. "The magic we made…"

He stopped. She heard his thundering heartbeat against hers. His hands gripped her tightly, too tightly. She winced.

"I'm sorry," he whispered, releasing her. His clothing and body armor reappeared as he straightened and moved away from her. "That was wrong of me."

"Why?" she asked, sitting up on her elbows. "Because it will strengthen the demon in your soul?"

"Because it will hurt you," he replied tensely. "You'll expect things afterward that will not happen."

She saw him there, in the light, Gifted king and isolated Guardian…and a person, just like her.

"You're afraid," she said wonderingly. "You've grown up believing in magic and duty. Pleasure is the best you've got. You've never been in love."

"It's not love," he said patiently. But she saw the uncertainty in his eyes.

"You never had anyone to fall in love with," she persisted. "No one in your entire world believes in love, either."

"I don't want to hurt you," he said again, shaking his head. His long curls trailed over his shoulders; in the soft light, he looked like a medieval warlord. Like a monarch. Someone set apart, never permitted the feelings she took for granted.

She smiled gently.

And when Isabelle smiled, something tugged hard at Jean-Marc's chest. She couldn't possibly be right about this love thing. Love was an illusion Ungifted clung to, to keep themselves from being afraid of the dark. A fairy tale the Gifted had long ago discarded. Respect and affection were real, and so was loyalty beyond the boundaries of death, but love was not.

"I am so sorry," he said again. "You're misinterpreting my behavior. I want you. This thing wants you, too. But true love is not my motivation for wanting to have sex with you."

Her smile grew. It was almost an aura, and he was startled by its intensity.

"All this talk of love, and sparing me…sounds a little bit like love," she said.

"I'm not a cold, unfeeling monster," he replied. "I would spare you from any number of things. I would spare you from—"

He caught himself, squared his shoulders, lifted his chin. He must not tell her about Caresse. He must tell no one.

"What is it?" she asked, pushing herself up from the bed. He was riveted. His body lusted for her; his hands needed to be filled with her. His tongue, to drink the nectar that was Isabelle.

The nightgown. It was the nightgown. It had been a mistake.

"What are you keeping from me?" she prodded.

Her foot came down on the sharp edge of rock; she winced and steadied herself with a hand on the bed, which brushed against the sword. Her eyes glazed over; her mouth went slack. She wrapped her hand around the sword and stiffened.

Tension thickened the air.

"Oh, no," she whispered. "Oh, my God, Caresse... I killed her," Isabelle gasped, sinking to the rocky cave floor. She burst into tears. "Oh, no, no..."

She read the residue of my thoughts off the sword, he thought. *Her Gift is returning. What a terrible way to discover it.*

"Isabelle," he began.

"Caresse is dead!" Isabelle wailed.

"Oh, how sad," Sange said from the mouth of the cave. Flanked by Jac and Louisette, the pair made long faces and slid their arms around her waist. Then the vampire queen ticked a glance over her shoulder at the burly man gaping in horror.

Andre.

His blinking eyes filled with tears. He reared backward as if someone had punched him. Throwing back his head, he howled so long and hard that pebbles dropped from the roof of the cave, falling like tears of stone. Then, in an instant, he transformed from man to beast. Where Andre the Cajun had stood, an enormous werewolf roared…and lunged straight for Isabelle.

Jean-Marc prepared a fireball just as Isabelle leaped to her feet—standing directly in his line of fire.

"Get out of the way!" he bellowed. "Get behind me!"

Andre was coming at Izzy in a whirlwind of fangs and claws. She scrabbled out of his path, landing on the bed, crawling like mad across it and then down the other side.

Magic fireballs erupted on her left and right. One landed on the mattress; the bed ignited. The ricocheting explosions sent showers of rocks cascading over her shoulders, smacking her shoulders and face. The werewolf roared and Jean-Marc shouted, and suddenly the cave was filling with men in the new Bouvard/Devereaux body armor, and then other men in armor she recognized as Malchance. And vampires she didn't know.

We're under attack!

She ducked as a geyser of fire roared straight up from the cave floor. A bullet zinged past her left ear. She remembered the ammo with magical payloads; if someone used 9 mm rounds, they could stop her heart.

My gun, my sword, she thought, but she was running barefoot for her life in a nightgown. A clear target, dead woman running, Andre was slathering at her heels.

Twenty yards ahead of her, the entrance to the cave was choked with soldiers firing their weapons—at her.

"Help me!" she screamed. Suddenly body armor enclosed her, and she had her Medusa in her hand. "The sword!" she shouted.

It didn't appear.

"Down, get down!" someone shouted. She thought it might be Dom. She fell to one knee, then whirled around. In full werewolf form, Andre sprang at her.

"Shoot it!" Dom bellowed.

A shot rang out from her left. It clipped Andre's left forepaw; yipping and growling, he landed hard, smacking the floor with his shoulder; then he threw back his massive head and roared with fury. His yellow eyes glared at her with inhuman rage. He pushed himself back up onto all fours, and prepared to spring.

"I don't want to hurt you!" she yelled, pulling the trigger.

Turning, she ran, not waiting to see if she'd hit him. If his heart had stopped.

A roar just behind her informed her that he was still alive.

A dark blue aura formed around her, marred by thick streaks of black. The streaks undulated for a second, then jerked, and pointed at her.

"Yesss, welcome," they hissed, snaking around her, looping around her wrists, her ankles. *"Here you are at lasssssssssst.*

"My sissssssssster."

"Look out!" Dom bellowed.

It hurt so badly. The pain was as if someone slid a knife under her top layer of skin and sliced…

Izzy stopped running and writhed in agony, grunting, panting, falling to the ground.

"Get her out of there!"

"*Sssssssoon I'll ssssssslice out your sssssssoul....*"

The pain ratcheted up. Izzy lost her breath.

Someone picked her up like a limp rag. White hands, white face, long, sharp teeth—

Then everything went black.

Chapter 15

Jean-Marc and his men pursued their quarry out of the cave and into the night, mowing down the enemy in their tracks. As he led the charge, Jean-Marc activated the scrying stone he had on Sange. It revealed Malchance soldiers surrounding the vampire queen, Jac and Louisette, as they dashed over a stream and disappeared up a trail. Then the scrying stone winked out.

Malchance interference, he thought.

A few more bursts of fireballs and bullets, and the firefight was over. The attackers had melted into the night—or had all died.

Dom and Lucky approached him with two vampires in tow. The vampires were strangers to him. Locals, in league with the Malchances.

"Any sign?" he asked his two men. "Isabelle? Andre? There was a sword—"

"Non," Dom said.

Jean-Marc ripped open a Velcro pocket and pulled out a bag of garlic. He pulled out a handful and crammed it against the face of Dom's vampire. The vampire screamed in pain as blisters and welts rose up. Dom held him tight. Lucky's vampire struggled angrily, hissing. He had a skull tattoo on the side of his face.

"Tell me what I want to know and tell me now," Jean-Marc ordered Dom's vampire. "Will they take Isabelle to the castle dungeon? Is that the altar room?"

"The werewolf got her. I saw it," the vampire said in a rush. His lips were swelling. "It ate her face off."

Jean-Marc nodded at Dom, who held the vampire even more tightly. Jean-Marc smeared more garlic over the wounds he had just caused. The creature shrieked and bellowed. Lucky's vampire hissed again.

"I'll tell you what you want to know," Lucky's vampire declared.

"Claude, *non!* She'll kill us!" Dom's prisoner pleaded.

Lucky's vampire—Claude—snorted with derision. "Stefan, she'll kill us anyway."

Spittle flew from Stefan's swelling mouth. "This was your idea, your stupid grab for glory—"

"Oui," Claude said dejectedly. He gazed at Jean-Marc. "We were only supposed to patrol the island. I saw you, and decided to attack." He shook his head. "I ask for asylum. In return, I'll tell you everything I know."

"Lilliane has a *demon*—" Stefan reminded Claude.

"The House of the Shadows has a demon as well," Claude retorted. "A benevolent demon. Do you not, monsieur?"

A neutral demon, Jean-Marc thought, as he silently nodded, refraining from mentioning that the Grey King was powerless to help either of them at the moment.

"Let's go," he said to Lucky. He nodded at Dom as he, Lucky and Claude moved off.

Stefan shouted, "Don't cooperate with them! Don't be a traitor, Claude! *Vive* Lilliane! *Vive!*"

Jean-Marc didn't so much as flinch as behind him, Dom pulled the trigger.

Adieu, Stefan.

Neither did Claude.

"Talk to me, Claude," Jean-Marc said. He looked down at his scrying stone, which was still black. "Where did they take her, what is the plan, and don't lie."

"Lilliane said she needed the full moon to raise Le Devourer," Claude said in a rush, as he stumbled over a tangle of vines. "She's been feeding him souls night and day."

Jean-Marc sincerely doubted the moon had to be full. After all, Jehanne had created the House of the Flames during a lunar eclipse. And she couldn't exactly wait four more days while she had attackers on her island—unless she took them out before, of course.

"Did you see the werewolf take down her sister, Isabelle?" Asking the question tore his heart out of his chest. By the Grey King, if she was dead, he would shatter this island with magic and send living men to the bottom of the sea…

"I did not," Claude informed him. "The last I saw of her, she was running away from it. She was putting a good distance between herself and it, but then body armor formed around her and it slowed her down. There were explosions. I couldn't see any more."

"Putain de merde," Jean-Marc swore. Had his attempt to help her by cloaking her with armor only made things worse?

"Will your mistress be able to feed Isabelle's soul to Le Devourer immediately, or does she need to make preparations?" he asked Claude in a calm, flat voice. For Jean-Marc's soul, she had performed elaborate rituals first.

"I don't know," Claude said again. "I've never seen her do it."

Expressionless, Jean-Marc inclined his head at Dom as he jogged along behind them. He hadn't replaced his revolver in his holster.

"By the fangs of the First One, I don't know," Claude said fiercely. "She didn't confide in me."

"But she slept with you. I smell her on you," Jean-Marc informed him.

"There is no bond between us. She loves screwing vampires. She always has."

"*Bon.* Dom, do it."

"Wait." Claude hesitated, made a decision, nodded. "Half her family wants her dead. A few of us have been plotting with them. We've been stockpiling weapons. They'll probably help you take her out."

That was excellent news. For him, and for Claude. "Can you put us together?"

The vampire nodded. "I'm yours now. I swear I am," Claude said. "My sire's not part of the plot. If you can find a way to spare him…"

So there's honor among vampires after all, Jean-Marc thought. He said, "Don't be naïve. If he's not part of the plot, he's on her side."

"Not necessarily." Claude began, but then he sighed and nodded. "Still, I ask for his life, if at all possible. He'll work with you. I swear he will."

"We'll see," Jean-Marc said.

"She has Gifted, *loa,* zombies. They'll be looking for you—for us. But there are many who oppose her. We have a real chance."

"Good to know," Jean-Marc said. He gestured to Claude's face. "Dom, give him some water.

Dom unslung a canteen from around his neck and handed it to the vampire. Claude unscrewed the cap and poured the water over his face. Then with a nod of thanks, he gave it back to Dom.

"*Oh-la-la,* if looks could kill," Sange gasped in mock horror as Izzy was thrown to the stone floor on the opposite side of what had to be a dungeon. The vampire sat on a throne of bones, human skulls topping two posts at her back. Torchlight cast orange light on her face. Jac and Louisette sat at her feet with Izzy's sword balanced on their knees.

Behind her, a row of filthy cells held gleaming knives and black-tailed whips; flat black braziers burning with white-hot coals and large buckets. A skeletal man writhed on what had to be a medieval rack.

Chained to the wall perpendicular to the row of cells, a man, a woman and two small boys—one just a toddler— gibbered and groaned. Foam dribbled down their chins. The littler boy convulsed and giggled.

The foreheads of the children and the woman bore wounds. The man's forehead was smooth. All of them had eyes of milky, unseeing white.

They had been unsouled, like the police officer back in New York.

They do this to children, she thought angrily, clench-ing her fists.

To the right of the quartet stretched a low black stone table loaded with skulls, dead birds and black candles… and in the center: a black goblet, decorated with red and black skulls. The golden hilt and first third of a jeweled dagger protruded from it.

"The Chalice of the Blood," Sange said. "Where your soul will float for just a few seconds, before your sister feeds it to her sweet demon mate."

Oh, my God, no. It's really going to happen. Her face prickled with fear—for herself, for Jean-Marc, as reality sank in. Just because she'd escaped death before, and she was a good person, trying to do something heroic, gave her no guarantees of escaping something worse.

"Ma soeur," said a familiar voice—her own voice. She gazed up fearfully at the figure swathed in layers and layers of black lace and crimson satin over a black leather bustier and a full skirt that covered her feet. A veil covered her face, and she wore a glittering crown of diamond and ruby skulls. With great ceremony, she gathered up the edge of the veil with scarlet fingernails tipped in black, and lifted it up. Then she smoothed it over the crown.

Izzy swallowed dark terror. It was her own face, and yet not: the features were much sharper; the hollows in her cheeks much deeper. Lilliane's eyes, the color of charred bone, were heavily lidded and thickly lashed. Her lips were fuller, and so red they were almost black.

"Ma soeur," Lilliane said again, saccharine sweetness dripping off each syllable. "It is I, Lilliane."

"I know who you are," Izzy said. "I've been hoping to meet you. So we could talk."

"Search her," Lilliane said to the overmuscled Gifted guard towering over Izzy.

The man reached down, clamped a hand around Izzy's bicep and dragged her to her feet so roughly her arm threatened to pull from its socket. She dangled like a puppet, her toenails scraping against the stone.

He patted her down, starting with her back. When he reached her parachute pants, he ripped each pocket open and grabbed her weapons in fist-sized clumps—her piano wire, her *sploders*, crosses, holy water, ammo clips, grenades. Everything clattered on the floor; the vampires drew back.

Next he ran his hand up each of her legs, up the sides, up the inseams, then he clamped his hand over her sex and ran his hand up her torso.

His hand flattened against the Medusa, lodged inside the armor. She didn't know how it had gotten there. By magic, she assumed.

Dark eyes met hers. He held her gaze, locked it.

"Clean," he said to Lilliane. Then he dropped her back to the floor.

He has to know it's there, Izzy thought, sprawling facedown on the stone. A rat scrambled up to her, squeaked at her and skittered on across the floor.

He must have felt...

Then it dawned on her that she had no way to shield her thoughts from Lilliane. She forced herself to wipe the image of her Medusa from her mind. Jean-Marc's face took its place. She couldn't think of him, either.

Hail Mary, full of Grace...

Then she remembered who she was...or rather, who she was supposed to be.

Je vous en prie, ma Patronesse....

An explosion rocked the dungeon. Lilliane blinked and cocked her head. "That didn't take long," she drawled, grinning at Sange. Sange grinned back, patting Louisette's head as the vampire scooted closer to her legs.

Lilliane smiled at Izzy. "But by the time Jean-Marc gets here, you'll be unsouled. And I'll be consort to Le Devoureur."

She gestured to the slimy floor on which Izzy sprawled. Embedded in the stone, a thick silhouette of a massive, horned figure nearly filled the space, extending its arms toward her, massive talons nearly touching her feet. Catching her breath, Izzy drew her knees beneath her chin.

"Please, Lilliane," she said, "let me talk to you."

"There's really nothing to say," Lilliane said coldly. She stood and gathered up her long skirt. She was barefoot. "Except, perhaps, *adieu.*"

"I didn't know about you," Izzy said. "I didn't know anything about the world of the Gifted. And I didn't know Luc was your husband."

Lilliane stared at her. Her shoulders began to shake, and Izzy realized she was silently laughing.

"So?" Lilliane asked. "You would have killed Luc anyway. And that's beside the point. The point is, you were dragged out of New York to lead the House of the Flames. But there won't be a House to lead, once Le Devourer and I get to work. The only House in the world will be House Malchance. Everyone else…" She raised her hand and snapped her fingers.

"So you really have no reason to live," Lilliane continued. "While I have an excellent reason to kill you."

"Le Devourer is quite a connoisseur of souls," Sange said from the sidelines. "A Guardian's soul is irresistible, *non?*"

Another explosion rocked the dungeon. Lilliane spread her bare feet apart and held her arms out from her sides, balancing herself on the shaking floor like a tightrope walker.

"Jean-Marc de Devereaux. Such a knight in shining armor. Soon to be a soul in a shining Chalice," Lilliane said. "I hope there's time to screw him. I missed my chance before." She pointed her toes like a ballerina and tiptoed back and forth. "Modern life is so rushed." She whirled in a circle. "Come out now, my priests and priestesses!"

From the darkness of the four corners of the dungeons,

fearsome figures in black robes and black half masks emerged. They bowed deeply to Lilliane, then to the silhouette as it stretched and shifted along the floor.

"I doubt you will have time to screw him on this night, either, Madame," said the tallest among them.

"Oh, Baron Noir." Lillian shook her head. "You're such a bore."

Lilliane flicked her fingertips. Red energy crackled from them as she extended her hand. The dagger in the goblet flew into the air, turned—and rammed hard into Baron Noir's chest. Blood spurted in a geyser from the center of his torso.

The others drew back in shock as sparkles of red covered his gasping body. He shook as if he were being electrocuted; lines of shimmering scarlet crisscrossed his face. His mask caught on fire; his body burst into flame.

Izzy yanked on the fastener that held her body armor together and dug her hand inside. She gripped the Medusa and made a tripod—arms straight and double-fisted, legs apart—and shot off a round at Lilliane.

Nothing happened.

Baron Noir's smoking body tumbled to the floor.

And Lilliane burst into laughter. "Oh, this is so sad!" she shrieked, covering her mouth with both her hands. "So very, very sad. *Blam-blam-ppft.* You poor thing!"

She whirled toward Izzy and snatched the gun out of her hand. "Of course I have warded this place. Dampening fields, my darling. Your magic won't work here. Neither part of it, Bouvard or Malchance. You can't conjure demons. But I can."

Izzy carefully screened out the answering thought that she had no Gift at her disposal. Sange didn't know. No one had brought the vampire into their confidence.

"Maybe you should try the sword," Sange said. "Oh,

wait. You can't. I have it." She tapped her cheek and narrowed her glowing red eyes. "You two are so arrogant, you and Jean-Marc. You had suspicions about me. But you let me come with you. I know why Jean-Marc did it. But it won't help."

Izzy didn't understand. Sange rose from her chair and reached for the sword. Louisette and Jac handed it up to her.

"Oof, heavy," she told Lilliane.

"You should do more exercising," Lilliane replied.

"Oh, I plan to. I'm going to spend a lot of time killing Bouvards." Sange wrinkled her nose at Isabelle. "Jean-Marc brought me here because he was worried about the people at the safe house," Sange went on. "What I might do to them. Left those men in charge—your castoff Ungifted—and still worried about *me*. He's a genius. He knew I was dangerous."

She ran a fingertip along the sword. A thin stream of blood welled along the skin, and she lowered it to Jac and Louisette, who lapped at it like kittens.

"You know, if that werewolf hadn't come after you in the cave, he would have quickly subdued those attackers. Ah, well, fate."

"Fate," Lilliane echoed. "Fate loves me."

"She'll turn on you, Sange," Isabelle said angrily.

"*Non,* sweet Isabelle," Sange replied. "She'll *reward* me. Lilliane is going to give New York to me, in return for everything I've done for her.

"By the way, *I* arranged for Caresse's death," she said. "It wasn't your Medusa, *ma petite*. It was Suzanne, your loving *Femme Blanche*. She wants to be a vampire. Who can blame her?"

Izzy gaped at her. "Wh-what?"

Sange pressed her hand in mock distress against her

chest. "Lilliane, how can it be that you're so wise, while your sister is such a idiot?"

Anger boiled deep down in Izzy's soul. She felt the darkness rising up inside her, the tendrils of evil, the legacy of her Malchance blood. Her heart was a boiling cauldron of wrath. She wanted to kill Sange, *kill her—*

Before she knew what was happening, a fireball erupted from her hands and shot across the room. It slammed into Sange's face and the vampire queen burst into flames.

Screaming, Louisette and Jac leaped to their feet. Jac started batting at her while Louisette screeched, "Put her out! Put her out!" She raced across the room, dragging the sword behind herself. She seemed to realize what she was doing and dropped the weapon, yelling and shrieking in horror as she ran down the line of unmoving, dark-robed figures.

"Guards, sh-show yourselves," Lilliane ordered, doubling over in hysterical amusement. Armed Malchance special ops clanged into the room from the passageway that led to the public square—ten, twenty, more, in full armor and helmets, weapons drawn.

Lilliane laughed so hard she tumbled onto the floor. She drew up her legs and put her hands around them, throwing back her head.

"Don't shoot until I give the word," she informed her guards.

Sange burned, a figure inside an inferno. Louisette ran in a circle around her, hissing and howling.

"Water!" Jac pleaded, tugging at the masked figures, who stood frozen in horror…and fear. Baron Noir lay on the floor, blood pooling over the stones. "Someone conjure water!"

"You're as pathetic as Sange is, Isabelle," Lilliane said, but her voice shook with fury. "I should have known I couldn't stop *your* magic from working in here. Your magic is my magic. Malchance magic."

Then Lilliane grabbed up her athame and advanced on Izzy. Izzy ran backward, trying to create another fireball. She was bewildered—and thrilled. There had been no warning signs, no preparation that she was about to perform magic. It had simply happened.

Her heel connected with the sword. She scrabbled over it, willing more energy into herself, begging her patron, the Grey King, anyone, to give her power.

Anyone? a voice whispered in her head. It was low and insinuating, alluring, sensual. It drew her mind to itself, and every cell in her body. *Even I?*

The silhouette on the floor stretched an arm toward her. She swayed, gazing at it. Something inside her reached for it, wanted it. The Malchance side.

I'll take that as a yes, said Le Devourer.

"You're more dangerous than I gave you credit for," Lilliane sneered at her. She seemed oblivious to the fact that Le Devourer was attempting to seduce her sister.

"Also, dumber. Why waste your surprise attack on a stupid vampire slut?"

Izzy tried to conjure another fireball, but she was losing track of what she was doing. The shadow on the floor undulated toward her.

Lilliane charged her.

Stop this, stop now! she told herself. She dropped to her haunches and grabbed the sword. The metal was icy. *Give me strength, let me lift it—*

With a roar, she hefted it over her head and balanced there for a moment, swaying beneath its weight.

Both sisters jerked, startled. Some of the robed figures took steps forward.

Others did not.

The guard took aim. Isabelle had to hurry.

"Ma Patronesse," she whispered, *"Jehanne.* Help me. My mother, forgive me. This is your child, but I have no choice."

Time moved all around her; she was in the center of a tragedy, a triumph. She was going to kill Lilliane.

The sword crashed down...

...and passed through Lilliane's body without harming one single hair on her head—as if it weren't there at all. The momentum brought Izzy to her knees, landing hard against the stone as the sword rang out like a hammer on an anvil.

"Don't hurt her," Lilliane snickered.

She pointed at Izzy and held her stomach, rocking uncontrollably back and forth on her heels. She looked around at the perimeter of black-robed figures and the crowd of guards. Baron Noir's body sizzled. Sange was a smoking pile of ashes, and her two vampire sirelings sat keening on the floor beside her remains.

Say the word, belle Isabelle, ma belle.

Le Devourer's voice crept like a velvet tiger inside her head. Through tearing eyes, she watched the shadow ripple and move toward her.

He is going to save me, Isabelle thought, mesmerized. Le Devourer can be my new patron, since the old one has failed me.

Yesssss, Le Devourer whispered. *I will not only save you, I will adore you and comfort you. I will set you above every other Gifted and Ungifted in the world. But you must invite me.*

"Now it's my turn," Lilliane declared.

Izzy's mind raced, working overtime to rationalize the choice she so desperately wanted to make. All was lost.

The sword had not saved her. Jean-Marc hadn't come. There was no one…

She smelled fire, felt heat scorching her skin. She thought of Jehanne, nineteen years old, burned at the stake.

I am going to die. Here, now.

You don't have to, Le Devourer promised. *Call me. Bring me to you.*

"No," she said aloud.

A pity, Le Devourer said without a trace of regret.

Apparently unaware of their exchange, Lilliane reached out her arms; red energy burst from her palms and flung Isabelle across the room. Her back smacked hard against the altar. She saw ribbons of gray dots.

Lilliane sniggered and giggled. She bent over Isabelle, singing and laughing.

"First, to make sure you can never come back," she whispered. Then she darted forward and plunged her athame into Izzy's chest.

It wasn't painful; it felt cold. There was terrible pressure. Reeling, Izzy stared down at the scarlet-ebony blood that branded her a Malchance dripping down her front. She couldn't breathe. She couldn't feel.

"Now there will be nowhere to put your soul, if someone manages to steal it back from us," Lillian hissed. "Your body will die, and your existence here will end." She put her hands on either side of Izzy's head, grabbed it and kissed her long and hard. Izzy swayed; she was freezing and sinking fast.

Her mind filled with the image of Jean-Marc's face. His dark, serious eyes, his square jaw, his lips.

I wish, she thought, *oh, my God, how I wish…*

Jerking back her head, Lilliane stuck her knife between her teeth like a pirate and chanted around it.

"*Barbaras est magnus,*" she sang.

Lilliane's crimson aura lit up the dungeon.

"*Cason magnus dux.*"

Her hands shimmered with scarlet. With a whoop, she plunged them into Izzy's skull.

Thepainthepainthepainthepainthepainthepainthepain.

New York City

The moon was the only normal thing in the sky. Beneath it, streetlights buzzed and the wind scattered garbage and trash over a human corpse—a homeless man, unlucky enough to make 108th Street his home.

Vampire minions swarmed from the burned-out tenement across the street, glowing greenish white in the field of Pat's night vision goggles. Their leathery wings enclosed grotesque white faces like picture frames. Their fangs chattered crazily, like toy windup teeth.

Beside Pat, his dreadlocks contained inside a midnight-blue helmet like his, Alain tapped his shoulder and pointed to the right.

Beneath the strobe-flicker of a semifunctional street-light, a trio of half-decomposed women staggered down the sidewalk. What was left of nice dresses—burial clothes—flapped in tatters over gray flesh.

"Zombies," Alain murmured. "Easy to kill."

Pat set his jaw and lowered his NVGs. How had this happened, and so fast? Had Jean-Marc known New York was about to be invaded by the dark side within hours of his leaving? Had he made up some crap story about going to Haiti to take Izzy out of harm's way?

If so, God bless him for it.

Sweat trickled down the side of Pat's face. Two of his

Bouvard men burst out of the tenement in black body armor, Uzis pointing toward the minion swarm as they ran toward Pat and the others. The three Devereauxes behind Pat hunkered down, alert, standing by for his order.

Blam-blam-blam, rest. *Blam-blam-blam,* rest. Minions started screeching and tumbling end-over-end from the sky. Their bodies thudded against the sidewalk, the street, on the tenement steps, on a Dumpster. The survivors swooped down on the Bouvards as they raced for Pat's group, long teeth, gargoyle heads, talons on their wings.

Blam-blam, and another minion dive-bombed to the empty street below, landing just in front of the trio of zombie women. The zombies tottered forward, stepping on it, then over it, unseeing, mindless.

In the broken tenement windows, pale faces framed by white hair appeared. Six vampires had made a nest there. Pat had obtained the information from that treacherous bitch, Suzanne.

Not pleasantly.

Sirens roared in the distance like terrified jungle cats. The police were out; the National Guard was on its way to the city under siege.

The vampires stared from the windows. Then the tallest one raised a rocket launcher to his shoulder.

"Hostie," Alain said. "RPG-7. At this range…"

"Grenades at the ready," Pat said. *"Izzy,"* Pat murmured. "Be well. Be safe."

The vampire fired the launcher.

A human woman burst out of the tenement, screaming.

Chapter 16

Haiti

Jean-Marc slammed Claude against the ancient rampart wall. Something slithered in the grass beneath their feet and Jean-Marc reinforced his aura. The poisonous *mambo* snake hissed and retreated. There were snakes everywhere.

And every sort of assault Lilliane could devise.

Jean-Marc's party had jogged for hours through the steep, rocky terrain. Now they were in Haiti's famed cloud forest. Charred mahogany and cedar permeated the air. Explosions of red light flashed through the lacy canopy, casting streaks of red war paint against the black camouflage on the faces of Jean-Marc and his men. Half the world was on fire.

"Look," Jean-Marc said, jerking his head up and sideways without breaking contact. "The sun is coming up. If we don't make contact with your fellow rebels in two minutes, I'll hold you here until you burn."

"I'm doing my best," Claude informed him. He was cool, composed, exhibiting extreme grace under pressure. He reminded Jean-Marc of Pat Kittrell.

Jean-Marc was past frustrated. After considering the risks, he had reopened telepathic communication and cast his mind above the island, searching for Isabelle. In the cave near the Jersey shore, he had flown with the gulls, but here, in Haiti, he flew with savage, mindless vampire minions hissing and darting through boiling clouds of smoke. He Saw the destruction below him. Huge swaths of landscape were ablaze. Fireballs and mortar fire had set off dozens of fires, and plantation owners, trying to keep the battle from coming onto their property, had started burning cane as a first line of defense. Then they rounded up their zombies and put them behind the fires, fodder to slow down the onslaught of the Malchances as they searched for Jean-Marc.

Malchance soldiers were swarming the island, shooting at anything that was not Malchance. Hapless civilians fled to the beaches. Voodoo drums rumbled like thunder. *Loa* raged in protest, creeping back into their snake disguises and escaping into burrows and the burning cane fields.

Above the lush canopies of trees, the vampire minions kept diving and circling. Vampires peered from treetops. A werewolf pack howled and flashed among the pines and rosewood trees, eager to tear apart Lilliane's enemies.

Jean-Marc sent out a prayer of protection for Andre.

Castle Malchance rose though the clouds like a hunch-backed gargoyle on the tallest mountain peak, a mono-chrome of evil washed with splashes of blue magical energy and smoke. Jean-Marc was well provisioned with weapons, but the castle was equally well warded. Barrage after barrage of his finest ammunition exploded against Lilliane's impregnable barriers.

At last he gave the order to stand down; all they were doing was revealing their location to her troops. Jean-Marc's side had sustained casualties—he was down to an even dozen men now, if that. Only one of his two search parties had reported in.

He needed a way in, and he needed it now.

Fury shot to the surface. He bared his teeth like a vampire minion. His anger was getting the best of him, the dark thing in his soul—

Kill them all. You're tired of this incompetence. Kill them and go to Lilliane. She has Isabelle. They both want you. The sisters Malchance; they will be yours.

His blood was boiling. He fought down his ferocity, balling his fists, taking deep breaths. He had to hold himself in check. The only two people on this island who had sworn to kill him if he got out of control were missing. He had to fight this thing alone.

"We're almost there. There's a tunnel," Claude said, bringing him out of his Seeing, and into his body. And back into sanity.

An explosion shook the ground. Another, another, five, seven, a dozen. As the wakening sun burned through the cloud cover, the minions overhead cawed like eagles.

If she's taken Isabelle's soul, there is nothing I will not do to her.

Jean-Marc and his company scrabbled along, ducking around boulders and under the trees, rushing. Time was an enemy. Flashes of red gleamed on the trees. *Onetwothree-fourfiveblamblam.* Closer, harder.

"Here," Claude said, racing to a large boulder. He called

out loudly, *"C'est moi, Claude! Avec Jean-Marc de De-vereaux!"* It is I, Claude! With Jean-Marc de Devereaux.

Immediately the boulder rolled forward. Faces peered out—Malchance humans and vampires. Uzis, pistols and revolvers were pointed straight at Jean-Marc and his men.

Claude moved between them. "These are Devereauxes and Bouvards, lead by the Son of the Shadows himself. I've promised my loyalty to Jean-Marc," he reiterated. "He wants what we want. To stop Lilliane. He has a dozen men, and good weapons."

"They won't do any good in here," said a tall, muscular man in old-style Malchance armor. His tawny-gold hair curled around his ears. He had blue eyes and tanned skin. He reached out a hand to Jean-Marc. "I am Armand de Malchance, and I'm commander of this company. The interior of the fortress is warded. Your weapons won't work. Ours don't, either."

"Then why are you leaving the castle grounds?" Jean-Marc asked.

"We have operatives on the inside," Armand said. "So far, they haven't been discovered. My counterpart is my cousin, Esmée. She's waiting for my signal. We're going around to the front of the castle to provide a distraction while she gets to work." He smiled sourly. "That would be the work of assassinating *our* current Guardian."

Jean-Marc raised a brow. "But how, if the place is warded?"

"Lilliane has allied us with dark magic, but some of her priests have obtained counterspells they hope to use against her. Esmée and her operatives will do anything and everything they can to render Lilliane vulnerable to attack, magical or otherwise."

"A suicide mission?"

"Are you referring to Esmée's mission, or mine?" Armand said wryly. "Monsieur, permitting Lilliane to live is a suicide mission. When we have more time, I'll fill you in on the details."

"Bon." Jean-Marc gave him a nod.

"Your weapons will work out here, then."

"Oui," Armand replied. "We'll attack the castle from without, whiles she attacks from within."

Brave, Jean-Marc thought admiringly.

"Do you know where her altar room is?" he asked Armand.

Armand nodded. "I know what you're asking. She took Isabelle de Bouvard to the dungeon. From what I've heard, that's where Lilliane communes with her new patron."

"I need to get there," Jean-Marc said.

There was a stir among Armand's people. "None of you will be able to enter the fortress," Armand asserted. "It's warded against non-Malchance. Once the vampires among us leave, they won't be able to get back in, either."

Jean-Marc frowned at Claude. "Did you know this?"

"We had hoped for a different outcome," Claude said, obviously distressed.

"Claude, we planted the counterwards, but they failed," Armand said.

"One hopes the counterspells will work better," Lucky observed.

"Nothing keeps out a Devereaux," Dom announced, striding past Jean-Marc and Armand. The Malchances and their vampire allies moved aside, and Dom made a half circle around the boulder.

At once, red energy snared him as if in a net, crackling and buzzing. Dangling in the air, he vibrated as if he were being electrocuted. Then he was flung backward, slamming hard against the boulder. Sliding down the uneven surface onto his ass, he groaned.

"Okay, *that* keeps out a Devereaux," he muttered.

The vampire Claude helped Dom to his feet. Armand looked from Claude to Jean-Marc, frowning thoughtfully.

"One ought to discuss what happens after we take that bitch out," Armand said, "but we'll have to do it later. Let's agree here and now that there will be no hostilities between us after it's done."

"Agreed." Jean-Marc extended his hand. They shook.

"*Allons-y.* Let's go," Armand said, raising his hand. His people filed out of the tunnel and started moving to the right, up a hillside.

Jean-Marc gestured for his men to follow. But something drew him back to the entrance. He turned back around, finding his footing in the moist earth, studying it as he approached. He reinforced his aura, then realized that that was the exactly wrong thing to do. He willed it to lie close to his skin. Then he stripped off his body armor, dropping it to the ground.

He took a tentative step toward the mouth of the tunnel, bracing himself for a shock such as Dominique had sustained. Nothing happened. He took another step. Another.

He was inside the tunnel.

"Jean-Marc?" Claude and Dominique stood five feet away, staring at him.

"The wards aren't working against me," he announced. "I think it's because of the contamination in my soul. I'm going into the castle."

"I'll tell Armand," Claude said. "He'll send someone with you. I would accompany you myself, but as he said, I'm a vampire and I can't go back in."

"*Merci.* We'll need weapons," Jean-Marc said.

"They must be conventional Ungifted. All magic is dampened," Claude said.

The vampire dashed away. Thirty seconds later, he was back with Armand and another tawny-headed, golden-skinned Malchance, this one wearing a skull-studded post in his left ear. He wore an Uzi around his neck and carried a second in his hand. Slung on his back with a black backpack decorated with a red skull.

"This is Paul," Armand introduced him. "He's got a full arsenal here."

Jean-Marc nodded. "You lead."

The two headed into the tunnel.

Darkness, and more darkness. The tunnel was brick and rock, reinforced with steel bars. Forced to crouch as he followed behind Paul, Jean-Marc raced faster than his heartbeat. He and Paul stayed low and hustled fast, fanning their Uzis upward, where vampire minions liked to cluster before diving down like bombs on their victims.

Shelling rocked the passageway, loosening stones that clattered on the ground, echoing against the hard surfaces. The fighting was intensifying. That was good. His people plus Paul's might tip the scales. If they could get in, find Lilliane and stop her, they just might win the day.

They ran over bone fragments and rusty chains, evidence of Malchance imprisonment and torture spanning the centuries. Around sharp corners into tight passageways. Jean-Marc had put his life into the hands of this stranger, and perhaps Izzy's life, too.

The smell of rot and burning permeated the tunnel. Crazy, uncontrollable laughter vibrated in the darkness. He tensed. He knew that laughter.

Paul halted. Jean-Marc did the same. Then the Malchance rebel made another quick right and knelt on his left knee. He moved his hand in a circle at some bricks covered with moss. Nothing happened.

Paul reached forward and pushed. A small door opened, revealing flickering light. The smell made Jean-Marc's eyes water—death, pain and evil.

An explosion rocked the corridor. He steadied himself with his hand against the wall. Then he heard the *ratatat* report of pistol fire.

Moving beside Paul he peered through the door.

They were looking into the dungeon from a vantage point of ten meters. He recognized it well.

A dozen robed, masked figures sprawled on the stone floor. A few were struggling and groaning, but most of them were silent. Malchance security ops stood over them, Glocks and Magnums drawn. Jean-Marc smelled gun grease and powder discharge.

Other robed figures were dipping brushes of rooster feathers in the blood of the fallen and painting a large pentagram on the floor. And in the center of the pentagram, an enormous shadow topped with horns moved beneath the stone floor like a newborn covered with the membrane of an afterbirth.

Le Devourer.

Jean-Marc's blood chilled. He remembered being with the demon, remembered the agony, the terrible inability to stop his own violation.

Le Devourer.

He looked away, hoping that the demon wouldn't sense his presence. He wanted to tell Paul they should back off, regroup, think it out—

—when Lilliane waltzed into his field of vision, holding the Chalice of the Blood above her head. She was naked, and her body was streaked with ashes and blood. She was singing tunelessly to herself and laughing, twirling past the robed figures who still stood upright, frozen and submissive before the ops and their smoking guns.

There was a row of cells. From somewhere inside one of them, a man groaned loudly.

"Tais-toi!" Lilliane screamed. She nodded at one of the guards. "Shut him up."

The guard nodded, but Jean-Marc detected the slightest hesitation before turning to carry out the order. Could that be Esmée, Armand's plant?

As if he had noticed the hesitation, too, Paul pressed his hand against Jean-Marc's elbow. Then he pointed to the ledge about two feet below them. It ran along the perimeter of the dungeon, and from their angle, at least, it was hidden by shadow. It would provide a second, maybe two, of concealment, and then they would be noticed.

Paul gestured to himself and pointed left. *You descend right, I'll go—*

Jean-Marc saw the altar.

Isabelle. Ah, non, non—

His heart stopped beating as he stared at her. She was naked like her twin. Spread-eagled, she was bound to the stone surface of the altar, surrounded by dead snakes and dead ravens, black candles and a skull. She was covered in blood. Too much blood. Her eyes were closed.

Too much blood. Let it be the blood of the sacrifices. Oh, by my patron, let it not be hers, or she is dead. No one can bleed that much and live.

But it was hers. It had to be. It was the deep blackish-red of Malchance blood.

He stared as the rage built inside him. *You failed; she*

is *dead; you brought her here for this; you knew that one of you would die an ugly death. And look who it is, Guardian! Not you. It's Isabelle, your little deranged half-breed. Make sure she's dead; she is evidence of your un-worthiness to live, much less to reign. Gun her down. Gun them all down and be done with the lot of them.*

Too much blood.

The world of the Gifted has thrown off its veneer of civility, and high time! You were French warlords, not dip-lomats. Burning saints and seeking glory on the battlefield. Those days have returned, and it's every man for himself.

You're a man, Jean-Marc.

Jean-Marc was caught in the thrall of the voice. He couldn't stop listening to it, agreeing with it.

His fingers moved to the trigger of the Uzi around his neck. Sweat poured down his forehead. He was trembling with fury. He couldn't blink his eyes.

Kill them. Let go of anything that stands in your way. She has been such a burden—

Jean-Marc. He heard her voice. Her mouth didn't move. He felt her words deep in his own soul; his broken, ravaged, tempted soul. Gripping the Uzi, he clenched his jaw and let his name, spoken by her soul, her precious soul, wash over him like a baptism.

Jean-Marc, where are you?

As if he hadn't used them in a hundred years, he forced his eyes to move to the left, to Lilliane, who was dancing with the Chalice.

She has her soul in there. She can't feed it to that thing. I won't permit it.

The rage built again. This time he took control of it, used it like any other weapon. He was in charge of himself; he, and no one else.

Paul crept to the opening and put out one leg, then the other, then dropped into a tight ball. No one below in the dungeon noticed. Jean-Marc remained crouched on the ledge, biding his time.

"Here she is, Le Devourer," Lilliane sang, as she held the Chalice between her breasts. She was thin and sinewy, like Isabelle. Her hair was long and curly, like *hers,* her features, those of his love. But her eyes were very different. Although they blazed with cunning and triumph, they were as cold and dead as the eyes of a dead woman.

Isabelle is not dead, don't let her be dead.

Another explosion rocked the dungeon. It was so violent that one of Lilliane's soldiers lost his balance, taking a step backward. The figure he had been guarding seized the advantage and rushed him, yanking a ceremonial knife from the pocket of its black robe.

Screaming, the figure slashed at the soldier's throat, but he missed. Another soldier opened fire and cut him down.

Another robe figure pulled out a knife and cried, "Die, Lilliane!"

He was gunned down, too, and the soldiers began to ring the figures as Lilliane cried, "Careful, careful, don't hit us!"

The shadow on the floor stretched a hand toward her. Then it shifted its attention upward—at Jean-Marc. And it smiled.

Greetings, it whispered in his head. *Well met, Jean-Marc. I've missed the pleasure of your soul. Hot and peppery. Such a sensation on my palate.*

Jean-Marc felt a shard of searing heat cut through his being; he felt the pull of evil dragging him off the ledge and onto the floor. He staggered to his feet and fanned the dungeon with submachine gunfire as Armand dropped down beside him.

"Fire fire fire!" shouted the same soldier who had hesitated to shoot the groaning torture victim.

At once, half the guards turned on the other half. *Blamblamblamrest.* So it was Esmée. Lilliane's side returned fire; soldiers scrambled for cover, delivering death as they made for the cells.

Blamblamblamrest. Lilliane raced behind her throne with the Chalice in her hands.

Jean-Marc willed his aura to grow and strengthen. It didn't work. He tried to form a fireball. Nothing happened. His magic was dampened.

So be it.

He ran toward the throne. Lilliane saw him and held up the Chalice.

"Too late," she said, putting the Chalice to her lips.

He was half a meter away; he sprang, hard—

—and was hit. The bullet didn't penetrate, but the force threw him off his trajectory, away from Lilliane—

—who had *also* been struck—in her right thigh. As reddish-black blood spurted from the wound, her aura blossomed around her, red and black in equal measures. Her eyes widened more in fear and pain as she shouted, "Who did that? No one should be able to do that! I have black magic! I am Lilliane, Consort of Le Devourer!"

Her eyes went completely black. Red energy crackled around her. As Jean-Marc scrabbled for purchase, he registered the flashes of red light popping all over the dungeon. The dampening fields had been lifted. Magic was in use. Jean-Marc strengthened his aura at once.

The shadow of Le Devourer undulated toward him, eagerly extending its hands, opening its mouth. Jean-Marc elbowed himself out of immediate reach. As he looked back over his shoulder, his hand came down on something sharp. It cut through his hand to the tendons, but he barely registered the injury as he realized what it was: Isabelle's sword.

Grabbing it, he formed a fireball with his other hand and hurled it at Lilliane. A stupid move; he could have hurt Isabelle's soul. She saw it and laughed, holding the Chalice to her lips as she easily ducked. Then she winced and caught her shoulder, nearly tipping the Chalice to the floor.

The huge shadow of Le Devourer swam through the floor over to her.

"Too late, Jean-Marc," she said, running her lip around the edge of the cup. "And that sword? Useless."

It is Isabelle's horrible death that is the price, said the thing inside him. It called to Le Devourer, pulled Jean-Marc toward it. Bleeding, his hand a ruin, he fought the call.

I am Jean-Marc de Devereaux, Son of the Shadows. I am not some lackey of a demon, a minion. I am a king.

In the chaos surrounding him—gunfire, flashes of red magic and now blue flashes, signaling that his men were here and the magical barriers were done—in the frenzy, all he saw was Lilliane with the Chalice of the Blood. As she held it to her black-red lips, the pulsing, golden mass of Isabelle's soul glowed like a halo.

"Come here," Lilliane said to him. "Let me have a little kiss before I drink her down." She flirtatiously wrinkled her nose.

"Non," Jean-Marc said. He reached out his hand. "I'll give you my soul in exchange for hers. Even if someone attempts to rescue me, I'll remain with you. I guarantee you."

She laughed. Covered her mouth and stamped her bare, bloody foot. "Oh, you're too much! As if I would ever believe that!"

"I swear it. You have my word," he said, preparing to drop the sword.

She laughed some more, silently, then shook her head. She raised the Chalice high.

Then she tipped it back and opened her mouth.

Jean-Marc! Isabelle cried in his head. Her soul was fluttering, weeping.

"No!" Jean-Marc yelled in a fury. He raised the sword over his head and charged her; then, at that moment, the black shadow of Le Devourer broke from the floor. A moving, shimmering shape of ebony, Le Devourer shot up behind Lilliane and pulsated behind her, from his torso to his chest, his horns breaking apart the ceiling. Huge chunks of stone rained down on the combatants. The shriek of incoming mortar pierced Jean-Marc's eardrums, overwhelmed by a great roar of delight from Le Devourer.

"You're free!" Lilliane cried. "A toast, then, to your reign!" She showed him the Chalice. He reached to take it as his other great, taloned hand extended to enfold her.

Jean-Marc lunged forward and slammed the sword into Lilliane's chest. It penetrated and slid all the way out her back—and into Le Devourer. Lilliane screamed; the demon roared and batted her out of the way, reaching for Jean-Marc. Jean-Marc ripped the Chalice out of her hand. Le Devourer's fetid breath coated his body with a waxy stench. He strengthened his aura as he held the Chalice protectively against his chest.

Le Devourer's brazier eyes blazed at him. His teeth glistened with glowing smoke. He was coming through Jean-Marc's aura, teeth ripping into the barrier. Closer, closer—

Jean-Marc! Isabelle screamed.

"Isabelle," Jean-Marc whispered. "I am here."

Then he placed the Chalice to his lips and drank her soul.

* * *

I am yours.

I am yours.

I am you.

Jean-Marc reeled, and then he wasn't Jean-Marc, he was Isabelle, and he was *we*. And they were joy. Pleasure such as they had never known filled them, welled up and overflowed. They had never known such a feeling of self-lessness, and rapture.

Their soul was full. It was healed. Their soul. By joining, dissolving themselves, giving more freely than anyone had ever given, their lives for each other, their very existence, for each other…

We are ours.

We.

He was himself again.

"I never knew," he whispered. "This is love. This is what we Gifted no longer believe in. What we lost when we became Gifted."

He picked up the body of his dying love in his arms. "You can't go now," he pleaded. "Now that I know I love you."

He was kneeling on the dungeon floor. Debris and dead bodies were heaped around him. Smoke and magic wafted around him. The Bouvards circled him, holding each others' hands and then Isabelle's, had attempted to save her life with field magic. But the one close to him sighed with resignation and lowered his hand.

"We have done all we can, Monsieur," he told Jean-Marc.

Jean-Marc went numb. Beyond the joining of his soul with hers, he didn't know where his body ended and Isabelle's began.

He tenderly laid her down on the floor and willed off his clothing.

He had not done all *he* could do. He was filled with her soul, and she wanted life. She wanted to be with him. He knew it.

"Clear the area," he demanded. Then he made his aura bloom around the two of them; a shield, a world. He kissed her blue lips and cupped her dear face. Then he went deeply inside himself and prayed.

Please, let me save her. Let this new magic be strong enough.

Energy surged inside him, pure and incredible and transcendent. It was the strongest magic he had known in his life. It crackled and pulsated, thrumming, sizzling, vibrating. It filled him, filled his sex.

He entered her gently, gazing down at her with the new magic he possessed—the magic only love can bestow. He thought of the miracles of her Catholic saints—magic performed not through the hand of their God, but the heart of their God. Life-giving. Life-restoring.

Make me an instrument of thy peace, he prayed. By my life, by my own love, let me do this.

He moved inside her, building toward ecstasy. Sex in his world was the strongest magic, but Isabelle had possessed a stronger magic. It was his now. He came, hard, inside his beloved.

As his seed flowed into her, he remembered the word on the sword: *beloved.*

It had been his sword to wield. He had been the beloved, and not understood the high honor being loved bestowed upon him.

Jean-Marc, her soul whispered, Je t'aime. *I love you.*

"I love you," he whispered back to her.

And that was the magic that was required. Her heart pumped in her ruined chest; color returned to her cheeks. She gasped and her eyes fluttered open.

"I…love…" she managed. "One chance to say it."

"I love you," he told her. "Many chances to hear it, please, Isabelle."

But she went limp in his arms.

"Non!" Lilliane screamed, as they grabbed her and dragged her out of the dungeon. She was bleeding to death, did no one see? Did no one *care?* Bouvards, Devereauxes, Malchances, her priests and priestesses! "Le Devourer, stop them!"

But he had sunk beneath the stone with a wail of fury. She couldn't even see his shadow. She couldn't sense his presence.

"If you kill me, I'll make you so sorry," she threatened.

"Shut up," said one of the soldiers derisively. It was a woman; she grinned at Claude, the vampire Lilliane had screwed, and then walked past him to Armand de Malchance, one of her most trusted advisors.

"Sir, I deliver your prisoner to you," Esmée said to him.

"I accept her."

"Armand!" Lilliane screamed. "How could you do this!" She surveyed the sea of faces as soldiers took off helmets and the priests took off their masks. "I am your Guardian!"

"Shall we kill her now, or later?" Armand queried the group.

"Le Devourer!" she screamed. But there was no reply.

For a full day, Andre maintained possession of the Zodiacs. Malchances lay dead on the beach as he patrolled in wolf form. He watched the crazy fighting all over the island and wondered who the hell was winning. *Merde.*

Then, as night fell, he changed back when he saw Jean-Marc leading a massive party of Devereauxes, Malchances and Bouvards. The strange little vampire pair, Jac and Louisette, were weeping among them, surrounded by un-smiling vampire guards.

"Jean-Marc!" Andre cried, waving his arms. "The beach is ours."

A smile flitted across Jean-Marc's features. "Thank the Grey King you're alive."

The two men embraced tightly. Andre was the first to pull away.

"Where is Isabelle?" he asked. "Ah, there!"

He gestured to the dark-haired woman in magical restraints, surrounded by rings of guards. She was gagged.

"That is Lilliane, her sister," Jean-Marc said. His voice was low, grief-stricken. "This is Isabelle."

He gestured, and two Bouvards approached with a stretcher between them. Isabelle lay on it, dressed in a white satin gown. A spray of lilies lay across her chest.

Her chest that barely rose and fell.

"She didn't kill Caresse," Jean-Marc said.

"I know." Andre pulled a cell phone from his pocket. "Alain called." He bent over Isabelle's pale form.

"Get better, you," he whispered.

She stopped breathing.

Epilogue

It had been a month since Jean-Marc's return to Haiti. Although Le Devourer had returned to whatever hell he inhabited, the world had been turned upside down. All that Lilliane had threatened had come to pass: Gifted warred on Gifted. Roving bands of Supernaturals preyed on helpless Ungifted humans. His own house, the House of the Shadows, was embroiled in a civil war, and New Orleans was in tatters.

Lilliane was imprisoned in the safe house altar room, magically restrained, crazy with fury. Jean-Marc found he couldn't kill Isabelle's sister. He simply could not, and his men were furious with him.

He had been warned by his spies not to go home. To everyone's surprise, François still sat on the throne, and he had put an enormous price on Jean-Marc's head.

Better to stay away and make plans.

"We have operating capital for the short-term," Michel said, as he sat with Jean-Marc, Kittrell and Alain in Jean-Marc's office. "Once we retake the Throne of the Shadows—"

"Why do that?" Kittrell asked. His face was leaner, his body more sinewy. He had become battle-hardened from weeks of street fighting. There was a cut across his cheek.

Jane, the woman he had rescued during a firefight with some vampires, was in his quarters now. She was nursing a graze she'd sustained during the evening's foray to kill another nest of vampires—and free some humans in the bargain. Claude and his vampiric followers had lent an assist.

Paul had elected to stay with Jean-Marc. Armand was back in Haiti, working to turn the Malchances away from the dark side. It would be a difficult, if not impossible job. His life might prove forfeit, unless he could consolidate his power base.

"Why do that?" Kittrell asked again. "Why try to reclaim the House of the Shadows? There's no official New York family. Why not create one? We have everything we need."

He nodded at Jean-Marc. "We have a leader."

He looked at Michel and Alain. "And advisors. We have tactical forces." Malchances, Devereauxes and Bouvards were garrisoned all over Manhattan.

"Create a new House?" Michel replied, looking pale.

"Yeah. We could be…the House of the Phoenix," Kittrell said, seized with inspiration. "Gifted and Ungifted, allied with vampires and werewolves…"

"*C'est fou,* crazy," Michel insisted.

Jean-Marc rose from his chair. "I'll be back in a moment."

"It's a good idea," Alain said. "Good for you, Kittrell."

"Insanity," Michel reiterated.

* * *

They argued as Jean-Marc crossed his office and opened a door. A waterfall of lavender mist descended upon him, cooling and healing. He walked past the statues of Jehanne and the Grey King, and knelt to them both.

"Thank you," he said. "I honor you both."

Then he softly opened another door.

He gazed in on his love.

Isabelle, his beloved, his mate, his soul. Asleep in his bed.

The queen of his new House?

Why not? We have everything we need.

He sat on the side of the bed and placed his hand on her abdomen.

We have everything, Including an heir. Our twin son and daughter, born of Flames, Shadows and Blood. The living symbols that love conquers all. As it has conquered me.

He leaned forward and kissed his new wife. Then he laid his head against hers on the pillow, and rested.

For just one moment.

To everything there is a season…

One sweet moment, all theirs.

* * * * *

The Colton family is back!
Enjoy a sneak preview of
COLTON'S SECRET SERVICE
by Marie Ferrarella,
part of
THE COLTONS: FAMILY FIRST *miniseries.*
Available from Silhouette Romantic Suspense
in September 2008.

He cautioned himself to be leery. He was human and he'd been conned before. But never by anyone nearly so attractive. Never by anyone he'd felt so attracted to.

In her defense, Nick supposed that Georgie could actually be telling him the truth. That she was a victim in all this. He had his people back in California checking her out, to make sure she was who she said she was and had, as she claimed, not even been near a computer but on the road these last few months that the threats had been made.

In the meantime, he was doing his own checking out. Up close and exceedingly personal. So personal he could feel his blood stirring.

It had been a long time since he'd thought of himself as anything other than a law enforcement agent of one type or other. But Georgeann Grady made him remember that beneath the oaths he had taken and his devotion to duty, there beat the heart of a man.

A man who'd been far too long without the touch of a woman.

He watched as the light from the fireplace caressed the outline of Georgie's small, trim, jean-clad body as she moved about the rustic living room that could have easily come off the set of a Hollywood Western. Except that it was genuine.

As genuine as she claimed to be?

Something inside of him hoped so.

He wasn't supposed to be taking sides. His only interest in being here was to guarantee Senator Joe Colton's safety as the latter continued to make his bid for the presidency. Everything else was supposed to be secondary, but, Nick had to silently admit, that was just a wee bit hard to remember right now.

Earlier, before she'd put her precocious handful of a daughter to bed, Georgie had fed his appetite by whipping up some kind of a delicious concoction out of the vegetables she'd pulled from her garden. Vegetables that, by all rights, should have been withered and dried. She'd mentioned that a friend came by on occasion to weed and tend it. Still, it surprised him that somehow she'd managed to make something mouthwatering out of it.

Almost as mouthwatering as she looked to him right at this moment.

Again, he was reminded of the appetite that hadn't been fed, hadn't been satisfied.

And wasn't going to be, Nick sternly told himself. At least not now. Maybe later, when things took on a more definite shape and all the questions in his head were answered to his satisfaction, there would be time to explore this feeling. This woman. But not now.

Damn it.

"Sorry about the lack of light," Georgie said, breaking into his train of thought as she turned around to face him. If she noticed the way he was looking at her, she gave no indication. "But I don't see a point in paying for electricity if I'm not going to be here. Besides, Emmie really enjoys camping out. She likes roughing it."

"And you?" Nick asked, moving closer to her, so close that a whisper would have trouble fitting in. "What do you like?"

The very breath stopped in Georgie's throat as she looked up at him.

"I think you've got a fair shot of guessing that one," she told him softly.

* * * * *

Be sure to look for
COLTON'S SECRET SERVICE
and the other following titles from
THE COLTONS: FAMILY FIRST *miniseries:*

RANCHER'S REDEMPTION
by Beth Cornelison
THE SHERIFF'S AMNESIAC BRIDE
by Linda Conrad
SOLDIER'S SECRET CHILD
by Caridad Piñeiro
BABY'S WATCH
by Justine Davis
A HERO OF HER OWN
by Carla Cassidy

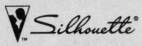

REQUEST YOUR FREE BOOKS!

2 FREE NOVELS PLUS 2 FREE GIFTS!

Silhouette®

n o c t u r n e™

Dramatic and Sensual Tales of Paranormal Romance.

YES! Please send me 2 FREE Silhouette® Nocturne™ novels and my 2 FREE gifts (gifts are worth about $10). After receiving them, if I don't wish to receive any more books, I can return the shipping statement marked "cancel." If I don't cancel, I will receive 4 brand-new novels every other month and be billed just $4.47 per book in the U.S. or $4.99 per book in Canada, plus 25¢ shipping and handling per book plus applicable taxes, if any*. That's a savings of about 15% off the cover price! I understand that accepting the 2 free books and gifts places me under no obligation to buy anything. I can always return a shipment and cancel at any time. Even if I never buy another book from Silhouette, the two free books and gifts are mine to keep forever.

238 SDN ELS4   338 SDN ELXG

Name	(PLEASE PRINT)
Address	Apt. #
City	State/Prov.	Zip/Postal Code

Signature (if under 18, a parent or guardian must sign)

Mail to the **Silhouette Reader Service:**
IN U.S.A.: P.O. Box 1867, Buffalo, NY 14240-1867
IN CANADA: P.O. Box 609, Fort Erie, Ontario L2A 5X3

Not valid to current subscribers of Silhouette Nocturne books.

Want to try two free books from another line?
Call 1-800-873-8635 or visit www.morefreebooks.com.

* Terms and prices subject to change without notice. N.Y. residents add applicable sales tax. Canadian residents will be charged applicable provincial taxes and GST. Offer not valid in Quebec. This offer is limited to one order per household. All orders subject to approval. Credit or debit balances in a customer's account(s) may be offset by any other outstanding balance owed by or to the customer. Please allow 4 to 6 weeks for delivery. Offer available while quantities last.

Your Privacy: Silhouette is committed to protecting your privacy. Our Privacy Policy is available online at www.eHarlequin.com or upon request from the Reader Service. From time to time we make our lists of customers available to reputable third parties who may have a product or service of interest to you. If you would prefer we not share your name and address, please check here. ☐

SN08R

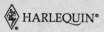

Inside ROMANCE

Stay up-to-date on all your romance reading news!

The Inside Romance newsletter is a FREE quarterly newsletter highlighting our upcoming series releases and promotions!

Click on the <u>Inside Romance</u> link on the front page of **www.eHarlequin.com** or e-mail us at insideromance@harlequin.ca to sign up to receive your FREE newsletter today!

You can also subscribe by writing us at: HARLEQUIN BOOKS Attention: Customer Service Department P.O. Box 9057, Buffalo, NY 14269-9057

Please allow 4-6 weeks for delivery of the first issue by mail.

IRNBPA108

nocturne™

COMING NEXT MONTH

#47 DEADLY REDEMPTION • Kathleen Korbel
Daughters of Myth
War threatens all the faerie clans. To help restore
balance, the queen's daughter, Orla, is sent to the enemy
clan as a hostage bride to Liam the Avenger. Now they
must negotiate their tempestuous marriage as they work
to save their world from destruction....

#48 THE NIGHT SERPENT • Anna Leonard
Lily Malkin is an ordinary woman—or so she thinks. Until
she's caught up in a ritual-murder investigation led by
Special Agent Jon Patrick, and Lily discovers she's been
stalked through her nine lives by the Night Serpent. Will
this life be her last?

SNCNM0808